ETHEREAL IMPRINTS

Book 1 *in* The Ethereal Chronicles

ELIZABETH WITTEKIND

ISBN: 979-8-9852145-1-2 (paperback)
ISBN: 979-8-9852145-3-6 (hardcover)
ISBN: 979-8-9852145-5-0 (ebook)

Book cover design and interior formatting by Miblart.com

Chrysanthe

The water was clear and smooth as I ran the fingers of my left hand through it, feeling the moisture soak into my skin, sinking into the pores of my extremity.

I stared at the liquid as my limb glided through it, studying the piercing, vivid blue color before I cupped my palm to the fluid, bringing it to my lips to drink. It was cool and refreshing as it slid down my throat, and I swallowed, my entire body immediately feeling rejuvenated.

The water tasted the way it always should be. At least, to me.

It tasted like it was enchanted.

The remaining liquid slowly dribbled from my flesh and into the stream as I turned my left hand around to look at the red chrysanthemum tattooed on the back of it, the green stem of the flower twisting its way around either side of my wrist.

The colors were incredibly bright, alternating hypnotically in the sunlight as I stared at the flower, slowly rotating my wrist to see the entirety of the whole tattoo.

I'd gotten it when I was a baby; the tattoo was given to me by an Oracle. Named after the chrysanthemum, she'd tattooed the blossom onto my skin.

My name is Chrysanthe.

I placed my damp arm at my side as I closed my eyes and tilted my head back slightly, soaking up the sun's warmth.

I felt mud seep in between my toes from where I was standing in the stream, and I welcomed it as I slowly opened my eyes again, taking in the lively world before me.

It didn't matter that my feet were in mud; they would never get dirty because of the water surrounding me. The fluid would clean itself before anything could taint it, all the sediment immediately going to the bottom once there was movement.

As I walked out of the stream and onto the green grass, nothing was on my skin.

My skin glistened as I found a place to sit, and I saw my feet start to shine as the sun's rays bounced off the tattoos, causing them to sparkle.

I smiled as I sat down in the grass, looking at my shimmering skin, watching all the various degrees of color upon my flesh.

More tattoos adorned my feet, starting on the top of my toes before spiraling, curling completely before stopping at the base of my ankles.

I wiggled my toes and watched the design seemingly dance under the sunlight, the memory of how I got them quickly entering my consciousness.

The tattoos on my feet were tree roots, and all of the symbols I had were of particular significance to me. They all determined my fate. They had all been given to me by the same Oracle.

The Oracle who had come to my parents before my mother had given birth to me, telling her she'd seen great potential for me with my future.

According to both of my parents, it was after my birth that the Oracle had returned to see me as a newborn, gazing at me before slowly picking me up and cradling me in her arms. She had rocked me back and forth, uttering a few soft words and muttering an incantation.

The designs had begun to show immediately, slowly growing all over my flesh; everywhere she touched became a canvas for the magical inked patterns.

The tattoos had been vibrant ever since.

Three of them took over my flesh.

There was a tattoo of a red chrysanthemum on my hand, twisting down on either side of my wrist. There were tattoos of tree roots extended onto my ankles. And then there was another set of exotic peacock feathers; they appeared at the end of both of my eye sockets. They settled on my nose before twirling and twisting. The multi-colored feathers took up the area of flesh near my eyebrows and extended to the left and right of my eye.

The skin around my face was saturated in the magnificent blue and green colors of the peacock's eye feather, making me look like I was wearing a permanent masquerade mask.

I'd always loved the tattoo resembling the bird's plumage the most; out of all the symbols I had, the peacock feathers always looked so unique to me.

A breeze kissed my skin gently as it blew through my braid, and I glanced down to see the strands of my blond hair moving along with the wind. The tendrils that had escaped from the braid were flowing in the current. I had woven tree vines throughout my hair.

They were at the base of my braid too, tied in a knot to keep the hairstyle together.

The wind blew through the ends of my dress slightly, causing it to flow up and ripple around my legs.

I watched the air twirl it, studying the colors swirling in the sunlight.

The multicolored dress I wore was a light, healthy, nature-green hue around the chest area, adorned with leaf and tree vine patterns before the material changed into an aqua color at my hips.

The bottom of the dress resembled the ocean, moving and rippling, while the top part looked like the Earth, the land, the trees, the plants. It was a combination of both the tide and the soil.

Both of which I looked after.

I closed my eyes again, absorbing everything; the sights, the sounds. I heard the air whistle around me, feeling it move through my hair, over my skin.

Everything in my existence was right here. The trees and nature; I loved it so much.

Hmmm, I thought as I lay against the grass, my back against it as I absorbed the sunlight. *Hmmm.*

I was relaxing when there was suddenly a soft rumble in the distance. A faint sound of paws interrupted my thoughts.

Huh? I immediately sat up and turned around; that was when I saw a large tiger slowly walking through the clearing, its amber eyes fixed on me, its brilliant, detailed coat shining in the sunlight.

Well, hello.

I felt another smile spread across my face as the tiger's ears swiveled slightly upon recognition, and I heard a broken, breathy rumble resonate from its throat.

The noise coming out of the tiger's airway didn't sound threatening; it was friendly.

"Hey, Caliya," I said, greeting her once I knew she could see me. "Come here, sweetheart."

Caliya's eyes were on me for a few heartbeats, and then she made her way over in two bounds. She moved her head to the side, attempting to graze it alongside mine as happy noises continued to shake through her throat.

Caliya was so powerful; she rubbed her fur against me, attempting to get me to show her attention.

I was never quite used to her being so strong.

She nearly knocked me over with her immense strength, but I laughed before I straightened myself up again.

She was so happy to see me.

"Hey, sweetie," I said, petting her, looking at her patterned fur, feeling the softness. "How have you been?"

Caliya moaned, the noise emanating from her colossal body sounding affectionate as she rubbed her body against mine.

"I guess well, huh?"

I laughed as I stroked her fur.

I'd always had a strong relationship with Caliya, ever since the Oracle brought her to me when I was a child, and she was a cub when the Oracle was training me. Caliya had become an orphan after her mother had died, so the Oracle gave her to me, teaching me to raise her properly so she would one day live in the wild.

She'd been on her own for a while now, and even though she was a wild animal, Caliya had always come to see me whenever I was nearby, always greeting me in the same manner whenever she saw me.

She would always act like a giant kitten.

The Oracle had taught me well; how to raise Caliya and be around nature in general. How to treat everything, from the animals to the flowers to the streams. I had to be respectful of it all, to help it become healthy so that I could protect it from harm.

That was one thing the Oracle instilled in me from the first day she'd begun teaching. If you are respectful to the environment, it will be respectful back.

The Oracle was good at saying wise statements and, now, I understood them as I rubbed Caliya's ears, watching as she closed her eyes in a relaxed state.

She'd laid down on the grass near me, her mammoth head in her paws, her body wrapped around where I was so I could lay against her, her mood suggesting she was going to fall asleep.

I watched Caliya blink slowly; my fingertips twirled around her ear absently, not paying attention to anything else.

I was focusing on Caliya, and I was in my happy place.

And that proved the point the Oracle had taught me.

I had liked her when I was a child; she was an exquisite teacher. She taught me so much, and I had heeded all the lessons and advice. Once she was confident that I had learned enough from her, she entrusted me with carrying on her legacy when she was gone.

It was such a great honor to hold onto it, but it was also a huge responsibility since she had a job that could be challenging at times, but since she wasn't guiding me anymore, it was all my job to do this.

It wasn't easy.

But it was enthralling.

Enthralling because the Oracle had entrusted me to be the Protector of the Earth.

I moved as I opened my eyes, blinking rapidly to shake the drowsiness from my brain.

The steady, methodic breathing of Caliya filled my ears as the rise and fall of her chest kept in perfect rhythm with it. The feeling was incredibly soothing as I twisted back to the position I was in before, my head moving in unison with her inhale and exhale.

I lay there, my ear pressed to Caliya's chest, the thumping of her heart sending a euphoric sensation through me. The organ pulsed in a rhythmic, healthy motion as she slept.

It was so calming to me, being with her.

I could spend eternity here, in the position I was in right now.

But, at the same time, I couldn't.

I took a deep breath, listening to Caliya's heartbeat one last time before finally pushing myself up and stretching.

I yawned and put my arms out in front of me.

"Caliya, wake up, sweetie," I said once I finished my yawn. "I need to leave, Caliya." She opened her amber-colored eyes sleepily, blinking before focusing on my face.

I laughed as I rubbed her ears, and a familiar rumble shook through her throat in response as she began leaning her head into my hand.

"Don't worry; you don't have to move."

I had been preoccupied with Caliya, and although falling asleep with her doubling as my pillow was a welcome distraction, it still took me away from things I needed to do today. I still had to look over the immense landscape, checking to make sure that it was healthy.

I straightened myself back up, studying the horizon and the turquoise blue sky.

The streams around me were crystal clear with nothing contaminating the water, the golden sun radiating light toward the Earth. The rays of light hit the streams, causing brightness to scatter across the clear, rippling liquid.

I smiled as I looked around at them, and the smile grew wider as I turned my attention to the plants around the edges of the brooks. Plants and life were abundant next to the small rivers. The flowers were bright, healthy, and colorful, while the grass, which covered the hard-packed dirt and soil underneath, was lush and bright green.

Everything around me was truly exquisite, and I had made it that way.

I admired how healthy my surroundings looked when I immediately noticed what appeared to be a dying flower.

I frowned as I watched it, seeing how sick the plant was.

Hmm. That's not how it's supposed to look.

I squinted, studying the blossom before reaching out and touching it, touching the purple, shriveled leaves, and gasped when the plant burst into life. The petals opened up, and it became beautiful and healthy once more.

I smiled at the change.

That's better.

I breathed in deeply, exhaling heavily and pausing for a few moments before glancing at the woods ahead of me. I caught my breath.

What the...?

I squinted, turning my head to the side slightly as I looked at the trees.

Huh?

The foliage, the trees, they appeared to be scorched. Like a wildfire had blazed through the woods, leaving a carcass of the vegetation behind.

I shook my head, puzzled.

The trees' bark looked like it was chipping off, while the other section appeared to be completely charred.

How did that happen? I thought as I took a step closer, my mind in a complete whirlwind.

The leaves and branches that were once a light, lively green were now a gross, brownish-black color. Their stems began to slump over, causing the entirety of the stalks to appear lifeless, dead. The wood on the trunks seemed to be hollow.

Empty and void of life.

Everything looked dead, disgusting, and rotten.

How did this happen?

I blinked, scanning the rest of the forest, and realized that the entire expanse of the woods appeared wholly burned.

I shook my head, confused.

How could this have happened? I was here yesterday *and* today, inspecting everywhere I walked; I made sure every part of the environment was healthy.

How could this have happened?

I glanced down at my tattooed feet, studying the design before an idea dawned on me.

Could it be that I...? Wait a moment.

I hesitantly took a step forward in the grass, looking behind myself afterward.

The greenery with my footprints embedded in it was already beginning to grow back; in the blink of an eye, everything underneath my feet was entirely back to the way it was before. It was as if nothing had touched it in the first place.

I smiled. My hesitation faded immediately.

Okay, so that's a good sign.

My ability still worked; nothing was wrong with my power. I could continue my duty and fix the forest that was now definitely in need of some attention.

I had the power to control and heal nature. I could regenerate plants, mend wildlife injuries, and take command of the weather.

I loved my talent; I'd had it ever since I was a child, and I wasn't the exception in my family. My parents were skilled as well.

They both had extraordinary abilities; my father, Viro, could control all the Elements; Earth, Water, Air, and Fire, while my mother, Thera, could heal anything or anyone she touched. She could also heal herself.

Every time I had a cut or a scrape as a child, she would touch the wound with her hand, sometimes whispering an incantation, and I would watch the injury as it slowly closed up, the pain leaving almost instantaneously.

I'd always envied my parents when I was younger, watching them use their talents. It always amazed me.

I'd watch my father create thunderstorms with his bare hands when the ground was parched and thirsty; I'd watch as he'd throw up his arms, causing the air to suddenly move and whistle, and it would soon be pouring down with rain. Lightning would illuminate the sky while thunder boomed across the landscape.

I would be observant of my mother as she would gently touch something that appeared to be incapacitated. Sometimes, she would cradle it in her arms for a short while before letting it go, any ailment the creature or Being had struggled with before entirely extinct.

It was not long after I turned four that I realized I possessed skills myself; I could bring the tree saplings that had died from lack of water back to life by touching them and also heal an animal's injuries.

There was one animal, in particular, I'd saved as a child. It was a tiny chipmunk with a fractured leg from accidentally falling out of a tree. The poor little one was so terrified, I remember, shaking like a leaf.

That was the first memory I had of myself having the ability to save creatures.

I'd saved the tiny little chipmunk by putting the small animal in my palms, petting its fur softly with my thumb to relax it before placing the rest of my fingers on its leg, holding it firmly but gently, before letting go after a few moments. It had scampered off, easily able to bound away.

My mother had seen what had happened. She had come right into view in the forest after the chipmunk had run away from me. I'd wandered away from her at the time.

She'd talked to me about the chipmunk, asking me questions, and, in a few mornings, the Oracle had returned, fully intending to train me.

Both of my parents knew I was ready for something extraordinary; the Oracle prepared to teach me.

It was when I was four that she had started taking me under her wings.

I shook my head at the memories as they all came back to me, laughing as I remembered them.

I'd certainly had an exciting life so far.

Barefoot as always so my powers would work, I made my way around the terrain in the woods, leaving a fresh growth of greenery behind me.

The tree roots tattooed on my feet sparkled in the sunlight, twinkling as I moved. I brought both hands up from my sides as I walked through the forest, my red chrysanthemum tattoo gleaming as I touched everything within my reach.

A singing bird flew overhead, and I felt a grin spreading over my face as the creature moved gracefully through the trees; it disappeared within a few moments.

I loved the sound of nature, how beautiful it was, and loved the fact I had this gift. The Oracle trusted me with all the responsibilities to take care of the Earth, and I loved it.

A quick movement out of my peripheral vision caught my attention, and I paused, turning to see a brown rabbit moving toward me, its nose sniffing the air nervously as it moved through the leaves covering the forest floor.

"Well, hello," I said as I crouched down to put my hand out to the rabbit. "You can't find a lot of food, can you?"

The rabbit tentatively extended its head out so it could sniff my hand, and it moved closer, becoming comfortable around me.

"There you go, little one," I said as it advanced. "There you go. You can trust me."

The creature was no longer nervous, now it knew I wasn't a threat, and it made its way in my direction, allowing me to pet its fur.

"Aww."

I rubbed the animal gently before picking up the rabbit with my left hand, cradling it in my arms, letting the creature rest while I continued to touch it.

"Aww," I said again, watching as it burrowed itself into the crook of my right elbow, snuggling down to sleep. "You're a cutie. Don't worry; I got you." I pushed myself up to my feet. "I got you."

I continued to walk through the woods, regenerating the foliage as I comforted the creature. I suddenly saw a multi-colored bird nearby, perched on a rock.

It turned its head in my direction, and I grinned as it flew from the rock and landed on my right shoulder.

I laughed; I indeed looked like I could communicate with creatures.

They sensed that they could trust me.

"I love you both." I moved my head toward the bird on my shoulder. Then I looked down at the rabbit in my arms.

You both are too cute.

I smiled as I made my way out of the woods to a meadow nearby; I was still thinking about my childhood. I thought back on the happier times of my existence, lost in my thoughts, when the colorful bird promptly flew off, taking off as fast as it could in the opposite direction.

What the...?

I stopped, and that was when I felt the creature in my arms squirming; the rabbit had woken up and wanted to get out of my arms as fast as possible.

"Okay, okay little one. Here you go." I crouched on my knees to let the animal down.

The rabbit bounded toward the woods as fast as it could.

Once the animal left, I stood there, dumbfounded that both animals that were by my side had gone away around the same time.

What the...?

Then it hit me.

Something was going on here.

Something big.

I turned around, and my feet became rooted in the grass, the smile dissolving from my face.

Worry crept through my brain as I looked ahead at the scorched vegetation. My mood quickly turned anxious.

I fixated on the charred trees and leafless limbs and branches in front of me.

The forest seemed to go on forever, and that wasn't good at all.

I twisted around to see all the work I had done, but instead, I only saw an empty, vacant, lifeless, dead carcass of trees behind me. All the blood drained from my face, and my insides felt like an inferno. I saw everything I had done, yet again, was destroyed.

No. No. No. No. No. No. No.

I turned back and looked at the large, dead cluster that seemed to be eternal.

No. No. No.

I had to figure out what was going on.

And fast.

If only I knew.

If only.

A sharp, piercing shriek abruptly ripped through the once silent sky, causing me to jump out of my reverie.

y eyes darted to the source of the noise as my heart pulverized my chest.

AHHH!!

I instantly stopped walking; my feet rooted to the spot as my head snapped upward. I stared at the sky, immediately attempting to locate the source of the noise.

What was that?

My eyes darted across the upper atmosphere, trying to find whatever caused the sound when the high-pitched interruption became louder and louder. The noise instantly morphed into a booming, thunderous clamor that threatened to shake the ground beneath me. As it got louder, the sky darkened, resembling the atmosphere before a thunderstorm.

What's going on here? I thought as I scanned the sky for the source of the racket. The loud sound engulfed my hearing, threatening to rupture my eardrums as I watched everything.

I finally noticed something in the distance of the sky, falling toward the ground.

It took a few heartbeats to realize it was the cause of the commotion.

It was because of this object tumbling toward the Earth.

It was falling incredibly fast; if my eyelashes would've fluttered and closed, I would've missed the entire thing.

I stared at the sky, fascinated. The loud noise assaulted my ears, and I quickly saw something strange.

Something appearing to be fire streaking across the atmosphere trailed behind the mysterious matter.

The object started lowering to the ground.

It continued to plummet, almost as fast as a hummingbird's wings, and I realized that whatever this object was, it was causing the sky's current setting. As it hurtled toward land, the sky's condition worsened, almost appearing like a gigantic tornado, with massive clouds forming above the object.

I'd never seen anything like this.

The object finally fell out of my view, slamming to the ground with a thunderous boom that almost split my eardrums apart.

I winced as it crashed into the Earth.

It took a few moments before I could move, and when I did, I was instantly light-headed.

"Ahhh," I whistled as I removed my hands away from my head. My breath squeezed through my teeth in a rush. There was still a ringing deep within the canals of my ears, pounding my eardrums.

I shook my head quickly before I stopped; even doing the most basic movement was nauseating.

I stood there in the grass, watching dust fly from where the object had landed. The remains of the dirt rapidly billowed into the sky and became a furious whirlwind.

Darkness draped everything in my view, coating me in a dreary feeling, blocking out the sun.

The healthy, happy emotion radiating from the Earth and the atmosphere had changed to a bad feeling immediately.

It took me several moments of blinking rapidly to realize there was something furry against my arm.

I heard a loud inhale and exhale, followed by a moan that reverberated through my bones.

I looked down to see Caliya beside me; her shoulder blade pressed up against my hand, her ears straight ahead as her amber eyes watched the clouds of sediment past the tips of the forest.

Hello there, sweetheart.

I watched her for a few heartbeats, studying her body language, noticing how focused she was. I wondered if the noise had affected her hearing.

"Caliya? Caliya, sweetie, can you hear me?"

She turned her head as she brought her attention toward me, blinking when she saw me smile.

"Hello, beautiful. I guess you can hear me. That was loud, wasn't it?"

Caliya scanned the woods.

I reached up from my side; my hand began to touch her fur as I looked at her; her eyes fixed on the foggy area above the cluster of trees, her body rigid and muscles tight.

I squinted as an idea popped into my head.

"Caliya?"

She twisted her gigantic, striped head around, looking at me with her amber eyes.

"Will you go ahead of me? Will you go see what happened?"

Her tail twitched, batting the air as she heard my words. She blinked, and I could see her attitude instantly change.

"Go on, Caliya, go look," I said, pointing in the direction of the commotion.

She turned her head, and I could see that she was following where I was pointing, over to where the racket was.

"Go on, girl." I leaned down, petting her head and scratching her ear as she stared ahead. "Go look. I'll be right behind you."

Her gigantic head twisted around toward me again, and I saw her throat tremble as I heard the breathy rumble shake through her muzzle. I laughed as Caliya's eyes fluttered, and she pushed her skull into my chin, her ears pressed against my airway.

"Awww, sweetie." She pushed her body into me. "I'll be alright." I kissed the top of her head and rubbed her ears. "You just have to go see what happened. I'll be alright; just run ahead, okay? Find out what's going on."

Caliya let out another breathy moan as she cuddled up to me but stopped when her eyes fell upon the commotion again. I stopped stroking her fur; I needed her to concentrate.

Caliya rumbled as she began to focus on what was in front of her; a deep throaty noise replaced the affectionate moan, her tail twitching. The sound carried through the air as she called, trying to locate anything in front of her.

Then she took off into the woods, in the direction of the dust cloud rising far into the atmosphere.

"Good girl, Caliya," I whispered as I saw her run off into the woods, her gigantic, striped body moving fluidly through the trees. "Go see what happened."

I watched her graceful frame move quickly through the dead-looking forest; she was quite a distance away from me. She was a fast runner.

Go on now, Caliya.

She probably would be able to find or hear something even I couldn't. After all, she was a tiger, she was a Creature of the Earth, so before I could do anything, I had to trust her, to see what she would or could be able to find.

The Oracle always taught me to trust nature if I ever hesitated about anything or got scared. She always said things would work themselves out; if they needed help, I had to use my abilities to save the Earth.

I heeded her words, but even as I did, it never hurt to use my powers to help nature in any way.

The Oracle was never against it either when I used my powers to heal the planet. She was always glad I was helping nature in any way possible.

That was what I loved about my ability, having the power to help, mend, and protect the Earth and its inhabitants.

Which was why what was happening right now was so frightening to me.

Here I was, a Celestial Being with enchanting abilities, a Protector of the Earth, yet I had no clue what was going on with the very Earth I was supposed to protect.

Calm down, Chrysanthe. Stay calm, and everything will be alright.

I took a deep breath once Caliya was out of my view, trying to steady my rising heart rate as I looked down at the grass. I watched my tattoos for a few moments before taking a step forward.

It's going to be okay. I walked ahead toward the trees.

The atmosphere continued to appear stormy and malicious as I paced rapidly through the meadow, through the long grass and flowers, determined to catch up to Caliya. My dress wavered slightly from the angry breeze that started blowing through the clearing.

I shook my head at the disturbance and continued moving as fast as I could.

I needed to see the extent of the damage, if I could repair anything.

I heard the grass rustling softly in the wind, and I glanced behind me to see that it was growing back as soon as my feet left it. For some reason, though, it was not growing as fast as it should.

I squinted at the greenery behind me, feeling bewildered. By now, I was in a rush to get into the forest, locate Caliya, and see if she possibly found anything, so I turned back around and kept moving.

My mind was still racing as I continued on my way toward the scorched trees.

The tattoos on my bare feet looked darker and gloomier as I advanced toward the deprived woodland area, and I held my breath as I finally entered the forest, stepping into the soil that was covering the ground.

My stomach dropped into my gut when I looked down.

My eyes widened as they followed the designs, which had begun to mutate, morph, and dissolve until they were almost a sickly smear engulfing my flesh.

My heart pounded against my ribcage as I watched my beloved patterns turning, changing into something appearing to look like thorns instead of tree roots. They were sharp, cutting and slicing into my flesh, leaving blood trails on my ankles.

Huh?

I quickly brought my hand up from my side, wanting to see the red chrysanthemum tattoo staring back up at me, but I gasped as I saw the design.

I closed my eyes, unsure if I was still mentally healthy or if I was losing my mind; I breathed rapidly. My entire body trembled as my mind scrambled to put together what my eyes witnessed.

It took several heartbeats to calm my nerves, and after I regulated my breathing, I opened my eyes and took in my left hand.

The blood left my face; I immediately felt bile rise from my stomach, lodging into my windpipe as I took a close look at my chrysanthemum tattoo.

Or, at least, what remained of it.

I was afraid if I continued to breathe, I would burst into tears as I studied the design.

The red chrysanthemum had mutated dramatically, the same way the tattoos on my feet had.

I stood on the soil, completely barefoot and nonplussed, watching the symbol that was now the opposite of what it had been before.

The beautiful, bright red chrysanthemum that had taken up the entirety of the back of my hand was now a deep, almost black purple. The entire flower had shrunk into the middle of my flesh and had shriveled up into nearly a disturbing ball of death. The petals were wilting and falling off.

It looked pitiful, and my heart pounded inside my chest.

The plant tattoo instantly turned; it quickly appeared depressed and hopeless while the stem of the plant looked brown and sickly as if it was rotting on my flesh.

No. No. No. NO.

The stem of the now rotting, dead chrysanthemum twisted around my wrist, slowly looking like it was cutting off the circulation in my hand.

I squinted, completely taken aback, and I observed my fingers; even they had begun to turn purple.

Okay. I was beginning to understand something *massively wrong here,* and I had to figure out what it was.

It dawned on me that it wasn't just my extremities that were turning purple; my entire body was beginning to look sickly since everything else on my skin had already turned.

My anxiety levels rose.

I struggled to breathe as my heart rate climbed; I felt my pulse beating through my skull.

Chrysanthe, it'll be okay. You will be alright.

I tried to slow my heart rate as I took in my new surroundings, trying to get a grip on what was around me as I trembled. At any moment, I felt like I was about to have a mental breakdown. For a Fantastical Being like me, that was almost impossible.

My body shook as I nervously glanced around, getting my bearings in this strange, dead place.

I gulped as I noticed my surroundings.

The dead trees around the area were completely rotten, some of them cracked and split in places, the bark completely stripped from the trunks. Every section of them was disgusting, with a sickening smell; the soil even had an overwhelming odor, almost like it had decaying matter mixed into it.

Ugh.

My nose wrinkled at the awful, unnatural scent.

There seemed to be no end to the woods as I looked ahead, in the distance of the dead forest, the eerie rotting place that was going on for eternity.

I shivered as I hesitantly glanced at my feet, looking at my morphed, sickly tattoos, and sucked in a breath as I tried to get my bearings. My insides froze, the blood draining from my face as I saw nothing growing where I stood. No leaves or foliage were beneath my feet.

It stayed infertile, arid, and deserted.

No. No. No. No. NO.

Something was *very* wrong here.

My abilities didn't work in this place; nothing could affect these woods, which was a problem.

This entire forest was like a graveyard.

Well, no.

It *was* a graveyard; everything here, everything I was surrounded by, was dead or dying, splintered or decaying.

Nothing was uplifting. Everything was debilitating about this particular area.

If only I could figure out the reason why.

A rumble echoed through the trees, breaking me from my thoughts; I shook my head slightly before twisting around, attempting to locate it.

Hey, Caliya.

I smiled as the noise echoed through the dead forest, floating through the air as the wind carried it. I looked up at the sky, finally locating the path where Caliya was from the debris that was polluting it.

That would be the easy way to find her. Just follow the cloud of sediment in the atmosphere.

Come on, girl, keep making noise, I thought as I began trudging through the disgusting soil, through the rotting, decomposing material. *Help me out here, sweetie.* I had to go down the path toward the sediment cloud, and then I would be able to see Caliya and find out if she found anything.

I was going to follow nature as the Oracle taught me.

I ducked beneath the low hanging branches and split twigs as I kept my eyes fixed on the atmospheric disturbance, Caliya's calls still shaking through the forest.

She was not far away. I could hear her; she was very close.

I stepped over a hollow log as Caliya continued to rumble, the sound shaking through the dead air, and that was when I paused to listen.

She was not far from me.

I looked at the fog that had now begun to engulf the barren forest, hanging over my head.

Where are you, Caliya? I wondered as I squinted, peering through the fog, trying my hardest to see in front of me. It had now become difficult to view anything; the clouds had dropped way below the trees, preventing me from seeing even my bare feet.

Now I knew there was something weird going on.

Something was wrong.

Get out, Chrysanthe, I said mentally as my body slowly began to feel damp; I was starting to feel like I was overheating from the inside. *Come on, get out of here. Get out. Get out. Get out.*

The miserable, gray clouds had completely taken over the entirety of my surroundings, making me feel instantly trapped, claustrophobic.

I scanned the area, instantly confused, and my head darted from left to right, attempting to find the path I'd been following.

Come on, Caliya. Where are you?

I stumbled blindly through the trees, unaware of where I was going when a loud huff of oxygen resounded to my right.

I stopped moving, freezing in my tracks as I squinted through the fog, now sure I had found her.

"Caliya?"

That familiar, breathy moan echoed through the air.

"Hey there, sweetie." I stuck my hand out, trying to see if I would be able to make my way through the low hanging clouds.

The dying purple chrysanthemum design smeared on my wrist as I kept my extremity out in front of me, the stem of the plant tattoo wrapping around it in an unsettling fashion, tightening around my flesh.

I felt my insides squirm as I saw the tattoo; my nervousness made me almost hit my breaking point when I heard Caliya moan again.

"Caliya, honey, I'm right here," I said as I finally made my way out of the dreary fog. I moved my hand back to my side as the low clouds disappeared, revealing the strange, disturbing forest once more. "I'm here, sweetie. I'm right..."

My words cut off in a gasp as my breath got trapped in my throat; I instantly felt as if lightning had struck me. I froze, completely unaware of what to do as I blinked, my eyelids fluttering as I took in what was in front of me.

Caliya was lying on the dirt, her mouth open as she breathed, her gigantic body sprawled out on the messy soil as her chest rose and fell.

Caliya had raked the dirt with her claws; she'd thrown it around with her muscles.

Huh?

She'd exerted herself since she was breathing so hard, and now she was exhausted.

But the fact she had overexerted herself wasn't the reason why I had stopped dead in my tracks as soon as I saw her.

It was because of what was beside her, clinging to her fur like a lifeline, grabbing her massive body to prevent falling back into the hole a little bit away from where Caliya was.

What the...?

It looked like an antelope or some other prey beside her chest as she lay there.

Utterly smothered in the dirt, filthy beyond belief, but as I started to look closer, I shook my head.

That would *never* happen. It wasn't like Caliya to show me what she was going to eat.

Something else was going on.

What is this, sweetheart? I thought questioningly, my brain not processing what was happening.

Wait.

It took me a few heartbeats to study what was going on, to understand what was in front of me.

Wait. What?

27

Dirt smeared across Caliya's fur as she huffed, air rushing into her lungs, and that was when I saw the grimy, soil-encrusted hand brushing against her body.

What the...?

My thoughts were whirling as I stared at what was in front of me, unsure of what was happening. It took several moments to realize what was beside Caliya, and when it did register, I gasped.

The hand with a firm grip on Caliya's body hit the soil next to her left paw, and I saw a disheveled, pathetic-looking face covered in filth staring at me, his dark brown eyes conveying complete defeat.

His body covered head to toe with sediment, his hair encrusted with dirt, with his eyes a deep, muddy, murky color.

But his attitude instantly changed as soon as he saw me; I could almost see the sparkle immediately appear in his eyes as they connected with mine.

The eyes were a deep, dirty brown but so familiar.

He blinked several times once he saw me, almost as if he couldn't believe I was real.

"Chrysanthe?" he rasped.

"**C**hrysanthe, is that you?"

I stared at him, completely caught off guard, my eyes still fluttering strangely.

"Chrysanthe, it's me." His voice sounded as if he had dragged his vocal cords across sharp rocks; they were so damaged.

I winced at the noise, at the pain he must've been feeling.

His dark brown eyes followed me as he attempted to bring himself up to a sitting position, dirt falling off his filthy body. "It's me," he repeated as if I couldn't understand him. "It's Celio."

WHAT? I screamed in my thoughts. I heard what he said, my brain seemingly transforming into mush as I struggled to contemplate what was happening.

Air soared through my lungs as I gasped, and I could see a tiny hint of a smile on his face.

"CELIO?" I said, taken aback. I scanned his body, which was now propped up in a sitting position on Caliya, looking at him from head to toe, but there was nothing distinct about him. His frame was utterly unrecognizable.

He was caked in filth, miserable, almost unnaturally, skinny, while he looked defeated.

And his eyes had changed color; now they were a disgusting, sickly brown.

Well, and most of all, he didn't have his most beloved, valuable possession. At least I couldn't see them anywhere.

I wondered if they still worked.

Without that and everything else, it all made him look incredibly weak, feeble.

Which I knew Celio wasn't.

"What the...? How did...?" I started but then switched to another question as I saw how messy he was. "What happened to you? How did this...?" Again, I trailed off, not able to finish.

I couldn't help but take a step toward him. My eyebrows raised in bewilderment.

Celio attempted a faint, shy smile, but it looked more like a grimace as he met my eyes. I felt my eyes soften as I looked into his.

Oh, Celio.

He took a deep breath before carefully exhaling; it was apparent he was hurting.

He gulped before he began talking, and even then, I could tell that was agonizing for him. "Well, I don't know exactly," he started, his voice still incredibly rough, his mud-colored eyes watching mine; I winced hearing how raspy and painful his voice was.

"I was just... guarding the Afterworld," he said carefully, in between breaths. "I was doing what... what Viro had commanded me to do long, long ago, and then... I don't know what happened. Something pulled me...," he cut off his sentence with a sharp gasp, and my eyes widened in worry as he stroked his arm, looking at it.

An extended cut across the top of his shoulder was spreading to his wrist, leaving a nasty bloody mark. He looked away, "...but something yanked me here; I crashed to Earth," he said, looking at me. "Once I crashed, I was trapped in the dirt. Well, until your trusty friend found me."

Celio grinned at the same time I did, lifting his dirty hand to thump it against Caliya's massive chest; I heard the friendly, breathy moan from her as she pushed her head into his palm, and he laughed weakly.

"Yeah," I said, smiling as she rubbed her skull on his chin, moaning sweetly. "She was here to save you."

It didn't take long, though, before my grin faded. My partly upbeat attitude quickly evaporated, becoming replaced by dread. And worry. It all hit me with the force of a hurricane.

Celio. It was Celio who had fallen from the sky.

Celio, the Protector of the Afterworld, had been thrown out. He had been given the position by my father, Viro, the Protector of Natural Elements. Celio had been thrown out of the atmosphere by an unknown force.

Like me, he was a Supernatural Being, but he was no longer in the area he was supposed to protect.

It was more like he had gotten torn out rather than thrown out; the World Beyond, the Afterworld, was more than a home to Celio. It was his whole being; it was who and what he was; it was everything to him. The same way Earth defined me. We were a part of the Realm or place we protected.

It made this whole predicament so heartbreaking.

I sniffled, blinking as it all suddenly hit me.

The fire that had trailed his falling form, the speed at which he had been descending. The *overwhelming* cacophony of noise when he was hurtling toward the Earth and when he crashed.

He had gotten forced out.

As I watched Celio absentmindedly, it all made sense as I watched him scratch Caliya's chin, play with her tail.

Celio didn't fall. He had gotten ripped out of the Afterworld. Out of the Realm that he protected.

Celio. The powerful Being I'd fallen for long ago, who had been my love many seasons back. He now looked drastically different, sickly, and skinny.

Celio.

He looked too unnatural, unhealthy, drenched with filth. Usually, he appeared so muscular and robust.

At least, he looked that way the last time I'd seen him before he became the Guardian of the Spirits.

I glanced at his severely emaciated form.

The worst thing, though, was that Celio didn't have his most valued possession.

The possession he loved and cherished; they were nowhere.

The thing that had also helped me fall in love with him long ago.

"Chrysanthe?" he rasped, his playful manner disappearing as he saw my expression, but I shook my head in response, my eyes already filling with tears.

"Where are...?" I began but then was cut off by a sob as he looked at me.

What had happened to him?

Celio swallowed, staring at me for a few heartbeats, squinting, seemingly knowing what I was going to ask, but he stopped before he could say anything.

I ran over to him and wrapped my arms around his body, embracing him in a hug.

Caliya huffed, a loud exhale that moved through her body as I walked up to Celio; he was still leaning against the tiger, and I felt her rub her head against my back as I wrapped my arms around him.

Tears ran down my cheeks as I embraced him, holding him tighter as my nervousness ultimately got a hold of me.

Oh, Celio.

I pressed up against him so much I felt his chest move against mine as he inhaled, ready to speak, but again, I cut him off.

"No," I said, my voice clear as I spoke into his ear. "No, don't. Don't strain yourself. Don't talk. Can you stand up? Where exactly are you hurt? Just point. I don't want you damaging your vocal cords now, too."

Celio nodded as I placed one hand around his hip while I put the other one under his arm, positioning myself so I could help him up.

Celio still had his back up against Caliya, and my arms grazed her striped bulk as I managed to get a good grip on him.

As soon as I could get him to his feet, I could quickly heal him. That wouldn't be an issue.

"Caliya?" I whispered.

Her ears twitched as she turned her head, looking at me.

"Caliya, help me here, sweetie. Push him up for me."

She huffed as she moved her front paws behind Celio before placing her skull behind his body. I kept Celio's frame steady, and I pulled his body simultaneously as the tigress pushed him.

Come on, Caliya.

Caliya's rumble shook through the ground as her head pushed against Celio's back and continued as she slowly got to her feet.

I smiled faintly at Caliya as I brought Celio upright, watching the tigress take her snout off his back as soon as I could stand with him.

"Thank you," I whispered. "You're stronger than I will ever be," I said, managing to move my hands around Celio's frame without losing my grip on him.

Breathing heavily as I moved Celio completely upright, my arms screamed from the effort. I held Celio tighter so he wouldn't fall over. I gasped from the strain but ignored the aching of my body.

Celio needed me. The pain didn't matter right now.

I felt something press up against my legs; I glanced down at the ground to see Caliya right below me, her amber-colored eyes steady and focused as I held Celio in my arms.

"Hey, Caliya," I said, my voice tight from the strain of my muscles. "Thank you, honey."

Caliya exhaled, and I felt the air exiting her muzzle hit my legs as she stood beside me. I noticed her watching Celio when I glanced down at her, and I smiled.

"Don't worry, honey." I looked back up at Celio for a few moments; he just stared at me with a look of utter astonishment, his expression full of wonder. "Celio will be fine."

His expression morphed quickly, and I couldn't help but smile. I still loved him.

I grinned back when I abruptly realized that I was feeling lighter.

What?

The heaviness, the aching of my muscles, was fading away, making me feel as light as a feather.

I shook my head, not understanding before I looked at Celio's face, and I gasped, astonished.

The color in his eyes was returning — the muddy, dirty, sickly tone slowly turning into a hazel hue. The filth covering his face and body slowly began to recede, revealing his peach-colored skin. It disappeared without a trace.

Wow.

The soreness of my frame was leaving, and as I took in what was going on with Celio, I realized it was because he was becoming healthier.

All of this was happening because I was touching him.

34

Within moments, he was completely clean; dirt and sediment got erased from his flesh as he stood on his own, straightening himself up, now able to stabilize himself without my help.

"Easy, Celio. Take it easy…"

Celio smiled, and I inhaled quickly at the powerful gaze he gave me; it wasn't long before I found myself staring at him wonderingly. However, the expression switched to a grimace when I saw the extended cut ripped deeply into his arm.

It stretched from his shoulder to his elbow, tearing his skin apart and leaving a long, thick trail of blood in its wake.

Ugh. My skin crawled, but I abruptly shook my head when Celio saw my reaction.

Alright, I thought as I looked at the gash. *I have to fix you up.*

I paused, looking up at Celio's throat for a moment.

Wait.

I saw Celio watching me from my peripheral vision as I slowly brought my hands up to his neck. I got taken aback momentarily, though, as I saw the tattoo on the back of my hand changing again; it was radiant and flowery as my fingers spread around Celio's throat.

I slowly moved my fingertips along his neck, being gentle, so I didn't accidentally hurt him.

There was a sensation of heat as my ability worked, and then there was an abrupt cooling one as Celio's throat healed entirely within a heartbeat.

I paused.

"How's your throat feel now?"

"Fantastic," he said in his natural, healthy voice.

"Good."

I slowly took my hands off his neck and turned my attention to his wounded arm, repeating my actions.

There was another feeling of heat radiating from my palms as I gently moved my hands along his body over his torn shoulder, moving to his elbow.

My fingertips moved slowly and methodically over the wound as I took in the severity of it.

I was relieved to see that as soon as my hands had touched his flesh, his skin started repairing itself, his muscle tissue and his outer layer of skin had become a suture; his body was sewing itself closed.

The cooling sensation signaled the aid was a success. I reached Celio's elbow, and I squinted, focused on repairing him.

As I moved behind Celio, I couldn't hide my horror at his back. It was mangled and covered in dried, congealed blood. *Celio, you poor thing. What happened to you?*

"I know," he said as he heard my gasp. "It feels pretty bad too."

Pretty bad. Well, that was a *colossal* understatement.

Celio's back looked like a slab of raw meat. It reminded me of when Caliya was young and learning to hunt. She would bring down prey, and marks and bites would cover them.

Celio's flesh unfortunately mirrored the appearance of Caliya's dinner before she ate it.

A mixture between a sob and a gag caused my throat to tighten, but I swallowed the lump lodged in my throat, taking a deep breath.

The wounds looked horrible and disgusting, and all of them were bleeding profusely.

"Isn't that... Isn't that excruciating?" I asked, dumbstruck.

"It is," he said. "But it's not as bad now that I've gotten healed a bit. They were unbearable before when I was tumbling toward Earth. I think I got marked up because I was falling out of the Afterworld, out of the World Beyond. The fact I fell out of my Realm caused everything to go wrong, and I..."

It was the Mark. The Mark told Celestial individuals they had failed their responsibility. There were situations where some Gifted Beings would lose their abilities if they failed in their tasks. They had gotten punished if they weren't doing tasks correctly.

There were multiple reasons for a Mark and numerous variations of them.

Sometimes they were scrapes and cuts, other times they were burns. The Marks sometimes were even outlines; the Fate Tattoos' remains torn from the Being's flesh.

I'd never actually seen a Gifted individual with a stripped tattoo mark, but the Oracle long ago told me about them when I was a child, and I knew what Celio was thinking.

"I can't... I can't move them," Celio said. "I got thrown out, and I can't move them. I tried, Chrysanthe, but it's so unbearable. I don't know what's going on, and I don't know what's happening with anything. Do you know?" he asked, his voice almost hitting a pleading tone. "What is happening here?"

I wish I knew.

"That's what's going through my head too, Celio. The main thing, though, is that you're still alive. I've found you and healed you for the most part. I'm going to see what I can do to heal your back. Right now, I need you to relax, okay? Let me see what I can do."

I closed my eyes, inhaling deeply and letting all the air out of my lungs before focusing on Celio's flesh.

It didn't take me long to clean up the majority of Celio's wounds. I repeated the same thing I'd done for both his arms and his neck, and I saw the blood and disturbing looking gashes disappear under my fingertips as I moved them along his flesh.

His blood smeared over my fingertips as I touched his body and then soon vanished.

I finally was able to see the gargantuan tattoo adorning his skin.

Black, defined eagle-like wings were over his flesh, the individual feathers looking incredibly detailed as the magical patterns took over his entire back. Part of the wings even stretched around his body to his ribs.

Beautiful, unique, and gigantic.

I grinned when I saw them.

This is what defined Celio.

"Hello." I took the wings in, admiring how stunning they were.

Celio laughed.

"You'll never get over those, will you?"

I shook my head, mesmerized.

"No, I never will."

I looked at the wings more critically; they had gotten clumped together, crushed over Celio's flesh. I frowned. The edges appeared to have escaped along his ribcage.

I am going to have to fix them.

The tattoo had gotten buried beneath cuts deep in his flesh; I knew by looking at them that they would take more time to heal than the other injuries since they were covering something *vastly* important.

I had to get to work.

But firstly.

"I need you to try to move them for me," I said as I looked at his tattoo, transfixed by it. "I *need* you to try."

"What?" Celio asked, bewildered.

"I need you to try to move them; I won't know what to fix until I see them." I watched the detailed, beautiful, midnight-colored tattoos. "Try to use them."

"I... I don't think I'll be able to."

"Just try, Celio. Please. I have to see what I'm working with."

"O...okay," he said hesitantly, nervously, and I saw him shiver as he closed his eyes tightly, focusing. I could tell by his tone that he was worried about anything regarding his Fate Tattoo.

He didn't want to lose them. He loved his ability. He would never want to lose it by doing anything to his Fate Tattoo that could strip him entirely of his power.

But Celio sighed, closing his eyes before using every ounce of energy into moving the ink.

There was a reason why the pitch black, eagle-type wings were so lifelike.

It was because they were.

Celio was a Protector of the Afterworld, the Guardian of the Spirits. Also, because of all of this, he was an Archangel.

5

I exhaled deeply, breathing out as my stomach tightened, my muscles clenching as I looked at the Archangel wings in front of me.

Come on, Celio. Just try this. I watched his back, looking at the detailed, black-feathered appendages tattooed on his flesh. *Come on.*

Celio slowly flexed his muscles, pushing them, and I began to see his wings bulge from his skin; the tattoo was starting to come out. Ink erupted, breaking through him.

Come on, Celio. Make this work.

The tattoo, though, as I'd thought, refused to break through his skin completely; the deep cuts were on him, on the wings inked onto his back.

It caused a weird motion once the appendages had begun to leave his skin as they snapped back into place.

They stopped a short while after they began; the wings created a strange lump beneath his flesh before entirely sinking back, the ink of Celio's Fate Tattoo settling back into his skin.

He exhaled loudly, frustrated.

"I can't... I can't...," Celio started, but I cut him off.

"You tried, Celio, and that's all that matters. Now that I know what's going on, let me try to fix you," I reassured him. "You'll be okay, I promise."

I pursed my lips and concentrated on the ink design.

"Just relax." I calmly placed my hands on his wounded back and quickly noticed that my chrysanthemum tattoo had begun to glow and sparkle when it touched Celio's Archangel wings.

I felt him shudder at my touch as I opened my palm completely, spreading my fingers wholly over his inked skin. I began to see the deep cuts vanish as his skin sewed itself back together.

His Archangel wings began to glow, the ink shining as the wounds disappeared.

I saw his flesh become clean, but, to my utter astonishment, that was when I began to see his body change, his muscles morphing.

Huh? My eyes darted from side to side, looking at him, watching as his physicality switched.

I watched, amazed, as Celio's flesh bulged, his skin distending. His body was changing as he stood there, his back to me.

What the...?

I stood there, breathless, as Celio's new muscle snaked through him. I was left speechless, and then, within a few moments, the process was complete.

I gawked at Celio's newly defined body. I couldn't believe what I was seeing; it was incredible.

The wings now covered his flesh, portions of them no longer twisting to the front of his body since he wasn't emaciated anymore.

His strength had returned, and the tattoo now covered his entire back.

The dark, torn fabric covering the lower half of his frame twisted around his hips, slowly repairing itself as Celio rolled his shoulders forward.

He straightened himself up, watching the sky.

I wanted — needed — to see what he was going to do.

I stepped backward on the grass, focusing on Celio, watching what he was doing. I inhaled sharply and gasped as I took it in.

Celio began to chuckle when he heard me, but I couldn't help it.

What was happening was breathtaking.

The eagle-like Archangel design was coming out of Celio's flesh, the ink morphing into actual wings. They slowly broke free as his back muscles flexed.

The wings were midnight black, feathered, and beautiful as they broke through his flesh. I was rooted to the spot in shock when I saw them in all their glory.

The wingspan was enormous, taking over the majority of the area behind Celio. The feathers flapped and kicked up dust as I stared, taking in how big they were before I couldn't help myself; I reached out and touched a feathered portion of one of the enormous wings.

"Celio…"

I heard him chuckle, and his body shook with laughter as I grinned; I realized my chrysanthemum tattoo was brightening.

I abruptly saw a small burst of light hit the ground then, from my tattoo, and we both paused.

The small light morphed into radiance as it hit the ground, and I gasped; the light bloomed across the land, bursting into greenery, transforming the entire place into a giant plethora of vegetation.

A smile took up my entire face as I saw the fantastic greenery.

It was us, both Celio and I. We were causing the grass to burst into life. It was because of both of our powers combined.

"Celio? Do you see this? Do you know what's happening here?"

He chuckled, and I felt his wings flutter as he looked at our now healthy, lush surroundings.

"Oh, wow. That's amazing. I wonder who did that," Celio said, a smile evident in his tone.

"We both did. It's our combined powers." I removed my fingers from the feathers, the gigantic appendages pulling in and up over my head. I giggled as the feathers grazed and tickled my cheeks; Celio brought his shoulders up, rotating them up to his ears, all while the massive wings arched up toward the sky.

He took a deep breath before turning around, looking at me steadily as I stood there, transfixed. I blinked as I took everything in.

Celio chuckled at my dazed expression.

"Chrysanthe?" he laughed, "are you there?"

I shook my head, coming back to the present. "Yeah, I mean, yes." I met his gaze that was suddenly so strong.

My heart started to pound against my chest, threatening to break my ribs.

He took a step closer, and I felt his breath soak my face as my heart raced; Celio blinked as he took in my features, his body within touching distance and his face inches from mine.

"I forgot how beautiful you are," he said softly, and I saw his gaze shift toward my eyes. I knew he was looking at the multi-colored peacock feathers adorning my flesh. "You've always been so unique and colorful," he added, the last portion of his sentence a whisper. "You do look like you are permanently a wild animal," he said, smiling.

I laughed, shaking my head slightly. "Thank you," I said. "You know, you permanently look like an angel." I winked playfully and brought my fingertips to his cheek, stroking it.

His demeanor instantly changed; his eyelashes fluttered under my touch while his eyes slowly closed. Celio watched me as he opened his eyes again, his face close to mine, his gaze seeming to burn through my soul.

Celio, I thought as he brought his hands up to my face, his fingers grazing my cheeks. He closed the gap between us and kissed me.

Goosebumps rose on my flesh as he did so, and I could feel my face burning up as his mouth began to move with mine. I couldn't resist him as I kissed him back, and I heard the rumble resonate in his throat.

Hmmm.

Celio's lips moved with mine as our breathing became intertwined; my heart pounded against my ribs, wishing this could last forever.

He took my face in his hands, and his fingers brushed through my braid before he moved one of his palms to my back, pulling me closer to him.

Celio.

I felt his wings brush against me; the vast feathers tickled my flesh as he embraced me.

I shivered and felt him brush my cheek with his fingertips, causing the shiver to flutter down my spine.

Celio, I love you.

I pulled my mouth from Celio's slightly, only to bite his bottom lip gently. His breath saturated my face as he kissed me again.

I didn't sense anything besides my insides becoming liquefied and my face heating up to the point where I thought it was going to burst into flames.

I brought my hands up from my sides, settling them on his broad chest, my lips breaking away from his again so I could breathe. I opened my eyes to see him looking down at me, an intense expression on his face as a tiny hint of a smile showed up on his lips.

Celio, I love you so much.

I took another breath before kissing him again softly and wrapped my arms around him, resting my head on his chest, so his heartbeat was right by my ear. I felt it rise and fall as he breathed.

Celio's hand brushed against my back as I hugged him, and I closed my eyes, mesmerized by the sound of his pounding heart and the smell of his skin.

A smile formed on my lips as I pulled Celio close to me, feeling as light as a feather as I heard his steady heartbeat.

I sighed; I was finally relaxed.

A blood curdling, gut-wrenching screech quickly ripped through the silence, causing my heart to almost tear through my chest.

"Please, please, no!"

I blinked, taken aback as my heart palpitated.

"Please, no! I love them; these are all of my existence. Please don't do anything to them!"

What?

My thoughts got cut short, though, as I heard the female screech; I clutched Celio tight.

"Please, not my ink! Not my Fate Tatt-!"

I didn't have much time to try to piece together what I had heard before a hair-raising shriek erupted again. I cringed a second time as my heart dropped to my stomach; Celio's arms tightened around me.

"NO! PLEASE, NOT MY WINGS!"

I gasped at the same time I felt Celio's body stiffen and his muscles tighten. I looked at him, only to see him turn away, so I couldn't see his expression.

"NO! PLEASE!"

Celio's body was now completely rigid, and I pulled away from him as my eyes watered, but he clutched me tighter so that our chests touched.

"No," he whispered into my ear. "Don't move."

"NO! PLEASE! PLEA-!"

But then there was an immediate bone crunching *crack*, and the female voice stopped.

"Celio?" I asked as I pulled away, removing my hands and looking at him. "Celio?"

He twisted away from me; his face was unreadable. But then a single tear ran down his right cheek, and I felt my heart sink.

Oh, Celio, I thought as he closed his eyes.

I reached up and wiped the tear away with my fingertip. "I'm so sorry," I said, gliding my fingers across Celio's face. "Did you know her well?"

He opened his eyes slowly and nodded, studying my features. His hazel eyes resembled liquid gold as we looked at each other. I held my breath as he answered me.

"Yes. Yes, I did, Chrysanthe." But then he was cut off by a choke of sobs building inside him.

He looked at the ground.

He sniffed before composing himself. "If only we could find the Being responsible for this—"

"Celio, that individual could be a long way away from here by now, and—"

"Help." A desperate, breathy, barely audible cry suddenly traveled through the clearing, cutting off my words.

Celio and I froze, looking at each other in utter shock when another plea made it to our ears. "Someone, please, help me."

The Archangel was wounded. Badly. I thought I'd seen the worst of it before when I'd healed Celio, but I was *very* wrong.

I'd never seen anything like this before; it made my heart pound against my ribs and my intestines writhe in knots.

Her enormous black wings had gotten wholly ripped from her body, blood streaming down her back where the tattoo previously was. It stained the pure, healthy vegetation covering the green grass underneath her crimson, and her wings were now bloody stumps.

Black and blue marks adorned her body, with large red patterns around her neck and ankles.

What happened here? I thought as I took in her appearance before wincing; I knew she was unhealable and that she would — and could — never recover.

I felt Celio stiffen beside me as he noticed the wounds and bruises on the dying Archangel. I heard a growl begin to rumble in his throat.

I took a few steps closer toward the Archangel, and then I saw her skin tone.

Her flesh, along with the black, blue, and red marks, appeared to be yellow and green, as if it was rotting.

There was so much going on with her. She had gotten so wounded; she didn't even seem to sense that anyone was there to help her. But we still approached in hopes of aiding her.

As I reached out and touched her hair, she gasped and opened her eyes wide.

Her brown eyes darted around before settling on both Celio and I. She looked at both of us, and her eyes narrowed.

"Celio? Chrysanthe?" she rasped.

I jumped at the sound of my name, astonished she knew it, but her eyes continued to dart between us.

Celio didn't seem as baffled as I was, but he did seem taken aback that she just kept looking between us.

"You both are who I needed to see," she started again. "But you must leave as soon as I finish talking to you both."

Celio and I shook our heads, not understanding, but then the Archangel rasped, "I can tell you the truth."

The truth? About what?

"What are you talking about?" I asked, bewildered.

I took a glance over at Celio, but he looked back at me, confused. Could we trust the dying Archangel's words?

"About everything," she said, her voice hoarse since she was so weak. "I'm talking about everything. I can tell you exactly what happened to me as well. I can tell you who did this to me."

"Okay," I responded. The Archangel sucked in a quick breath as the pain overwhelmed her, and I maneuvered my hands under her head, trying to calm her down. Her sweat pooled around her hairline as I stroked it, her flesh hot and sticky.

I didn't care about my beautiful green and blue dress becoming soaked with the Archangel's blood.

"Who did this to you?" Celio asked, finally able to form a question. "Who took...," Celio paused as he gulped, "your wings from you?"

The Archangel sighed heavily, and I could see that the color was leaving her face.

She stared as I brushed her hairline softly. I peered down to see a fresh wave of tears overcoming her features. It took her a few moments to calm down, but she continued to stare at Celio when she did.

"She calls herself the…. the Phantom," she breathed the words out painfully.

My heart sank, and I was finding it hard to keep my emotions in check.

"The Phantom?" Celio repeated. "Okay, well, that's a start," he glanced over at me before continuing. "What else do you know about her?"

"She's the reason why you're here, Celio, and not in the Heavens anymore. She traveled to Earth by trapping another Archangel in Hell, using his blood to use a spell, enabling her to go across the Realms, but only once. She's the one who threw you out of your Realm." I felt all the blood leave my face.

Celio gritted his teeth, suddenly enraged.

"She wants every Being out of their Realms, so they're weak," the Archangel continued, "and then she… she… rips their tattoos out as she did with… with me. It was just a bonus that my tattoo was already extended out into my wings when she broke them off."

Both Celio and I winced, and I felt my body freeze up as the sound of her screech resounded in my memory. Celio's face hardened and contorted with anger.

"Celio…" I started, reaching my hand out to calm him, but I pulled it back when I realized it had gotten soaked in blood. "Celio, this is a good thing; now we know what's happening. Wait…"

I stopped talking, thinking.

If the individual who harmed the Archangel also took Celio out of his Realm, that meant that she wanted to hurt me as well.

The Phantom.

This Phantom was the reason why all the trees looked dark, dead, and charred. It had been all *her* doing.

Celio glared as it hit him as well, and I watched his wings bristle in agitation.

"We have to stop her," he said, his features hard against his face.

I knew he was upset, as was I, but I quickly interrupted him.

"It won't be easy, Celio." I looked at his stiff expression. "She's stronger than you are, than both of us combined; how are we going to defeat her?"

"You're going to have... to... trust what... I say," the Archangel said before any word could come out of Celio's mouth.

"You're going to help us?"

"All you... you are going to have to do is-"

She started coughing. I tried straightening her up so she wasn't lying down, but it was fruitless; she continued to cough heavily.

It was at that moment I truly knew; the Archangel was dying before my eyes.

She stopped coughing enough to finish her sentence in a hoarse whisper.

"Just... just follow... the... the... outline, and you can save everyone."

I shook my head, immediately confused.

The outline? What outline? And to save everyone? What did she mean?

"What?" I asked, gazing into her now dimming, darkening eyes.

"Follow the outline," the Archangel whispered again. "You have to save them," she murmured.

She inhaled slowly, exhaling in a broken, uneven manner.

"Take care of them," she said before taking her last breath.

Her eyes became still, and her hands fell to her sides.

She was gone.

The Phantom.

I looked at Celio, feeling baffled.

The Phantom was the reason everything had seemingly gone wrong. The trees, the Earth, and the fact that Celio had fallen out of the sky. And now, to make things worse, there was this, an Archangel's death.

The only good thing about the situation was that we both finally discovered *who* was doing this damage. We just had to figure out *how* to defeat the Phantom.

My mind roamed to what the Archangel told me, and that was when it began to whirl.

What exactly was going on here?

Celio broke me out of my thoughts as he leaned over me, brushing the Archangel's hairline with his fingertips, gently pushing her hair back behind her ears, closing her now still eyes.

"Chrysanthe," he said, "we can't leave her here. I have to make sure she goes to the Realm of the Souls; if not, she'll go to the Abyss and live in eternal damnation, and we don't want that."

I nodded before taking my hand off her forehead.

"Okay," I said, slowly beginning to stand, letting Celio grasp her shoulders and pull the Archangel up so I could get to my feet. I had tucked my legs underneath her body.

When I was on my feet, I realized the Archangel's blood was all over me.

My dress was a mess, while my arms and hands were soaked in bodily fluid, making me look like I was part of a massacre. It was a disturbing look.

I glanced behind me to look at Celio, watching as he slowly got on one knee, his head bowed low. He muttered an incantation; I couldn't make out what he was saying, but I knew they were the words that would carry the Archangel to the Realm of the Souls, to the Afterworld, where she would be forever.

She would be where she belonged.

A few moments later, her body evaporated, turning into dust before completely disappearing, and I knew then that she was now in the World Beyond.

Wait.

I walked toward Celio.

"Celio?"

He turned his attention to me in response.

"What did you mean by that?"

"About what?"

"About her living in the Abyss. About eternal damnation."

"Chrysanthe, if she doesn't go into the Afterworld, she goes into the Abyss. Thankfully, she's not going to go to the Abyss, so that's good, despite being touched by this Phantom..."

He paused, and I saw it coming together inside his head at the same time as me.

"The Phantom," we said together.

As the Phantom was the reason for all the damage in this Realm and Celio's, as well as the Archangel risking eternal damnation, that could only mean one thing: that this Phantom wasn't just anyone, she was the Queen of the Abyss.

Blood drained from my face as the realization hit me. My insides felt like they were burning, and sweat poured down my face. My breathing became uneven, and I realized I could barely see Celio, even though he was right in front of me.

I suddenly couldn't see him as I slowly began to lose my grip on reality.

"Chrysanthe?"

I could barely understand my name; it started to sound garbled and jumbled.

"Chrysanthe?" Celio said again.

But I couldn't respond as the land around me spun, making me feel queasy before I lost my grasp entirely on everything and plunged into darkness.

The warm feeling of fingers brushing my cheek and a breeze kissing my face caused my eyes to open, a voice slowly swimming into my consciousness.

"Chrysanthe?"

My eyelashes fluttered at the tone; it instantly calmed me. It was a kind, female voice; kind, and yet so familiar.

"Chrysanthe? Sweetheart, are you awake?"

Yes, I thought as I took a deep breath and exhaled. Then I took in my surroundings.

I quickly attempted to scramble.

I was on a cliff, my body tucked into an opening in the rock face. I blinked as I realized I was pretty close to the sky; thick clouds almost obstructed the bright sun that was softly cutting through the rock opening.

How did I get here?

It took a few moments to get my bearings before I realized I had been asleep. I didn't know for how long, but what I did know was that my head was in someone's lap.

Not just someone.

I knew this female.

"Chrysanthe, honey, wake up."

I slowly looked upward, being patient so I wouldn't get startled.

I jumped, though, when I saw her.

My mother.

She gazed down at me; her bright blue eyes and long brown hair shimmered in the sunlight.

"Hello, honey." She grinned down at me, her beautiful smile radiating the air around us.

I straightened myself so I could look at her.

"How... how are you...?" But I couldn't finish the sentence as my words got choked.

My mother had been gone for the past four seasons, along with my father. They'd both left to the Afterworld after deciding they were ready to leave the Realm.

My kind lived for millennia, but we still could pass away if we chose to.

That had been Thera's final wish, as well as my father's, to finally leave Earth and go to the Realm of the Souls.

But it still didn't explain how Thera was here with me right now.

"What the...?" I continued to gaze at my mother, who seemed healthier than ever. I couldn't believe that she was here. With me. Holding me.

My heart began to pound my ribs in surprise as I watched my mother, saw her blue eyes hold mine, and then I noticed her appearance.

Her thick brown hair hung long past her ribs, with the top half of it pulled back into a bun. Her deep purple dress flowed in the breeze, rippling as if it was swimming in water; her monarch butterfly tattoo on her wrist shone brightly in the sun.

There were no signs of aging — no wrinkles, nothing to betray her actual number of seasons she'd been around. It was like she had found the Fountain of Youth.

"How are you here?" I asked her, finally able to form a question. I was beyond bewildered, and my mind still had not comprehended what was going on.

"I got granted permission," she said.

"From who?"

She beamed knowingly, her eyes were bright as she threw her shoulders forward, and I saw the gargantuan, ink-black wings protruding from her back, brushing slightly against the rock surrounding her.

I smiled, instantly understanding what was happening.

Thera caught this and winked.

"You know who."

I shook my head in disbelief, and Thera gazed into my eyes before she reached over and grasped my right hand, squeezing my wrist gently. She applied pressure to my wrist with her thumb.

I didn't yank my wrist away because I knew there was a reason she was doing this.

A few moments later, Thera took her thumb off my wrist. My mother had tattooed a beautiful, colorful, blue butterfly onto my flesh when I looked down; the creature's wings appeared to be in flight.

Thera looked straight into my eyes; her blue eyes bright.

"Come find me, Chrysanthe."

I awoke with a start.

"Chrysanthe? Are you alright?"

I glanced up at the sound of my name, only to see Celio steadily watching me with his hazel eyes, a worried tone to his voice.

"Chrysanthe?"

"Yes, I'm okay," I replied groggily.

"I was wondering when you'd come back to me."

Wait. What?

"Have I been out long?" I asked, peering around at my surroundings to get a feel for where I was.

It took a few moments; the sun had almost entirely set now, leaving very little visibility.

I twisted around, only to feel arms holding me tight, a pulse against my skin, and a steady heartbeat in my right ear.

Celio was carrying me.

"What was that?" I asked him as I met his eyes for a second time. "Was that a dream?"

Celio chuckled.

"Yes, Chrysanthe, it was."

"But...what...? Was that her? Was that *really* Thera?"

"Yes. It was."

I shook my head, amazed. I never had one where I reconnected with my relatives who had passed into the Realm of the Souls. Passed away into the Heavens.

"But how...?" I started and then quickly stopped.

Wait, how did Celio know of my dreams? How did Celio understand? I felt groggy from just waking up, so anything could've come out of my mouth, but how would he know about my dream?

"Wait... how do you know....?"

"How do I know about the dream you had?" Celio asked. "I know about it because I created it," he answered confidently.

"You *created* it?"

"Yes, I did. I figured you needed to see your mother, so I granted her permission to see you. The only way to do that is through your dreams. What you saw and experienced was real, Chrysanthe."

"It was?"

"It was," he replied.

That meant I *was* speaking to Thera; I had been talking to my mother.

"Wow," I said, not fully understanding what was going on. "Wait a moment..."

Celio stopped walking, confused, as I brought my right wrist up to my face -the one Thera had touched in my dream- and examined my flesh.

I gasped.

I heard Celio chuckle as I stared at my wrist.

There was an enormous tattoo of a magnificently colored blue butterfly, the wings of the creature taking up both sides of my wrist. Upon closer inspection, though, I noticed something was different.

"What?"

There was a lot of detail inside the design, a lot more than a typical Fate Tattoo.

"Huh?"

I squinted at the ink in confusion, but as I looked closer, I realized something.

I remembered the Archangel's words, and I gasped.

The outline. Follow the outline.

I finally understood what was on my skin.

It was a map.

The tattoo grew as I slept once more. I couldn't see it all in the moonlight, but I made it out as the sun rose in the morning, bright and lively and beautiful as the rays warmed my skin. It was only then that I could truly see what was on my flesh.

I was blown away by everything; the butterfly tattoo had grown from my wrist to my shoulder, the ink being that of Archangel wings.

Big, thick, black, beautiful wings took up my right arm, while the other portion of the tattoo grew to the palm of my right hand, becoming a pale orange skull on that portion of my skin.

I stared at the colorful ink, mesmerized.

I stared at it closely.

The map was incredibly detailed; every part of my World mapped on the tattoo.

I hadn't seen any of this the night before since it had been dark. But now, I could fully see everything in the daylight.

"Chrysanthe?"

I looked up from my tattooed right arm, only to see Celio walking toward me.

He stopped as he saw my expression, and there was a worried tone in his voice.

"Are you alright?"

I nodded. "Yes, I am. I was looking at the map," I said, extending my right arm out to show Celio the design. "It's grown since last night."

I looked at it once more, admiring the map of my World; it was as if everything was alive. The detail of the ink was exquisite.

A hand gently grasped my right, and I glanced up to see Celio staring at the ink that now adorned my right arm.

"Wow," he breathed; his fingers lightly brushed across my skin as he studied the tattoo. "How did this happen? When?"

"I woke up, and it was already there. This map is what the Archangel was talking about," I said. "This is the outline. She said, '*follow the outline, and you can save everyone,*' she means this, this map, Celio."

Celio looked up from my skin and blinked, his hazel eyes abruptly changing to disbelief as realization slammed into him. His attitude instantly changed.

"You don't know what you're saying," he said abruptly.

"What?" I asked, confused by his statement and the tone of his voice.

"You don't understand."

"What?"

"Chrysanthe, the Archangel... she wants us to go to Hell. She wants us to go and confront the Phantom. It's why she said what she did. It's making sense now; that's why this map is on your skin. It's showing you the way to the Underworld."

A shiver rattled through my body, and Celio grabbed my wrist again, his eyes burning with sudden fury.

"Chrysanthe, you can't do this. I won't let you leave me. You know I won't be able to come with you to the Abyss.

It is forbidden for us Archangels, since we are the Protectors of Souls, and I can't leave you, not after I have found you again, not after all this time."

I was amazed by what he was saying, but another thought hit me as I studied his face.

"The map, Celio, it was from Thera, from my dream. She put the butterfly on my wrist when I saw her after I passed out. I remembered what she said, too."

But then my face grew pale as her words returned to my memory.

"She said, '*come find me, Chrysanthe.*'"

I gasped as it all truly hit me, as I finally knew what was going on.

My mother, Thera, was trapped in Hell.

I don't know how long I sat there, staring at Celio as it all unraveled around me. It all made sense, and I finally understood what was happening. I had to rescue my mother, and I couldn't have my love with me.

Celio gritted his teeth together and continued to stare at my face; his expression was no longer calm.

"Chrysanthe, we *cannot* go to Hell. It's forbidden, for me, as well as you."

That much was true.

Not only for Celio, because he was an Archangel, but for me as well, being a Celestial Being.

I could lose my Fate Tattoo permanently; I could get a Mark. The Abyss was so dangerous, and I would have a scar from my tattoos being ripped forcibly from my skin.

Or I could also die.

It was all very dangerous.

My mother, though. She needed me.

Panic started to pump through my body as I immediately visualized my mother in Hell, with the Banshees and the Wraiths.

The Banshees could signal death by wailing and screeching, and the Wraiths could suck out souls.

I shivered at just the mere thought of all the creatures being around her before I came back to myself, looking at Celio.

"We have to save her. Thera needs help, and she's trapped. We have to save her. *I* have to save her."

My heart was battering my ribs, my breathing rapid.

I had to save her. I just had to.

"And how are we going to do that, Chrysanthe?" Celio was frustrated. "How are we even going to *get there?* After we follow the map, how exactly are we going to get in the Abyss without losing our tattoos, or worse, dying?"

I paused to take a deep breath, ready to respond when a voice suddenly piped up out of nowhere. "I can help."

I turned around, startled, only to see a beautiful woman who was pale white and completely transparent floating nearby. Celio and I gasped at the same time.

She was an Apparition.

Apparitions were Beings who were pure but had sacrificed themselves for specific reasons. Because they were respectable, they could never go to the Underworld, but because the Being had gotten killed on purpose, they couldn't go into the Heavens.

They were Floating Souls, in between Heaven and Hell.

The Apparition looked to me before glancing at Celio, advancing closer toward both of us.

"I've been an Apparition for a long time, Chrysanthe. I figure I could help you, possibly find a way to save your family, and hopefully get on the good side of someone who can finally help put me to rest somewhere. I've been wandering around since before you were even a thought in your parent's minds."

I blinked. My parents had been gone for four seasons now. That meant the Apparition had been a Floating Soul for a long time.

I brushed past this thought as I watched her. She looked at me, studying my face. "How can you help us?" I asked, ignoring Celio as he was about to talk.

"I can help you get to the Underworld so you can save your family. I made a noble sacrifice, or so I thought, once upon a time, but now I regret it. I can easily help you save your family."

My family. My family. Not just my mother.

Wait.

"What do you mean by my family? Only my mother is in the Abyss," I said.

"She's not the only one there," the Floating Soul responded, and I felt the blood drain from my face. "The Phantom you seek took more than one member. I saw her do it myself, although I could do nothing because they were in Heaven when it happened."

"Do you know who else there is?" Celio asked as I gasped, unable to fathom what she was saying.

The Apparition looked at him, knowing he was hesitant to ask her a lot of questions.

"Chrysanthe's mother, Thera, has been taken, along with Viro and Sybella, also known as the Oracle."

I sucked in a breath, unable to believe the Floating Soul's words. But I knew she couldn't lie.

Everyone I loved, cared about, respected; they were now in the Underworld. Tricked by the Phantom who had thrown

Celio out of his Realm, poisoned mine, and murdered another Archangel.

I felt as if a giant rock had suddenly been pushed against my ribs, making it impossible to breathe.

I glanced up at Celio, who was slowly watching me. I looked at the Apparition as tears began to form.

"You can help us?" I asked as one escaped my right eye, running down my cheek. "You can help us get to the Underworld?"

"Indeed, I can," she said.

"Okay," I said before glancing over at Celio, who now seemed to understand how important this all was. He stared at me, his eyes like liquid gold, and held out his hand. I grabbed it, holding it close to my heart. "Help us get there," I told her. "Help us go to Hell."

10

Thana

The faces swirled underneath the water beneath me, their expressions contorted in rage.

I smiled as I stared down at them from the black rock poking out of the water. I appreciated the fact that they were writhing in their own misery.

They deserved it; they were finally paying the price for what they did up on Earth.

The Ghost's faces had gotten contorted as I fell to my knees, leaning forward to glance into the fluid. Their realistic faces stared, and I realized some of them were coming up out of the liquid; arms and hands reached out as if to grab me. I stood back up on the rock at the edge of the River.

The Ghost's extremities became wisps of smoke as they rose out of the water. They disappeared after that, going deep into the liquid, knowing they could never reach me.

I smirked.

The Dead couldn't get to me; after all, I was their Queen. I was the Queen of the Abyss, and no one who was in Hell would ever be able to confront me; I faced and controlled them.

I walked along the rock bridge that surrounded the River, breathing in the old, musty death-scented air as I watched the Ghosts in the water scream.

They realized they were trapped forever; they could never escape.

"Sucks for you." I looked at the faces in the River as hands attempted to reach for me again. To grab me.

Instead, I made my way along the bridge to the large expanse of rock, and I saw the orange 'sky' above me.

It was really the remains of the Ghosts, leftovers from their bodies, turned into smoke and fog, clouding the air. There were so many remains that it had turned everything above the Inferno River orange.

It was the reason the air smelled musty, old, and dead.

I was literally breathing in the Dead as I passed by.

I finally made it to the expanse of black rock when a growl reverberated through the air, followed by a grating whine.

I looked over to my right side at the noise, only to see my gigantic Hellhound approaching me.

My Guardian to the Gates of the Underworld, Morgeran was massive. He was as tall as a horse while his thick muscles poked through his matted fur and decaying flesh. His skin was black underneath his mangled coat, with the ligaments and tendons partially poking out.

He turned his head to the side, expecting me to pet him.

I stroked Morgeran's fur, feeling the rumble from his throat shake through my bones as the sound echoed throughout his body.

"Good boy. Good boy." He pushed his head into my hand, and I stumbled on the rock I stood on. "Good boy," I repeated as I straightened back up.

I looked at his black fur; his black hide was underneath, and I saw the entire left side of his jaw.

It was exposed; the wolf's razor-sharp yellow teeth and deteriorated gums were visible on the left side of his face, leaving the hound with a terrifyingly emaciated look.

But that was the point. He was a Hellhound.

He was the Guardian of the Underworld, while I was the Queen. We ruled together, and I loved Morgeran.

I stroked the rough, matted hide behind his ear, and his red eyes opened. He stared at me with an interesting look; I studied it, starting to smile. It was as if he was trying to tell me something.

I felt another rumble shake through my bones as he turned around; I took my fingers off his ear as he walked off, but Morgeran stopped and twisted his body around again. I knew as he stared at me with his blazing red eyes that he wanted me to go after him.

"Okay, I'll follow you."

Morgeran disappeared into the mist.

The mist that was the Dead.

For the Ghosts, it was either stay trapped in the Inferno River forever, screaming and wailing in misery for all eternity, or become the smog that enveloped my world.

I smirked at the thought of the Ghost's fate, particularly the ones who tried to grab me earlier. I stood there on the rock, thinking, before I followed Morgeran into the thick fog, knowing where he would be taking me when I started following him.

The gate that stood in front of us was colossal. It stretched above my line of view; the top of it was covered in the orange clouds of fog floating around us.

Morgeran twisted his head around once he came to the entrance, his red eyes staring at me, and I walked forward, extending my arm out to touch the barrier.

It was rough, cold, and had an off-white color.

I stared at it before leaning forward and examining its structure; my hand touched the outside of the passageway that meant that I would be visiting the prisoners.

I stared at the entryway and felt the cold knobbed edge of the design.

The structure of the gate wasn't stone.

It was the bones of the Dead.

I sneered as I held my left hand out and watched the skull tattoo on my wrist.

"Time to open up," I said to the bone encrusted passage. I brought my hand to my chest, where another crow tattoo was with its left wing extended.

I glanced down at the ink before bringing my fingers to the crow's feet that were positioned on my ribs, bringing them up so that I grabbed at the tattoo on my skin.

I grasped my flesh, my fingernails scraping at the crow design, and pulled the key to the gate from my body.

The key was hidden inside my tattoo so that I could always have it.

I brought it to my face to examine it.

It was also made of bone.

But this key wasn't made up of just anyone's bones.

The key was *mine*.

I wiped it on my deteriorating black dress before placing it into the appropriate slot.

The gate creaked open.

I stepped forward, and Morgeran followed, as silent as a Ghost as he padded after me.

11

Chrysanthe

attoos had always been a part of my existence. They had always been a part of the Celestial Beings' existence; tattoos were also crucial in the presence of the Archangels. Not only had they determined our fates, but they also *defined* us, who we were as individuals, who we were as a part of our World.

Tattoos were essential to us as a society, and to think there was a Phantom from the Underworld who was taking the unique, magical ink from others was enough to make me sick.

And now I learned that she had taken my family. The family I thought for so long had been in Heaven, protected from the evil demons of the Abyss.

And now they were in danger.

It made me want to curl up and sob my heart out.

It took several moments for me to take control of myself after I'd heard the Apparition's words. Tears rolled down my cheeks as I thought about everything she had told me.

Celio stood in front of me as his eyes fixed on mine, an anxious expression taking over his face.

"Chrysanthe?"

A sob made my throat close, so Celio leaned forward and pulled me into a hug.

I lost control once more and cried into his shoulder. I cried for a long time.

Celio's hand caressed my face and brought me back to reality. I brought my head up from his shoulder, my eyes feeling like raw meat.

"Oh, Chrysanthe," Celio said as he looked into my eyes, and his fingertips brushed my cheeks. "Everything is going to be alright. We have someone who can help us now."

"You want to help find my family?" I questioned.

It seemed like he didn't want to before, but it was because he was forbidden to do so. It was prohibited for both of us to enter the Abyss. But what other choice did I have? I had to rescue my family; I had to get them back.

I just kept having the mental images of my family getting tortured, their souls being sucked out by the Wraiths while I sat here, trying desperately to get help to try and save them.

I would travel down to the Underworld, no matter what it took; it was a good thing we'd found help through this Apparition.

Still, I didn't know if Celio wanted to help or if he was just trying to calm me.

"Of course, I do," he said. "But I can't venture into the Underworld; I would lose my wings."

The Apparition spoke up.

"That will not happen, I promise." She glanced at Celio. "They are precious to you, your prized possession, as well as your identity. As long as I am here to guide you and show you the way to the Underworld, you will not lose your wings."

Celio considered her for a moment before turning back to me.

"Everything's going to be okay, Chrysanthe. We have help so we can now find Viro and Thera, as well as the Oracle."

I sniffled, a tear running down my cheek as I regarded Celio; I turned my attention to the Apparition, who watched me closely.

"I will help you get to your family, Chrysanthe. But we do have to move fast before it gets dark. If we are to go to the Underworld, we must leave now."

I nodded in acknowledgment.

I felt Celio's warm hand in mine. He was staring at the Apparition, watching as she made her way over to us. Her transparent body hovered as she approached.

"I will gladly show you the way, Chrysanthe."

She held her hand out as if to take it.

"I will guide you so that you can save the individuals that are dearest to you from the Phantom. I must warn you the journey is dangerous, and I will be unable to protect you since I am already dead."

"Okay," I nodded. "I understand." I was just grateful that she would be able to help me. I needed to save my family from Hell.

"I understand," Celio said as the Apparition looked to him.

"Okay, well then, let's get going," she said. "We have far to go before nightfall."

Celio and I stood up and glanced at each other.

I was nervous, and I could sense he was also. An Apparition was guiding us to a place that was forbidden. But I had to trust her. I had to save my family from the Phantom of the Abyss.

12

Thana

A snarl ripped through Morgeran, cutting through the silence like a knife.

I paused, and a growl rumbled in my throat as I felt the Hellhound's body language. I straightened when I heard the flapping of wings in the distance.

I blinked in surprise.

It could only mean one thing; my messenger had found something.

"Thana?" I heard a croak as I saw the pointed, bat-like wings through the fog. "My Queen, where are you?"

Morgeran snapped viciously as I heard the clicking of claws against the rocky surface. I brought my right hand out to his hide, petting him to calm him down as I advanced toward the voice in the mist. I breathed in the smog.

"What is it, Damon?"

It took my eyes a few moments to adjust before I saw him.

He was all black and utterly hunched over and emaciated; his pointed wings resembled those of a bat. Damon was a former Archangel who had fallen from his perch in the Heavens.

He'd failed his duty in Heaven when he volunteered to help me in the Abyss, so Damon had been thrown out, but I had saved and altered his wings once he had gotten into Hell. He was now my messenger; he could travel between Earth and the Underworld.

Damon appeared shriveled and haggard now, resembling more of an ink-black, withered, wilted creature with a hunched, spiny back. He was no longer an Archangel; he was my loyal servant.

His orb-like, dirt brown eyes stared back at me once I appeared through the mist. The tips of his wings clacked on the rocky ground as he glanced at Morgeran, who stood his ground and growled at Damon as he stared at him with his blood-red eyes.

Damon finally spoke.

"My Queen, I am glad you are back; I'd grown worried."

"Did you find anything?" I asked.

I wasn't going to waste my precious moments thanking him for the fact he'd gotten worried about me; that wouldn't help me get information out of him about *her*.

Damon brought his eyes to the rocky ground; his body language told me immediately that he had not discovered anything.

The claws on the front portion of his bat-like wings continued to click on the rocky surface, causing it to echo through the Abyss.

"I-," he started, but I cut him off, growing angry.

"You found nothing?"

Damon looked up at me, his already enormous eyes growing wider in fear.

"I tried! I swear, Thana. I tried to find anything I could about *her*, but I lost her trail!"

My teeth gritted, and I snarled.

"What do you mean, you lost her trail? Were you even *looking* for *her*?"

"Yes, I was! And I found her, along with another Archangel; I think he was the one you threw out of the Heavens when you traveled to Earth. I found them; they were both with the

Archangel you tortured; she died in *her* arms, but as soon as I tried to get closer to both the Archangel and *her* to hear more of the conversation, I suddenly couldn't. I suddenly couldn't see either one of them. I tried following them, though, I swear!"

He sounded terrified; he was shaking, but I didn't care.

I snapped at him.

"So, you *lost* her?"

Damon looked meek, and Morgeran snarled behind me. He licked his lips, his face contorted in a scary expression when I looked behind me. His eyes fixed on Damon.

Just one command, and Morgeran could shred Damon to pieces.

But I knew better.

"No, Morgeran," I said, turning toward the Hellhound. "Shhh..."

Morgeran stopped snarling at Damon within moments, although his eyes were still on him when I turned back around to talk to my messenger.

"I'm in the Underworld after I ripped that Archangel's tattoo and threw her out of the Heavens and tortured her. She wasn't telling me anything, so I most certainly did kill her; she bled to death after I cracked her wings; I understand that part of the information. As well as the part where I threw the other Archangel out of the Heavens," I growled at Damon, pausing when I felt the pressure in my head rise.

I glared at him, and he retreated several steps.

"But what I don't understand," I seethed, "is how after I come back to the Underworld, back to where I've gotten cursed to live for all eternity," I swallowed my disgust, "how after I sent you, you couldn't find them at all! *I saw* the Archangel's blood ooze from her back after I left her to die. Right after I came back to the Abyss, I sent you to find them! You are a messenger, are you not? *Why don't you have anything for me!*"

"I did find them-" I slapped him though, hard, cutting him off.

My long, black fingernails dug into his leathery-feeling cheek.

Damon howled in pain as I struck him but stopped immediately as my face contorted into a murderous expression.

"Shut up, Damon, and find them!"

He looked terrified as I stood there snarling at him, so enraged I thought my head was going to explode.

"Find them now!" I screeched, my blood reaching a boiling point.

Damon then promptly twisted around and flew off without another word, his leathery, bat-like wings flapping awkwardly into the sky before he disappeared entirely into the fog.

13

Chrysanthe

The oxygen was refreshing as it entered my lungs when I rose to the surface of the water to breathe. The air tasted sweet.

I shut my eyes at the feeling and welcomed it, running my hands through my blond hair, wetting it again as I felt the cool, crisp wind slowly brush my skin.

The map that had led me to the cascade of water glittered in the sunlight. It shimmered, and I smiled as I glided through the enchanted water, welcoming the clean feeling that washed through my body.

The enchanted ink had brought the Apparition, Celio, and I to the magical liquid, so we had taken advantage of the opportunity to bathe in it.

The Apparition had a point when she'd mentioned there was no reason to make the trek if I had gotten covered in the Archangel's blood; I would be attracting the wrong kind of attention.

She had disappeared as we bathed.

The fluid from the Enchanted Cascades did its job and helped us to feel refreshed.

I looked ahead of me, only to see the waterfall. The water's motion caused a rainbow to form, scattering colorful light across it and the rocks, making a dazzling display.

"It's beautiful, isn't it?"

I turned to see Celio beside me. I hadn't heard him enter the water.

"Yes, it is."

"I thought you might like it."

Wait.

"You've been here before?"

"No, I've seen the waterfalls though, from Heaven. As well as their rainbows."

I smiled. "Well, the rainbows are gorgeous." I was in awe. Celio focused his eyes on mine as he edged closer to me in the water.

"As are you," he said.

His arms encircled my body, and he pulled me close as the water sloshed along.

"Now," he breathed into my lips, and my heart pounded against my ribs. I studied the trace of his mouth, which was so close to mine. Water dripped from his hair and onto my skin. "Where were we, before we got interrupted by all this?"

The smell of the enchanted water filled my senses, making me feel intoxicated with its scent. The taste of Celio's breath made me feel dizzy.

I leaned forward and kissed him, the sensation dissolving into my heart.

I don't know how long we were in the magical waters; it could have been moments, it could have been mornings, or it could have easily been seasons. All I knew was that I loved Celio, and I couldn't stop tasting his breath as it intermingled with mine; I couldn't stop feeling the warmth of his skin through the liquid that surrounded the both of us. The feeling seared its way into my brain, leaving a mark on it that would never, ever leave.

Celio's lips broke away from mine slightly, and I felt the droplets of water fall onto my tongue from his face.

Celio.

I couldn't help it as I felt the liquid drip on my tongue; I kissed him deeply, all the heat in my body rushed to my head as I felt him slowly caress my cheek and felt his defined body against mine.

His hands moved from my cheeks to my head, and he took it gently into his hands, running his fingers through my hair. He tried to move closer to me than he already was.

Celio.

His breath tasted delicious, his skin feeling so warm.

The sound of water hitting the rocks was what broke us apart.

I walked out of the water; the fluid droplets caused goosebumps to appear on my flesh.

The water soaked through my undergarments before abruptly evaporating, disappearing from my skin within a few moments.

My hair was different, as it wouldn't bother me when it was wet. It didn't dry quickly, although the enchanted water did cleanse my hair, so now it was fresh and rejuvenated.

I went over to a rock where my clean clothes were and quickly got changed.

The Apparition had somehow found both of us extra sets while we cleaned up, so we could be in new clothing when we went to the Underworld, which was refreshing.

I squeezed my hair to shake the moisture from it and ran my fingers through it, attempting to get out all the tangles.

That was when I suddenly felt eyes looking at my body and twisted around to see Celio staring at me. His eyes were on mine, and the water dripped from his well-built body.

A shudder rippled through my system as I stared back; I couldn't stop looking at his muscular physique when Celio's hazel eyes met mine.

My thoughts began to morph as we watched each other, but then the rough sound of hooves hitting the grass made me jump out of my thoughts; I turned toward the noise.

"Celio? Chrysanthe?" I heard as I twisted toward the trees, over where the sound was.

I squinted in confusion for a few moments, but I smiled as I saw two beautiful horses galloping toward me.

One was white as snow, the other black as night.

The black stallion was thicker, much more muscular than the white mare, who, I realized when I advanced closer, was a Unicorn.

I sucked in a breath in shock and awe; the mare looked right at me, and I noticed that she had a blue eye and a brown eye.

I felt Celio walk up behind me, and I saw him exhale in a gust.

"Wow," he said, looking at the stallion, who was now grazing. "He's a beauty."

"They're for you."

The Floating Soul came back from the woods, making her way toward us.

But that wasn't what made us blink back our surprise.

"What?" we both said simultaneously, wondering if we both had heard her wrong.

"The horses are for you both. Chrysanthe, you get the Unicorn mare, while Celio, you get the black stallion," she said, before adding, "Celio, you might find something interesting about your mount." She winked.

As soon as she said that, I thought I knew what she meant, that something was interesting about that horse.

Sure enough, when I peered closer at the stallion, who now had its head up from the grass, who was now staring at Celio with chocolate brown eyes, I saw he had an outline on both sides of him. It was as if he'd been shaved a bit on either side of his body.

It was an outline of wings.

The black stallion was a Winged Horse.

Winged Horses were rare creatures, creatures that only existed in the Afterworld since they had wings like the Archangels who rode them.

"Go on, Celio," I said, turning and looking at him as I saw him stand on the grass, taken aback. "Go on," I said before bringing my gaze to the Apparition.

"Where did you find them?" I asked, taking a moment to look into the woods before I walked up to the white mare, who sniffed my hand when I held it out.

I knew that Winged Horses came from the Afterworld, but I didn't know how the Apparition had found one since she couldn't go to the Heavens.

I also wondered where she'd found the Unicorn, who was now rubbing her head against my body, wanting to be petted.

But the Floating Soul just chuckled.

"That is information I cannot tell you. Now go, get on; we have far to go, and we must leave now."

14

Thana

 y green eyes stared back at me as I studied my reflection in the Inferno River, as I knelt to see the image in the murky, blackish water.

I'd gone over to the liquid after yelling at Damon and needing to calm down.

But as I saw myself, my face paled, and I gasped at what I saw.

I didn't know what I was expecting, but it most definitely was not this.

My intestines began to writhe in loops, grabbing my heart and dragging it downward.

My eyes looked sunken in as I peered in the murky, ghostly fluid, almost appearing dead. My long brown hair seemed incredibly matted into clumps, while my skin seemed to be a greenish-purple as if someone had beaten me up.

Either that, or it was as if I was rotting from the inside out.

I snarled as I took in my appearance in the unpleasant water. I was both unnerved and enraged. I seethed.

It made my intestines churn, made me sick to my stomach as I saw my face mingled with those who were eternally lost. A Ghost gave me a sinister smile.

I glared as I finally yanked myself away from it and looked away from the River and toward the Death Fog surrounding me.

I started walking away from the River and onto the black rock.

I growled again, repulsed by my reflection. I was determined to harm the individual who made this all happen.

She had done this all to me. *She* had made me look this way, act this way. *She* had made it, so I lived in the Underworld for all eternity.

And I hated her for it.

I knew what to do.

Damon needed an extra pair of eyes and ears.

I didn't trust him alone. He'd failed me, but now I was giving him a second chance. He was going to have the crow with him, seeing anything he wouldn't, or couldn't, see.

My teeth crunched against each other as I put my skull tattooed hand on my heart, over the crow design. My fingernails scraped against the ink.

Within moments, I felt the crow leave my skin, and I smiled as I looked down at my chest. The tattoo had become alive, the design morphing into a real crow as it jumped onto my arm.

The crow flapped its enormous wings and landed, watching me intently, waiting for a command.

I reached out and petted the crow's feathers and leaned forward, so my nose touched the bird's beak.

"Go find *her*," I seethed to the crow.

And with a caw, it took off, flying away into the fog and out of my view.

I watched the crow leave silently, knowing that it would come back with valuable information. Something Damon hadn't done.

I stalked off after watching my crow leave me, disappearing into the mist. My footsteps echoed across the Abyss as I stepped on the rock that was the ground of the Underworld.

There was green grass on Earth, leaves to sink into, and dirt you could feel underneath your bare feet. However, in the Underworld, there was just a large, hard expanse of black rock that bordered the Inferno River.

I stomped through the mist, determined to get to my seat close by, and then eventually got fed up with walking and stopped in my tracks, flexing my back muscles.

I felt the gigantic bat-like wings push out of my back before I heard them flap; I looked to the side, seeing the sheer range of them.

They were enormous, the wingspan bigger than Damon's.

They took up space behind me; the bottom portion scraped the rock I stood on.

I hoisted myself up into the air and immediately flew off, away from the Inferno River and to the other portion of the Underworld. That was where my Throne waited for me. It was buried in the rock and was so dark only thousands of glow worms lit it up.

I had only just arrived at my Throne before Gog appeared from behind a corner, wishing to speak to me.

I saw him approaching before he looked up and watched as I flew toward him.

I acknowledged him with a nod, although I knew he couldn't see my face while I was high in the air.

Gog greeted me with a low bow. My pointed wings flapped as I landed on the rugged black stone.

"My Queen," the Goblin straightened up. "There is much to discuss."

"About?" I pulled my wings into my back.

"About your...monster..."

"What about him?"

I'd left the Goblin in charge of the beast. It was hard dealing with my monster, and Goblins were known to be very resilient, so I'd put Gog in control of the creature.

"He's growing restless," Gog said.

"And?" Of course, any creature here would become restless. I mean, it *was* the Underworld.

"He's also hungry."

"Hungry?"

"Yes," Gog replied, being careful with his words. "He needs more food."

"More food?" I repeated.

My creature was always hungry, he still needed to feed, and I would not let him starve.

I'd fed him the Archangel I'd trapped down here with Damon's help.

But now, it seemed the monster required more food.

"Thank you, Gog."

The Goblin nodded a farewell before he disappeared into the darkness.

I went and sat down on my Throne, my eyes adjusting to the blackness as my thoughts moved around in my brain.

Then I smirked, the expression taking over my entire face.

My creature needed to feed, and I knew exactly how to satisfy him.

15

Chrysanthe

A sob built in my throat as I looked at my father's face, his blue eyes, and his powerful build as he stood in front of me. I couldn't help but let a tear escape as I walked over to him, enveloping him in a hug.

"Oh, Chrysanthe," he said, his gigantic hand moving along my back in a comforting gesture. "You'll be alright. You're young; you have your entire existence ahead of you. We're just going to another Realm, that's all."

I knew what he was saying. It was just that I was sad at seeing them go; I would never see my parents again, not on Earth, anyway.

My father pulled away from me to see my expression and wiped away the tears I couldn't hold back. His long blond hair and beard blew around as the wind traveled through it.

Viro looked like he hadn't aged at all when I took him in. He still looked fit, healthy, and mighty. But then again, he was the King of All Celestials, with my mother, Thera, being his Queen.

"You'll be alright," Viro said as I blinked, focusing on his words before stepping away from him and twisting around when I heard my mother's footsteps.

"He's right, honey," Thera said as I saw her, her thick brown hair in a ponytail as her purple dress flowed in the wind.

Both appeared to be made for each other as I watched them, studied the way they looked at each other for a moment. They were still in love after all the seasons they'd been together, through the millennia.

And now they had chosen to cross over to the Realm of the Souls together.

My mother put a tree-tattooed hand over my father's heart as their eyes met, and she leaned forward, kissing him softly.

My father seemed to relax automatically, all the tension in his body disappeared as they focused on each other, and I blinked, my eyes hitting the ground as the moment was for the two of them.

"We'll be alright; we have each other," Thera said after she broke apart from him, her eyes still on Viro. She brought a hand up to his face, her fingertips grazing his neck before she turned her attention toward me again.

She reached her other hand out as she watched me, her blue eyes bright.

"Come here, Chrysanthe," she said, her palm extended.

I walked over to my parents, and they watched me lovingly. I hugged both of them harder than I'd ever hugged anyone.

I felt Viro's face bury into the crook of the left side of my neck while Thera's face got buried on my right.

I squeezed them hard as I sobbed into them; I was going to miss them both dreadfully.

I pulled away and stared intensely at their faces.

Viro still had violent claw marks on his neck as his tattoo, while his broad, built body still conveyed strength and power; even though he was crossing to the Afterlife, he was still intimidating. Thera always looked healthy and graceful, her brown hair thicker than ever as her purple dress blew in the wind, her figure in the shape of an hourglass. Another tattoo of a monarch butterfly graced her wrist.

They both appeared to be ageless.

Ageless and perfect beyond recognition.

A bright light appeared behind Viro and Thera, and I blinked several times as the rich illumination partially blinded me. I saw my parents smile when the brightness slowly died down, and then I saw the figure that accompanied the glowing light.

His thick, black wings flew from behind him as he landed on the rock Viro, Thera, and I were on. My heart pounded against my chest, pummeling my ribs.

It was Celio.

It took a moment for my eyes to adjust, and I saw Celio's hazel eyes staring at me, a powerful gaze taking over his face as he watched me.

I couldn't help it then; I ran over to him, throwing my arms out to hug him as well.

"Hello." I squeezed his body tightly and felt his feathers tickling my back.

Celio held me tight, and then I pulled away from him, staring into his hazel eyes.

"You're the Chosen One to bring them?" I asked, watching him closely.

He nodded.

"Yes. Yes, I am. I promise I'll watch over your parents."

He broke his gaze as he looked behind me; I turned around to see them holding hands, their eyes fixed on Celio.

"Are you both ready?" he asked, bringing his hands to his sides.

My mother and father nodded.

Celio glanced at me for a few moments before he walked over toward my parents.

I watched him silently before he paused, touching both of their arms.

He closed his eyes and said an incantation.

Both of my parents watched him closely, and it took a few moments for me to catch on to what was going to happen.

Once he finished, he stood in front of my mother and father. His massive wings were flapping behind him as soon as he'd said the magical words.

I gasped suddenly; he turned around toward me, a chuckle building in his throat as he began to smile.

There was a glowing brightness on both Thera and Viro's backs; within a few moments, I saw black, feathered wings appear on their skin, through their flesh.

"Celio..." I said, my words coming out in astonishment.

But he smiled.

Thera smiled at me as well, her eyes connecting with mine.

"We'll be okay," she said, walking over and giving me another hug.

Viro exhaled in a gust as his massive wings flapped behind him, and he twisted around to look at my mother and I.

"Chrysanthe," he said, seeing my tear-stained face. "Everything will be okay, I promise you." He walked over to me and embraced me yet again.

I glanced over at Celio once Viro pulled away from me. I went and grabbed Celio's hand.

"Please take care of them," I said, even though he'd just promised me moments before.

Celio stared at me steadily before he grasped my face in his hands, leaning forward to place his forehead on mine.

"I promise you," he whispered, and his breath hit my lips as he spoke, "with all my heart, I will watch over them."

I ran my fingertips across his cheek as his feathery wings tickled my back.

"Be safe," I said.

Celio pulled his face back a little so he could kiss my cheek; it instantly felt warm as his lips touched my flesh gently.

"Goodbye, Chrysanthe," he breathed.

I felt Celio's feathers pull away as he walked toward my parents, and I stood as all three of them strolled over to the rock bridge in front of us, the bridge that would lead straight to the Afterworld.

All three of them — Celio, Viro, and Thera — turned back to look at me as they stood on the bridge.

I grinned through my tears as I watched their faces, my eyes meeting Celio's as water continued to gush down my cheeks.

He studied my face with a piercing gaze when his hazel eyes met mine.

"Take care of them," I said, even though I knew he wouldn't be able to hear me since my voice was barely a whisper.

I saw him nodding gently as if he understood my words before he twisted back around, extended his black angel wings out, and took off into the brightness.

Viro and Thera followed him after turning around and looking at me one last time before extending their thick black wings and taking off into the Illumination behind Celio.

16

"Chrysanthe?"

I blinked, coming back to the present, taking in the setting sun.

I'd drifted off as soon as I had dismounted the Unicorn mare.

"Chrysanthe?"

I shook my head slightly before turning my attention toward Celio, who was beside me, observing.

"What are you thinking about?" he asked curiously once my eyes met his.

I shook my head tearfully before the truth spilled out of my mouth.

"The day you took Viro and Thera to the Afterlife." As I said this, my throat closed with emotion.

"The day I promised you nothing would ever happen to them," he said; his voice drifted off as the memory took over.

I nodded again as I watched his face, and his eyes connected with mine.

"Chrysanthe, I'm so sorry." He brought his hand to my cheek and wiped the tears with his thumb. "Truly, I am."

He kept his hand on my face; his fingertips grazed my neck as I inhaled quickly, attempting to regain my composure.

"It's okay, Celio. It wasn't your fault. It was the Phantom's. You did promise me until you got thrown out of the Afterworld. You did keep your word, Celio."

"I tried," he said, "and I failed you."

"No, you didn't, Celio," I jumped in before he said anything else. "You did, no matter what you say. You kept watch over them, and that's all that matters right now. You watched over them and did your duty. None of us saw this whole thing coming with the Phantom, Celio. Everything's going to be okay now that we've got the Apparition to help us. As well as some horses that she found. We'll get them back. You tried your hardest, Celio; you kept your word. That means something to me."

I kissed him, breaking away after a few moments to gaze at his face.

"I love you, Celio," I said as I watched his eyes that were now seeming to burn into mine. "I love you so much."

The Floating Soul's voice caused me to look away from him.

"We have to keep going," she said. "We're close to where we need to be for the night. We'll be there by the time the sun goes down, so we must leave. Go on, mount your horses."

I looked at Celio quickly before I walked over to my Unicorn and got on her.

Celio did the same thing, going over to his stallion before the horse snorted, taking off into the woods, with me not far behind.

Leora came to a stop as I pulled slightly on her mane, right in front of a body of water.

The Unicorn mare was very well behaved. She twisted her head around, and her blue eye was visible as I carefully dismounted. I petted her sleek white coat and talked to her softly.

"Hey there, Leora." She brushed her head up against my chest.

Leora meant *light* and fitted her since she was a stunningly creamy color with an excellent temperament.

Celio had named the Winged stallion Maximus since he was so large, not to mention very muscular.

Celio came up beside me as Maximus snorted; his thick tail swatted the air as the Archangel dismounted. Celio walked over the healthy grass, making his way to the lake.

"Here we are." The Apparition lowered and stopped in front of the water.

She had been above us as we'd rode on, ensuring there was no danger, which, so far, there hadn't been any. We had been lucky, but I had a feeling that it wouldn't all be this simple.

"The Psychic Lake," she said, twisting around toward the pool of liquid.

I squinted for a moment before looking down at my right wrist. Sure enough, there was the Psychic Lake, all drawn out and illustrated on my flesh, with a crystal ball being on my skin and blue liquid partially filling the ball up. It all symbolized the Lake.

I turned my attention back to the Apparition.

"So, we have to look into the water? To see Thera, Viro, and Sybella?" I asked.

The Apparition nodded.

"Yes, Chrysanthe. This lake will help you see the Beings who have gotten taken from you. It will help show you them; that way, you won't worry as much," she responded.

93

I nodded for a moment before I glanced back to my wrist, truly understanding what the Psychic Lake was as I studied the drawing.

It clicked inside of my head.

The Psychic Lake helped Beings see the past, present, and future, as well as anything we Beings would want to see. Anything we commanded would show up in the Psychic Lake waters, making it one of Earth's most influential water bodies.

I looked back up at the Apparition, suddenly realizing how mighty the Lake was, and put my hand back to my side, my dress flowing and rippling as the wind picked up.

I could see the Apparition looking into the fluid; I walked over to where she was.

I glanced over at her as our eyes met, and she watched my expression and nodded, encouraging me to investigate the waters.

"Go on, Chrysanthe," she said.

I took a deep breath, exhaling in a gust before peering into the Lake, certainly not expecting what I saw next.

17

Thana

A growl rumbled in my throat, and I sneered. I stared at the gigantic monster that was chained up.

I was in the other portion of the Underworld, away from my Throne. I now breathed in the scents of the Dead as the Ghosts wafted above me.

I'd come as soon as Gog had told me about my monster; I was determined to see the creature.

It was enraged. The beast was fighting the chains that were around its neck and nailed to the floor. Ropes were tight around its front limbs and were becoming strained as the creature pulled against them.

Wow. The beast continued to tug on its restraints. It was so mighty, so muscular, and intimidating.

It took seven Goblins to keep control of its head alone as it swung around, swiping the air with its horns.

Gog noticed me watching the monster as he held the ropes to contain the beast. He walked over through the Goblins that were fighting to stop the bull-like creature. Gog spoke in a croaky voice.

"Thana, my Queen, your beast is hungry. He needs to eat."

A loud bellow erupted from the monster, as my attention had gotten diverted. The noise drowned out the rest of Gog's words, and the creature quickly locked eyes with me. Its eyebrows were crinkling into its forehead; its horns were as sharp as knives.

The deathly scent of it drenched me as I held my ground, and my fingernails dug into my palms.

The beast's horns nearly gored me as he quickly twisted his gigantic head around. The Goblins tugged on the metal chain around his thick neck, and I took several steps back, away from it as I exhaled at the close call.

I continued to stand my ground against the beast.

He roared again in frustration, standing up on two feet and rearing himself. His black muzzle covered in blood, his coal red eyes fixed on me as I backed up slowly, keeping my eyes on him.

I backed up before I walked off.

The monster needed to eat and was furious because he was so hungry. I was going to have to fix this. And quickly.

And I knew *exactly* what to do.

The battered, pulverized Being was curled up on the rock-hard floor as I entered the area made up of bones. The site was encrusted with skeletons of the Dead. I noticed the red mark on the Being's cheek, the black and blue spots around his eyes.

He stood up as I entered, delirious and not aware of what he was doing as he scrambled up from the ground, automatically wincing when he did so.

His expression was distant and his eyes vacant since I'd kept him chained up next to a Wraith.

A Wraith who had slowly been sucking out his soul.

I mocked the Being. His expression was blank as he blinked, trying his hardest to look at me.

I laughed at him as he tried to focus but couldn't.

He was undoubtedly my prisoner.

I twisted my head toward the pure black, hooded Wraith who was keeping him contained. The Wraith was floating above the ground, and I nodded as I saw the cloaked figure turn its head in my direction, ignoring the Being who was groaning in pain.

The Wraith lifted a scabbed, ink-black hand as it turned its attention toward me. It brought its hand across its body and reached for the sword inside the sheath.

It quickly sliced through the metal chains holding the Being with one mighty swipe, causing the Being to fall to the ground again with a groan.

He moaned in agony; I leaned down to grab him by the shoulder, my dark black fingernails digging into his flesh as I dragged him away from the Wraith and along the hard rock.

He'd been my prisoner for a while, and now he was going to be food for my Beast.

I gripped him hard as I yanked him along the rough floor, glad he wasn't fighting back.

The Wraith had sucked out most of his soul. It would now be quicker and easier to feed him to the creature because he wouldn't fight back.

It was the ultimate punishment for what this Being did, to be eaten by my Beast.

This Being had betrayed me, and now he was going to pay the price.

He was going to be eaten by my Minotaur.

18

Chrysanthe

The water in the Lake rippled, causing the image to become distorted entirely before it finally settled down; the liquid turned smooth, and I could see it completely.

I was taken aback at the reflection, and I felt Celio come up beside me, looking into the still Lake.

I smiled as I saw what was in the fluid.

It was both of my parents at the time of my birth. My mother held me, and she was still in the bed she gave birth in. She appeared tired as she looked down, sweat pooling around her temples as her attention turned to me. Her hair was slightly messy as she smiled.

My father was right behind her, leaning in and over my mother to see my face. Both watched me and beamed. They looked so happy.

I had gotten wrapped in nature-colored blankets, and I reached up with a tiny hand to touch my mother's cheek, cooing as I did so.

My mother grinned, the smile taking over her entire face as she looked up at my father, whose expression was the same.

The Apparition, who was still beside me, sighed as she saw the image. I exhaled again before I focused entirely on the memory, trying to understand what was going on.

I wasn't expecting what came next out of the memory in the Lake.

"She's so beautiful," my mother commented to my father, staring at me with a loving expression. She put one hand underneath my tiny body, holding me tightly against her chest. "She's so sweet."

"Yes. Yes, she is," my father replied, bringing his hand up to brush it against my cheek; I moved slightly at the touch. "She sure is a beauty."

He smiled as he looked down at me, and I opened my eyes widely, taking in the look of him. His long blond hair and beard hung over my face.

"Hi there, sweetheart." My mother looked deeply into my eyes.

I looked at her for a few moments before I yawned, reaching my hand up and touching my father's face with it, my tiny fingers grazing along his beard.

He grinned at the touch and smiled gently as my fingers moved across his face.

I grabbed his beard for a few moments before letting it go. My fingertips curled into a fist as I studied both of my parent's faces before closing my eyes again.

"Aww, you sweet thing. Welcome to the World, little one," my mother said before she handed me to my father, who put me in the tiny baby bassinet close to the bed. "Welcome to the World."

She watched my father put me down, but then she cried out sharply; her slightly swollen abdomen, which hadn't adjusted to my birth yet, had abruptly started to move.

My mother had an expression mixed with shock and awe on her face.

"It cannot be." She blinked, but the assistant Being who had helped with my birth joined her. The Being touched my mother's arm.

"It is," she told her, reaching out and grabbing her hand. "My dear Thera, you were pregnant with twins. Get ready to push again."

"What?"

Viro looked at my mother in shock as Thera struggled to process what was happening.

She winced as her body prepared itself for another birth.

"My Queen, you are going to have another baby; get ready," repeated the assistant Being. "Get ready," she said a third time, squeezing her hand before going and sitting down to see the baby being born.

The Being put her hand on my mother's leg as my mother winced again. That was when the Being looked up at her from where she was sitting.

"Go on, Thera. Push!"

The water rippled again; the memory disappeared into oblivion as I blinked, unable to understand what had just happened.

I heard Celio gasp, and he turned to look at me out of the corner of my eye, but I couldn't bring myself to look back at him. I was in too much shock.

The water abruptly stopped swirling and stilled again. Another memory then started in the Psychic Lake.

The Oracle appeared in the room soundlessly. She walked past the door and headed over to the bed where my mother was sleeping.

 100

My twin had just been born, and she was in the bassinet with me. She slept as the Oracle approached my mother.

She'd pulled the top half of her blond hair back in a bun; the rest of it hung long. Her teal dress moved with her as she walked; she knelt to see Thera.

Vines and multicolored flowers decorated her hands and arms. Peacock feathers on the front of each hand glowed stunningly in the sunlight as the brightness illuminated through the window. The light made her blue eyes appear almost hypnotic.

The Oracle looked to my mother, who blinked at her presence.

"May I see them?" she asked Thera.

Thera continued staring at the Oracle and nodded. She blinked as she put her head on her pillow, her body and mind exhausted.

The Oracle leaned down, looking in the baby bassinet where my twin and I had gotten wrapped in blankets.

She picked me up and cradled me.

"What is her name, Thera?" the Oracle asked as she twisted her body around to show my mother which baby she was holding. "She's beautiful."

"Chrysanthe. The baby's name is Chrysanthe," my mother said, leaning back against the pillows once more.

"Well, I know what to give you as a tattoo," the Oracle said, smiling as she looked down at my tiny face. "And what your fate will be," she continued. "You will help heal the Earth, and help it blossom and be as beautiful as you are. You will help heal wildlife and the Earth and take control of the weather as your father does. You will be the ultimate protector of nature." The Oracle muttered an incantation, bringing her head close to mine.

The tattoos then appeared on my flesh, the tree roots, the red chrysanthemum, and peacock feathers. They inked my skin with my fate.

A small giggle made its way through my tiny body as I saw her long hair graze my skin, and I grabbed hold of it as she brought her head away from me.

"Hi there, sweetheart." She smiled as I observed her face, letting go of her hair.

The Oracle glanced at my flesh, which had gotten adorned with the tattoos.

"They're perfect," Thera said, smiling from her bed as the Oracle turned and looked at her. "They fit her, too," she said.

"I was hoping they would," the Oracle said, grinning while she put me back into the baby bed. "Now it's her twin's turn."

The Oracle, still leaning over, reached down to take my sibling, but then she stopped immediately, pausing in shock; her hands froze before she could touch my twin's flesh.

"Something's not right," she murmured as Thera sat up in her bed, feeling worried at the Oracle's expression.

"Is everything alright, Sybella?" she asked, suddenly scared.

"No," the Oracle said, her face frozen, her eyes wide and alarmed. "No, it isn't. There's something wrong with this young one; I can sense it."

"What do you mean?" Viro entered the room and went to Thera's side. "What do you mean by that?"

"I mean that I see great darkness in her future," Sybella replied, pointing a finger to my twin. "This one, we cannot trust her. There is evil in her future, an evil I cannot protect you from," she said. "Evil that has to become contained."

My twin began to cry.

Sybella blinked at her as the noise grew, and that was when her eyes widened.

Somehow, even though the Oracle wasn't touching my sibling's skin, my twin had started to get her tattoos.

This time it was an ink-black crow on her chest, the wing portion of it extending up toward her throat, while there was an orange-yellow, disturbing looking skull, which appeared on her wrist.

The Oracle inhaled sharply before shaking her head, taken aback.

"I hate to say this to you, Thera." She twisted around and faced my mother, who looked beyond exhausted and confused. "But your daughter is pure death."

My father and mother looked at each other, completely bewildered.

"She is an omen for great evil." Sybella took in my twin sister, who now was moving around uncomfortably in the bassinet. "I have to take her with me; I have to take her somewhere where she won't cause any harm."

"Cause any harm?" Thera and Viro asked at the same time. "What do you mean?"

"She could destroy everything you hold dear," Sybella said, looking down at my sibling, who was now pouting. "I have to take her with me," she repeated.

"Take her with you?"

Sybella looked at both Viro and Thera with a stern expression in her turquoise eyes.

Her tattoos twinkled in the sunlight, and her teal dress moved as she reached down to grab my sister.

"Yes. I'm going to have to."

"Where are you taking her?" Thera asked, her voice on the edge of panic.

Sybella turned as my sister began crying; she was still wrapped in the black blanket as Sybella watched my parent's faces with a grim expression in her eyes.

Sybella's voice was cold as she answered my mother.

"I'm drowning her in Hell."

19

"**W**hat? No. No. NO!"

My mother was so stunned by what Sybella had just told her that she couldn't form a coherent sentence. My father shook his head, and his arms stayed at his sides while he clenched his fists.

Viro's blue eyes pierced Sybella's as she held my twin sister, and she retreated several steps as his lip began to curl and quiver, exposing a disgusted look from my father.

"Viro," Sybella started, trying to speak as the baby bassinet I was sleeping in began to shake, "Viro, I have to take her; she could destroy everything."

The bedroom darkened as the sky became overcast; the sunlight disappeared as Viro lost his temper, and the wind whipped through the area from outside.

"Give me my daughter, Sybella! NOW!"

The Oracle jumped and jostled my sister.

My father was beyond enraged, and my mother couldn't stop crying.

"SYBELLA!" he roared as the Oracle watched him with wide, open eyes.

She began to shake, shudders ripping through her body, and walked over to my parents.

"Here," she said, partially shoving my twin sister into my father's arms. "Here's your daughter."

Viro's eyes were slits as he glared at Sybella, but they softened as he looked at my mother, who was now holding her arms out, wanting to have her child.

"Here she is, my love." Viro handed her my twin.

My sister cooed as she realized her mother was holding her; she reached a tiny hand up as she stretched and yawned in her blanket.

She opened her eyes to reveal they were light green. My mother gasped at the vivid color and leaned forward to nestle her head against my twin's body.

My mother appeared so peaceful when suddenly she shrieked. It was an abrupt, piercing sound of pain.

Viro blinked before stepping back, his eyes meeting the Oracle's in shock, who had appeared apprehensive the whole time my twin had been out of her arms.

Now she stared, wide-eyed, as Thera screamed.

My twin sister had brought her tiny hand up and outside of the blanket. She'd reached up and touched my mother's cheek with her bare skin, causing instant agony for Thera.

My sister's yellow-orange skull tattoo on her wrist began to glow as Thera continued to screech. It was soon interrupted as Viro quickly grabbed my twin, shoved her into Sybella's arms, and turned to my mother, who had become silent.

She looked at Viro in shock; sweat began to pool around her hairline, her chest heaving as she breathed.

What had just happened had shocked everyone. Thera's ability was healing, and she had instantly shrieked in pain by my sister's hand.

It seemed that my mother understood what had to happen as she stared at the Oracle. My sister was wrapped back in her blankets so no one could touch her.

"I... I'm... I'm sorry Thera, and Viro," Sybella said as she looked at both of my parents. "I'm going to have to take her

now; she's already caused great harm for you, Thera. I'm sorry,"
she repeated as my mother cried. "I truly am sorry about your
daughter," she said as she pulled my bundled-up sister to her chest,
making sure she had a good grip on her. "I have to take her."

Sybella held on to my twin when she started wailing loudly.

Within moments, gigantic black wings flew out of the Oracle's
back, appearing through her flesh. Sybella took one last look at
Viro and Thera before walking to the nearby open window.

She twisted around, my twin in her arms.

"Goodbye," she said as her wings flapped, and then she took
off into the sky, my parents staring after her.

Air struggled to get into my lungs as I attempted to breathe,
so shocked by everything I had seen. I could barely feel
Celio's hand on my shoulder.

I couldn't believe it.

I also didn't want to believe it.

My intestines writhed in knots as I tried breathing, which
made me almost sick to my stomach. I retreated a few steps
before I finally leaned down, bringing my head in between
my knees as I crouched over the grass.

It wasn't real. It *couldn't* be real.

But I knew, somewhere deep in my gut, it was real; it
was true.

I had a twin sister.

Not only that, I had a twin sister who was wreaking havoc
on the Earth, but now I knew exactly what she wanted.

She wanted me, and she was willing to kill anyone and
everything to get to me.

The Phantom, this, well, *evil,* was my sister.

Wow.

Suddenly, there was a noise in the distance, of tree branches moving, and I looked up to see a peculiar looking black figure flying off.

And that was when I realized that we were getting watched.

20

Thana

I squinted as I watched the black beetle walking across the hard rock. It was oblivious to the danger. I studied it for several moments, observing its movements, before I quickly crushed it between my fingers, smirking.

"I got you, you little pest," I said as it got squeezed under my palm; I squeezed the life out of the insect, enjoying the sound of the hard crunch of its shell, meaning the death of the beetle.

I laughed at the dead bug; I was glad I had killed it. But then, I had an idea.

"Wait... Hmmm..." I said out loud before I brought my hand up from the dead bug. "I wonder if that'll work...."

Using the hand with the skull tattoo on my wrist, I held it above the dead beetle. I moved my index finger and thumb away from each other, causing the beetle to become extended, longer, and straighter.

I chuckled and moved my index finger and thumb slightly, causing the insect to squeeze against itself; its head touched its rear end.

I looked at the ring the beetle had become before I poked it. I slipped it on my left ring finger before I smiled; I had just made my own jewelry.

It fit incredibly well, and I began knocking my new ring against the rocky floor a bit to see if it would break; it didn't.

"Ahhh," I extended my hand out to look at my new beetle-ring that was around my skin. "Durable and easy to make. Hmm."

My gaze shifted to the Ghostly region of the Abyss. I stared at the Inferno River, lost in thought.

I was thinking about how I'd gotten here, how I'd become the Queen of the Underworld.

How I'd gotten forced to rule Hell while my twin sister was on Earth, on Earth saving its inhabitants.

I growled, seething, my teeth gritted into my skull. I became enraged.

My *perfect* twin sister, who could do no wrong.

A familiar clicking sound on the rock followed by heavy breathing made me twist my body around, and I blinked, taken aback.

It was Damon, looking more ragged than he usually did.

He breathed in a gulp of oxygen before sputtering.

"My Queen, Thana, I found them," he said.

I froze, looking him in the face, wanting to know the truth.

"Are you certain?" I asked. I didn't want to get my hopes up.

He knew this was the type of news I was anxious to know.

He nodded, his wide, dirt brown eyes appearing even wider as he smiled, finally able to give me the good news.

"How?" I asked, not entirely convinced.

The last time I wanted him to find my sister and the Archangel, he had said he had *lost* them.

"I saw her tiger, the one she loves so much. It was following closely behind them. They didn't see the tiger, but I saw it moving along with them. Once I was able to see the tiger, I came across your sister and the Archangel. There were some horses as well."

"Where were they?" I asked harshly, tapping my new beetle-ring against the rock.

"They were at...at the Psychic Lake, Thana, my Queen," he said.

"The Psychic Lake?"

"Yes, Thana."

The way he said it made me squint.

"How do I know you're not lying to my face, Damon?"

"Because I am not, my Queen. I am telling you the truth." He looked nervous, and I couldn't blame him.

I looked at him for a few moments before getting up and approaching him.

He retreated several steps as his claws clacked against the surface of the ground.

"I promise you, Thana, I am telling you the truth," he said.

"You'd better be," I said as I walked past him and yelled. "Gog!"

The Goblin appeared from behind a hard rock wall; he bowed low.

"Yes, my Queen?"

Damon seemed to be stunned, looking from Gog to me and back again.

I ignored his confused look and saw Damon gulp hard.

"Gog lead the way; I want Damon to see my Beast," I said, staring at Damon the entire time I spoke.

"Yes, Thana, my Queen. Follow me." Gog walked in the direction of my Minotaur, who no doubt was craving more blood now that he'd had a taste of it already.

Damon's eyes were now vast in fear, but I ignored his expression as I walked right by him. Instead, I followed the Goblin.

"Come on, Damon, you have to see him." I wanted Damon to have fear.

There was a clacking sound as he moved his claws on the hard rock, and he took off, flying behind me. An apprehensive breath escaped his lungs as he did so, causing me to grin.

He was now beginning to understand what his fate would be if he failed me.

The Minotaur's breath was red hot as it escaped its mouth and brushed against my face.

It snorted, enraged, and I smiled.

The Minotaur snorted again before throwing its head back and roaring.

I wasn't afraid of it, though, as I watched him.

On the other hand, Damon was, and I heard him falter in the air; his wings stopped flapping as he saw the Minotaur.

His claws clicked against the rock as he landed on it.

I twisted around to see his reaction when his eyes met the Beasts'.

He saw the Beast as I observed and he began to hyperventilate as the bull-like creature locked eyes with him, licking its bloody muzzle as it did so.

The Minotaur bellowed in Damon's face as he stood frozen with fear. His withered body appeared haggard as he took in the Beast's muzzle and coal red eyes.

"Thana," he said, sounding almost close to tears as he saw the creature, "Thana... My....mmm...my Queen... I promise you; I am telling you the truth! I swear! This time I found them!"

"Where is your proof?" I tapped my left hand against my right palm idly.

Damon's dirt-colored eyes widened as he stared at me with tight lips. It looked like he was going to start crying as his gaze hit the floor.

Tears started escaping, staining his rough hide.

The marks from my fingernails were still embedded in his flesh, looking excruciatingly painful.

Not that I cared for him.

Right now, he needed proof that he had found my sister but looked fearful as he watched the floor.

"I don't have any," Damon said, gulping down oxygen quickly as he averted my gaze.

"You don't *have* any?"

"No. No, I do not, my Queen."

"Hmm," I said, watching him. "Well, that is unfortunate." He still wouldn't look at me. He knew that he had failed me once more.

I heard flapping in the distance suddenly; I looked up and listened to a loud caw.

It took me a few moments to realize that it was my crow tattoo flying toward me.

I grinned maniacally as the crow neared, and I extended my arm out.

Caw.

"Do you have any important information for me, I wonder?" I asked the crow as it landed. "Well, let's find out..."

I brought the arm where the crow perched over my heart, and the black bird extended its wings, flying back into my skin and becoming absorbed in my flesh.

Since the crow had left my skin, it had picked up memories that had now been transferred to me, since I had reabsorbed it.

It was time to view them.

21

My name isn't Thana.

I don't know what my real name is, the one I was given at birth, or if I even have one at all.

I was taken from my parents by the Oracle, who had named me. My name means *death*. She then drowned me in the Inferno River, the River which led me down below to the Underworld; this is how I got condemned to death there, how I had gotten forced to rule Hell.

I ruled Hell, drowning in the depths of the Inferno River, ruling over the Deathly Beings; the Banshees, the Ghosts, and the Wraiths. However, my sister was on Earth. She was able to communicate with the Archangels, the Prophetic Beings, and the Earth's Creatures.

I *hated* her.

Chrysanthe protected the land and the wildlife, and the weather. She watched the Earth while I had the potential to destroy it.

She had the blessing from my father, Viro, to rule over a portion of the Earth, the part only for Celestial Beings. This portion was shut off to mortals so they would not know of our existence.

There was an invisible barrier created thousands of years ago that protected the Celestials on the Earth from mortals.

The Immortal Lands, Viro called them. The Immortal Lands was the portion of the Earth Chrysanthe was allowed to rule since her power helped replenish it.

The Celestial Beings really live high in the sky; their original homeland was in the Clouds, near the Archangels, residing in the Ethereal City. Once a Being had a ceremony where Viro would proclaim them Ruler of a place for all eternity, the Celestial Being had gotten a permanent home.

Viro helped Chrysanthe ever since the Oracle had made her the Protector of the Earth. Helped her control the Immortal Lands, and because of that, Chrysanthe's permanent home was on the Earth, living among the Life she protected.

I gritted my teeth together, jealousy flooding my system at the mere thought, and I swallowed hard against my throat.

My lip curled upward as I snarled in disgust.

I hated my twin. *I hated her.* I hated Chrysanthe and the fact she was so nauseatingly perfect.

Respected, pure, and oh so *perfect*.

I watched every one of her accomplishments, as I had gotten forced to see her succeed from the Inferno River.

Not only did the River contain Ghosts and was the main entryway to Hell, but it was also my torture, my only way to the outside World.

It was the only way I could see anything, view anything, on Earth, in the Immortal Lands, or the Ethereal City.

It was all in the poisoned Water, all there so I could see it.

But I couldn't touch it; I couldn't change it. I couldn't communicate with anyone.

All I could do was watch.

That was what I was sentenced to, what I had gotten condemned to, for all eternity. To watch every other Being excel and advance, be excellent, and grow up to be powerful, while I had gotten cut away from the World, forced to grow up in the Darkness.

That was how I had lived for millennia.

I could feel the 'thoughts' of my tattoo being absorbed into my brain as I stood in front of Damon.

I clenched my teeth together as I saw the mental images fly through my mind.

It only took a few moments to view everything.

Those moments were all I needed.

I was sure I had found Chrysanthe; I had found my twin sister.

"So, it turns out you were right, Damon. She was there." I looked at the former Archangel, who was now viewing me with wide, fearful eyes.

He still had tears drying on his cheeks.

"I know she was," he retorted, his voice shaking slightly. "I told you, and am telling you, the truth, Thana. I did find her."

"Yes. Yes, you did," I said before turning around and beginning to walk off. I paused to twist around and glance at Damon. "Well, come on." I beckoned him forward. "You don't want to stay with the Beast, do you?" I asked him, and he immediately flew away from the creature, who was still fighting the chains around its neck.

"Come on, Damon," I said before twisting my body back around. "You don't need to be near here anymore. We're going to go on a walk."

And with that, I began making my way down the dark hallway, over toward where the Gates were. My footsteps echoed as I did so.

22

Chrysanthe

 rumble ripped through the ground beneath me as it began to shake; the entire Earth reverberated underneath my feet.

I looked around me, at the grass and the dirt; I realized in the now fading light that the sediment beneath us was disintegrating. It was because of the tremors that were darting through the hard-packed ground.

I took a deep breath, trying to steady myself, but it only made the tremors worse until the shaking made the landscape genuinely separate.

I was the cause of this; my powers were becoming out of control.

I tried to steady my breathing as my heart battered my rib cage, and I gulped as I tried to stop the sediment beneath me from crumbling. But it was to no avail.

The Earth was breaking apart; cracks ruptured through the ground, which caused the tree roots to become visible as they tore through it.

I stared, petrified, as the Earth disappeared beneath my feet. I glanced over at Celio, whose wings were now out and flapped behind his body. He lifted himself off the Earth.

The Apparition blinked several times before looking at the surrounding destruction; she took off immediately, and her transparent body seemed to fly off into the trees.

I heard Celio flying above me; his hand extended out so that he could grasp mine.

"Chrysanthe, we must leave now! Come on, grab my hand!" he yelled over the roar of the destruction.

I grasped my lovers' hand right as I felt the dirt beneath me fall apart entirely, leaving nothing to stand on.

I grabbed Celio's hand at the right time.

He lifted me and pulled my body to his.

Celio's arm wrapped around me protectively, keeping me from falling. I grasped his body tightly as we flew higher and higher. We flew away from the cracked and crumbled soil beneath us. I didn't know what caused it; I had never had my powers stray before.

A lump formed in my throat. In the distance, I heard a whinny, and I turned to see the Unicorn mare galloping into the woods as the ground beneath her broke apart.

I watched her disappear into the trees, my heart breaking into pieces at the sight.

It was all my fault.

I felt a tear run down my cheek, and I sniffled; Celio held me closer, and that was when I heard a crunch.

I looked down to see the Earth completely broken. The roots of the trees showed through the dirt that was now completely exposed.

Oh, no. No. No. No. No. No.

I attempted to breathe, but every time I did, there was a tightness in my chest, which caused it to catch in my lungs.

I had done this. I had destroyed the Earth. I had torn everything apart.

My heart was suddenly in my windpipe.

I couldn't move; I couldn't breathe.

My pulse pounded in my eardrums as Celio quickly helped me to my feet.

A gulp escaped my throat as I glanced at both the Apparition and Celio. I watched their nonplussed faces as they stood on either side of me.

There was so much information to soak in.

The powerful and awful thought that came to me about my abilities suddenly wreaking havoc on the Earth wasn't a good thing either. Was it a premonition? Would I cause the Earth to shatter?

It took several moments to figure out how to breathe again, and even then, it was hard for my intestines to stop squirming; they felt like liquid. I had found out so much about the Phantom. About my twin sister.

Celio's hazel eyes met mine, and I quickly turned toward the Apparition, who seemed to be panicking.

She stared at both Celio and I, giving us an anxious look.

"We must leave, now," she said. "The enchantment I had put over you both is now gone, so we must go. Right now."

"Do you know what that figure was?" I asked her. "The figure that flew off, what was that?"

"That was your twin's messenger. Your sister sent him to find you. I managed to keep him away from us with the enchantment, but now it seems, somehow, he broke through."

What? I thought, not wholly understanding. *My twin has a messenger? There are a lot of things I am learning about today.*

"How?" I asked her. "How did the messenger break through the enchantment?"

But then I realized the Apparition was probably thinking the same thing.

"Right now, it doesn't matter, Chrysanthe. Right now, all that matters is disappearing from this area. We must get out of here, before the messenger, or your sister, shows up. Let's go," she said, and when I caught a glimpse of her again, I saw a tear cascade down her transparent cheek.

23

I sighed as I petted Leora's neck, cooing as she nickered. She tilted her head to the side once she could hear me.

"Good girl, Leora. You've been such a good girl." She brought her head close to me once I began to dismount, and I brought my hand to her ears so I could play with her mane.

She snorted at the sensation of my palms running through it, and I laughed.

"You're such a good Unicorn."

"She's brought you all this way, which is a good thing. You should praise her," the Apparition said. "She's been an excellent mount."

I nodded, agreeing with her. She was right. The Unicorn had brought me a long way; she deserved the attention.

We had continued to move after spotting my sister's messenger and managed to get to the edge of a forest in the darkening light.

It was almost nightfall, and my eyelids were drooping. I was exhausted.

There was an abrupt rumble from deep within the forest as I looked around, trying to find an area to go to sleep. I perked up immediately, though, as I heard it, instantly alert.

The darkening sky bled into the forest as I scanned my surroundings. The horses stomped the ground nervously, walking in circles.

What? I thought as I quieted Leora.

"Shhh." I tried to calm the Unicorn. "Shhh, Leora. Wait..."

It wasn't until a few moments later that I recognized the rumble, as another one broke through the silence.

So breathy and relaxed, but still familiar.

It was Caliya.

The tiger had followed us.

A smile spread across my face, and I inhaled quickly before calling her name out.

"Caliya! Come on, girl! Come over here, Caliya!"

I heard her moving as she ran to me, and the horses spooked, galloping away from the moving tiger.

Caliya ran straight to me, moaning and rumbling as she rubbed her body against mine happily.

Celio laughed as he saw me fall over due to Caliya's strength. He walked over and pulled me to my feet.

"Up you come, Chrysanthe," he said, a grin on his face as he put his hand on my back so I wouldn't fall.

I laughed, looking up at his hazel eyes once he pulled me up to his chest. He leaned forward and kissed my cheek.

"Thank you, Celio."

Celio looked down at Caliya as she rubbed her head against his stomach, circling him as she continued to moan.

"Hey there, Caliya." He watched the tiger and petted her fur.

I laughed as Caliya's breathy, friendly moan radiated through her throat. I laid down and stroked her ear.

"Good girl, Caliya," I told her. "You're such a good girl."

I was praising all the Creatures today.

Caliya pushed her gigantic head into my chest affectionately. "Aww, Caliya."

Celio laughed from above me.

A second laugh came from the Apparition. I twisted my head to look at her.

"How long have you known her?" she asked me, looking down at Caliya.

"Since she was a cub," I replied. "Her mother had gotten killed, so the Oracle gave her to me to raise."

"Hmm…" the Apparition replied. "We could use as many eyes and ears as possible to get to our destination. I think your tiger could be valuable."

I peered over at Caliya, who was now flat on the ground, her tail twitching in the air as she breathed in a relaxed manner. I knew the tiger would never leave my side; she was still so attached to me, as I was to her. I guessed she was valuable to what we were doing because she was a Creature of the Earth.

I glanced at the Apparition again and nodded.

"Yes. Yes, Caliya can certainly help us."

I tugged on Celio's arm.

"Come here, Celio," I said, while Caliya emitted a breathy moan, glancing up at him. He grinned before crouching down and petting Caliya's head gently.

"Hello there, sweetheart," he said, laughing as Caliya answered him in a rumble.

I smiled as he did, and he twisted his head toward me.

"Hello, Chrysanthe," he breathed before he kissed me in a way that made my insides melt.

I pulled him close to me for a few moments before I broke away.

Caliya had settled down to sleep, and she looked utterly relaxed as she put her colossal head on the grass. Her amber eyes blinked before she shut them and disappeared into a slumber.

I wasn't far behind her as I extended my arms out to stretch before I yawned and put my head on her massive body.

Celio leaned forward and kissed my cheek before going over to a nearby tree and leaning on it.

I managed to catch his wink before I shut my eyes completely.

A branch breaking in half above me caused my eyes to snap open, wide and alert.

For a moment, I scanned my surroundings and wondered if something had happened while I had been asleep, but I relaxed when I realized that it was just a tree branch snapping in the wind.

I blinked away the bright light as the sun shone above us; it took me a few moments before I saw Celio; his back was to me. He took off his shirt and threw it to the ground, his winged tattoo glowing on his skin.

He rolled his shoulders forward and stared at the sky as the wings started to protrude from his flesh, and I watched them unfolding. They were beautiful.

Then he twisted around to look at me.

"Good morning, Chrysanthe." He smiled.

"Good morning, Celio."

He walked over to me and extended his arm out; I took it before I stood up and stretched. I didn't think I would sleep as well as I did.

"So…where do we go now?" Celio continued to look at me.

I shook my head. I had no clue. The Apparition was our guide, and right now, she was nowhere that I knew of.

Apparitions didn't sleep, so I had no idea where she was at the moment.

"I guess we could look around for a while," I said, glancing at Celio.

He nodded.

"Yeah," he said. "Let's do that."

We then walked toward the forest; the sunlight cut through the branches and shone on the leaves as we did so.

We had just reached an old-looking tree when I spotted something that instantly sent a chill rattling down my spine.

24

The old, withered tree had a large rock underneath it, almost like the tree was perched on the hard surface.

"What the...? What's this?" I wondered as I slipped my hand from Celio's so that I could examine it.

I gasped, though, as I noticed charred bits of bark surrounding the outside of it.

That was when I realized the design was...was...was...

Air soared through my lungs as it all came together, as I started to understand what was going on.

The design on the bark of the tree was a skull.

My twin sister had been here. She had touched this tree.

But how she'd left the burn marking on it had me confused.

I touched the design on it, feeling the ridges of it and the charred, scorched bits of bark, when suddenly there was a deep, Earthly rumble that shook the ground.

I stepped backward and turned around to see Celio, who was as concerned as I was.

What the...? I started but got cut off as I saw the rock below the tree suddenly move. A gigantic blue eye opened from the side of the 'rock' and narrowed into slits as it stared at me in anger.

What? I thought in terror as I saw that the 'rock' rose out of the ground. The tree was the back of the beast.

The 'tree' flapped down over the spine of the beast as it came alive; the 'roots' came out of the ground on either side of Celio and I. That was when the creature rose to its full height, towering over the both of us.

The creature was colossal, and I stepped back, surprised and in shock at what had just happened and also the beast in front of me.

There are a lot of things I had known about since I was the Protector of the Earth. But I had never seen anything like this before. Ever.

Wait a moment, I thought, squinting as I looked at the beast.

I remembered hearing the Oracle talk about creatures who lived among nature, who lived among the Earth, like this one.

It was a troll.

The troll leaned forward and sniffed us tentatively. It brought its massive head towards us; its nose almost poked us as it smelt our bodies.

I shut my eyes as the creature's breath doused me, as I felt its body close to mine. That was when anger instantly blistered through the troll, and it roared straight in my face. It caused my blood to run cold as the troll threw its massive, root-like limbs out, attempting to knock me over.

I ducked just in time so the 'roots' wouldn't hit me; a spine-chilling, guttural roar burst out of the troll as it saw me block its attempts to get me.

It stared right at me with blazing blue eyes as it attempted to get me again, but to no avail.

First, it attempted to hit me with its left limb, and then with its right, but I ducked yet again, so I had gotten missed...yet again.

Dirt hit my face in clumps as the limbs attacked me, and I spit it out.

"Chrysanthe!" Celio screamed.

I felt a quick brush of air against my cheek and face as Celio rushed right in front of me, throwing his wings out and staring at the enormous beast.

The troll stopped and glared at Celio angrily.

I finally managed to climb to my feet and grasped onto Celio's shoulder to regain my balance. The troll took a deep breath after a few moments, and then I could see its eyes soften as it continued to stare at Celio. Instead of the dark slits, they were not so tense anymore.

I inhaled deeply before I began walking over to the troll. I ignored Celio's worried look and approached the beast.

The troll stared at me as I watched it, exhaling in a huff; its colossal chest was heaving with the effort, but the creature made no attempts to hurt me as I walked closer to it.

It's alright; I'm not going to hurt you, I thought as I made my way closer to the troll, walking carefully. *You don't have to be afraid.*

The blue-eyed troll looked at me right as I stopped in front of its enormous chest, looking at the skull that had gotten burned into the creature's skin.

The beast put its head down then, looking down at the grass before turning its head back up toward me, gazing into my eyes.

It's alright. I waited calmly; I brought out my hand so that it could sniff my flesh again, and the troll leaned forward, bringing its massive head toward me.

It sniffed my hand tentatively before the troll let out a moan that was enough to make the ground beneath me rumble.

I brought my hand back down to my sides; the creature just watched me after that; all the anger and the ferociousness was gone from it.

That was when I knew that the troll wasn't going to hurt me now. It had just been frustrated before.

I gazed up at the creature and spotted the skull burned onto it from my twin sister, right where the creature's heart would be.

Oh, you poor thing.

The troll paused and allowed me to put my hand on its flesh.

The beast's blue eyes closed as it relaxed, and I smiled when it opened them again, almost resembling Caliya after I rubbed her ears.

It watched me intently and then attempted to look at the burn mark on its heart. Another moan escaped the creature, and it blew air over me as it exhaled heavily.

"Oh, you poor sweet thing." I neared the burn mark and reached up on my tiptoes so I could reach it. I lay my hand on it, and within moments I felt the heat radiating from my palm, healing the skull burn.

The skull burn entirely disappeared from the flesh of the creature.

The troll sighed in delight as it healed, but that was when I quickly heard a loud shriek from the sky; I jumped and twisted around, only to see the atmosphere instantly change.

The sun went behind the clouds; the skies immediately turned gloomy.

A tremendous black cloud made its way toward us, looking very ominous.

I squinted, confused, but then I saw the crows flying along with the cloud, and my heart began to pound against my rib cage.

"Oh, no," I mumbled as the black cloud approached us.

It was not going to be good, what was going to happen.

It was not going to be good at all.

Thana

I stared at the splatter of discoloration on her skin and noticed the purple-blue bruising over her right eye. The skin and the tissue had swollen shut so that she couldn't see properly.

Her lips had parted slightly, and her mouth opened, but only a moan escaped.

My lips curled, revealing my teeth as I snarled at her. She tried to see me with her one good eye, but it was clear she was in pain. It was then I saw her black, disheveled wings.

They were disintegrating.

They were utterly decomposing now that she was in the Underworld and not in the Afterlife anymore.

"Please, please, please..."

I walked around and ignored her. I heard a growl and saw Morgeran behind me.

He stared at her; his hackles raised as a deep, throaty growl rumbled through his body. His teeth were exposed as he snarled viciously.

I smiled at Morgeran before twisting back to face her battered and bruised body.

"Please... Please," she continued, trying to stop me from torturing her.

I was angry at her and gritted my teeth.

She deserved it. She needed to feel the pain I felt, not only on the outside but also on the inside.

How dare she let the Oracle drown me in the Underworld?

How dare she let me live my life in complete misery, meanwhile my twin sister, Chrysanthe, had everything?

It was her fault. It was all her fault.

And now she was going to pay the price.

Morgeran snapped at my mother; his razor-sharp teeth looked deadly as he stalked around her body.

Morgeran looked at me, waiting for a signal, and I raised my arm high; he tensed in anticipation, but then suddenly, a blood-curdling scream erupted from her. It was so loud and so full of distress it even made *me* pause.

"PLEASE, MY DAUGHTER! NO!"

I stopped. She had never referred to me as her blood before. She hadn't mentioned my name either. It was the first time she'd acknowledged me as one of her own kin.

That statement made me pause.

I lowered my hand in a way so Morgeran wouldn't go straight for her throat. My mother had tears rolling down her cheeks, and she let out a small, pained moan.

"Please, no, my daughter! Please, don't do this!" she wailed as she looked at me, her eyes squeezed shut.

I hadn't let Morgeran attack yet, but it didn't mean that I wasn't going to.

The Hellhound stared at me, knowing he couldn't go after my mother.

A rumble blistered through his body as he was displeased, but I ignored him as I yelled at my so-called mother.

"Why? Why shouldn't I? You left me with the Oracle who drowned me and left me in Hell for millennia! Millennia! She left me to drown in the Inferno River while I was an *infant*! Letting me grow up and watch my twin through the Waters; watching her grow up and become so spectacular! She gets everything, and I get nothing!" I screamed, anger boiling inside me.

"Yes, yes... Yes... You do," my mother stammered through her agony. "You have abilities like no other Being in any...any... Realm. You had...have...the love of both of your parents, which strengthened once you were in the Abyss. We missed you, Calla, we missed you so much, Calla."

My breath caught for a moment.

Was that my real name? Was my name Calla?

"C... Calla, please... Don't continue this. This isn't...the way I wanted my daughter to act. Even though you have the potential to harm, you shouldn't. You've always been Calla to me, always have been...have been...beautiful... Even when you had gotten trapped in the Underworld. Even when the Oracle took you and gave you the name Thana."

I had gotten taken by surprise.

As I stared at her, I realized she was telling me the truth. My name was Calla. I finally knew, after all the millennia, what my real name was.

And now, I knew I'd always been with her. I'd always been in her thoughts, even when I was in the Underworld. She had cared.

A sudden, quick, squirming movement within my chest made me glance down at my crow tattoo. It was becoming real, protruding from my skin to perch on my arm.

Caw.

It looked straight at me with small, beady eyes.

It opened its beak.

Caw. Caw. Caw.

It was trying to tell me something.

Caw. Caw.

It threw its head back, and I turned around to see what it saw.

Outside where my mother had gotten tortured was the Inferno River. A Wraith was beside it, drifting above the hard, rocky ground.

I saw a black, scabbed hand sticking out from underneath its cloak. I stared for a few moments before I realized the Wraith was beckoning me forward so that I could look into the Inferno River.

Something was going on. And I wanted to find out what.

I approached the Wraith and stared into the water.

It was Chrysanthe.

She was very close, but thankfully, I knew exactly where she was.

And I knew precisely how to track her down.

I glanced over to my crow.

"Find her," I commanded before it flew off into the darkness and disappeared.

I looked over at Damon, who had been out by the Inferno River, keeping a healthy distance from my mother.

I looked straight into Damon's dirt-colored eyes.

"Find her, Damon. Find Chrysanthe. Once you do, I will come and follow you."

"What?" Damon asked, dumbstruck.

Never before had he ever questioned me, but I had never requested anything like this back.

"Find her, Damon," I said. "Find her, and I will follow you so I can see her myself."

Damon stared at me for a few moments before he nodded and flew off into the darkness.

I twisted my body to gaze at my mother, whose face was an utterly swollen mess.

"Well, I guess today is your lucky day," I told her as she watched me with her black and blue eyes. "Your life has been spared, mother."

I walked off across the dark, black rock, following the Wraith as it drifted across the ground; Morgeran followed softly behind me.

26

Chrysanthe

Thunder cracked across the sky as the cloud neared unnaturally, causing shivers to rip through my spine.

I shook as I saw the black cloud and heard the loud noise, as well as the cackling crows.

"Chrysanthe!" I heard Celio yell, and I looked to see him running towards me; his wings were outstretched, ready to flap. "Chrysanthe, hang on!"

As lightning erupted across the sky, he reached me and threw his arms around my body; he lifted me from the ground and into the air.

Within mere moments, we were flying.

He held me tightly as he navigated through the forest to get to the open air and toward the clouds. But that was when another lightning strike caused a tree branch to fall from its perch. It landed right in front of us.

NO!

I screamed as it collided with Celio. The branch scratched my arm as we plunged toward the ground; it was incredible how far we were from it after only a few moments.

Luckily, we never hit the grass. The troll roared as it reached out and caught us in its palms before we plummeted to the Earth.

It lightly put us on the ground, moaning sweetly, and exhaled in our faces.

I felt my body shake as I stared ahead. Suddenly, I started hyperventilating.

And I, a Celestial Being, *never* got afraid. So, it was a first for me.

I felt Celio's arms wrap around me as lightning struck a tree not far from us. The weather was becoming too dangerous to fly in. Unless....

The troll in front of me roared as it stared ahead, seemingly unfazed by the danger headed in our direction.

The ground started shaking.

The Earth trembled underneath my feet, ripping apart in places as I looked down. Mesmerized, I turned my attention toward the forest, which, to my shock, had vines snaking around the trunks of the trees. The branches moved as the rocks on the ground shifted.

The troll roared once more and stared ahead. I quickly understood that the creature controlled the greenery.

I smiled, finally convinced that it was good.

What if we used both of our powers?

"Stay back, my love," I said to Celio as I broke free from his arms, ignoring the cautious look he gave me. "Celio, I have to do this."

He let me go then, seeming to understand.

Thank you, I thought before I looked over at the troll.

Bringing my attention to my feet, I saw that grass was rapidly growing beneath me.

I still have it, I thought. *I still have my powers.*

And now I was going to use them, all of the abilities I had, to protect the Realm I called home.

I glanced behind me, watching the vines snaking around the trees' trunks and the roots getting pulled from the ground.

I was so ready for this.

I threw my arms up, sending the tree roots towards the cackling crows. I made a full-grown tree appear, which blocked the blackbirds, but lightning quickly struck the tree, and it snapped in half.

The troll abruptly roared so loud and with so much force that the ground shook.

It sent shockwaves throughout the Earth, and I saw the vines from the forest trees moving toward the now dead tree. It wrapped around it before a blood-red rose formed at the top of the dead tree. All while a large black cloud was nearing us.

I heard the beast exhale as the forest quickly began to move. Trees attacked — growing taller. The roots sprang from the Earth and struck the crows as they bound themselves to the dead tree.

The tree roots choked the crows; the roots wrapped themselves around their necks, the greenery squeezed the life out of the birds before the crows disappeared, evaporating into smoke.

Wait a moment.

These weren't ordinary crows. These were enchanted birds created by my twin.

Of course, she was still hunting me.

There was a loud shriek suddenly, so loud it almost made me jump out of my own skin. I heard voices getting carried by the wind.

What the...?

Was I going crazy, or was this real?

But the answer came quickly to my mind as I saw the orangish-red smoke come closer.

It was real.

The voices were *in* the smoke.

What is going on here? I thought as it hurtled toward me.

There was an eccentric laughing that ripped through the air as it quickly surrounded me.

I'd never heard or dealt with anything like this before.

I glared, angry as I squinted through the fog; I threw my hands up so I wouldn't be driven mad by the noises. I waved my extremities around and caused the weather to change instantly. The smoke disappeared, sunlight beaming down.

As the clouds dissipated, the blood-curdling screams cried out.

What is going on here? Who or what was screeching?

I found myself screaming as I became aggravated.

"GET OUT OF HERE!" I shrieked at the wind.

As if on cue, the troll beside me roared so tremendously and so profoundly that it seemed like the entire forest shook.

Then I remembered Celio, and turned to see how he was doing. But when I turned around, I immediately felt the blood drain from my face.

He wasn't there.

My heart started to pound as I became scared and anxious. Celio. Celio. Where was he?

"Celio!" I yelled, but he didn't yell back. "Celio!"

That was when I spotted a single, long, black feather on the ground.

No. No. No. No. No. I leaned forward and picked up the feather.

I was desperate to find him, but then I noticed what was in the sky.

I saw a winged, emaciated looking black creature fly off into the atmosphere.

It hit me quickly.

Celio had gotten taken.

"NO!"

27

Thana

 chorus of blood-curdling shrieks caused me to blink, breaking me out of my reverie.

Gog ran up; his Goblin features were contorted with overexertion as I sat on my Throne, sitting contently and petting Morgeran.

"Thana, my Queen. It is..."

"THANA! WHERE ARE YOU, MY QUEEN!"

Another screech.

I stood up straight in my seat and squinted as I heard the shrieks for a second time.

It was the Banshees. The Banshees had seen something.

"Thana? My Queen?" Damon's voice carried over the Abyss loudly. "I have something that is of great value to you."

I looked over at Gog, who was clutching his side, and he nodded in agreement with Damon.

I had my doubts, though.

Damon? Finding something of great value? For me?

The withered former Archangel must've lost his mind.

"What is it, Damon?" I shouted over the Abyss.

"Come and see. You'll love what I found for you." His voice carried over to me.

Damon's statement was enough to make my eyes roll. I stood from my Throne, ignoring Morgeran's snarl.

He was upset that I had stopped petting him and looked at me disdainfully.

Damon. Damon. Damon, I thought. *You pesky former Archangel. I wonder what you have for me.*

I opened my wings and flew off to see what Damon had found.

Morgeran's snarl tore through the Abyss as I landed on the rock.

My neck twitched at the sound, and it took me a moment to realize Morgeran had made his way over to Damon, and he was unsupervised.

No, Morgeran, I thought, knowing what would happen next. *No, Morgeran, no!*

I rushed around the dark, dank area, running toward the Inferno River, when I heard Morgeran's teeth snap. He growled so loud, and so viciously I felt the tension in his muscles, all the way from where I was.

When I turned the corner to the Inferno River, the Ghosts hit me square in the face, which caused me to stop. The old, musty, dead smell of them erupted. I could taste the Dead on my tongue, and I grimaced as I made my way over toward my Hellhound.

I saw then that Morgeran's hackles had gotten raised, his teeth exposed as he continued to snarl.

But when I saw what he was looking at, I smirked.

Damon stood there. But that wasn't what held my attention.

It was that Damon had an Archangel with him.

I couldn't speak for several moments.

I walked forward, staring at the Archangel before I saw Damon grinning broadly.

"What do you think, Thana?" Damon asked, a giddiness in his voice. "You didn't even have to follow us; we found him with your twin," he said, beaming.

I soaked in the information as I approached the Archangel.

I watched him silently and studied his features.

He was incredibly defined, his bare chest muscular, a lot more muscular than I would've imagined. His short, dark brown hair was slightly damp with sweat. His eyes were to the side since he wasn't looking at me, and his massive, black angel wings flapped behind him.

I paused, becoming still as I stared at him, and addressed Damon as we watched each other.

"Damon, you have been a good messenger. You have gotten the Archangel my twin sister cares so deeply for."

Then I locked eyes with Damon.

"You will go lock him up until he is ready to talk. Right now, he doesn't want to do a thing, but I'm sure since he guards the Spirits in the Afterworld, he'll find great company with the Ghosts."

I looked at the Archangel again and walked forward, grabbing and tilting his chin upward so that he faced me.

He gritted his teeth but still looked me in the eyes.

"Let's see if you are a match for *my* creatures," I said, bringing my face as close as possible to his. "Let's see what Chrysanthe thinks about that."

28

Chrysanthe

"*NO!*"

I twisted around rapidly, shaking. I panicked as I searched my surroundings, hoping that Celio was near me. But it was futile.

Celio was gone.

"No. No. No. No. No. *No!*"

I shut my eyes and blinked away the tears. I tried to steady my breathing and calm down; after a few moments, I lifted my hands and opened my eyes. I angled my palms and healed the Earth, which had begun to crumble into disarray because of my anxious state.

It worked immediately.

The Earth began to mend itself; within the blink of an eye, the ground was entirely back to the way it was before.

Healthy, green, and beautiful.

But even though I smiled at the greenery, it faded as I realized what had happened.

Celio was gone.

He was taken, taken by my twin, taken by her messenger.

Taken to the Underworld.

An Archangel in the Underworld.

I had to get him back. *I had to.*

"Chrysanthe?"

I turned at the sound of my name.

Who was that?

But then I saw her, floating through the trees quickly, making her way toward me.

It was the Apparition.

"Chrysanthe?" she asked again.

My eyes were raw. I'd been crying so hard in my distress, and I knew they were incredibly inflamed.

"What happened, Chrysanthe?"

"Celio... Celio... He...he...got taken. He got taken by the messenger of my twin. He's...in the Underworld." I paused in between breaths, struggling to steady my breathing. "I'm trying not...not to...lose control either because it will damage the Earth."

The Apparition took in everything and calmly spoke.

"Look at me," she said, and I glanced up from where I was studying the ground. "We are going to get Celio back, okay?"

She paused for a moment before continuing.

"We will get him, I promise, but it is not going to be easy. We are going to have to travel to another Realm to get the help we need before we go to the Underworld."

I blinked in surprise.

What?

"Another Realm?" I asked.

"Yes," the Apparition replied. "There, we can get the help we need so we can rescue Celio."

"What is the name of it?"

"The Flourishing Realm," she said.

A soft brush underneath my palm quickly made me look down, only to see Caliya brushed up against my hand. Her striped fur was smooth as it stroked my skin.

"Oh, Caliya." I leaned down so I could pet her head. "I love you so much."

"Chrysanthe?" the Apparition asked, grabbing my attention once again.

I looked up at her and then nodded, understanding what she was saying.

"Okay, let's go get Celio," I said.

I gazed around at my surroundings, looking for Leora, but couldn't see her anywhere.

I whistled before I saw her gallop out of the forest.

The same forest where the troll was.

Where is the creature? I wondered; I tried to catch a glimpse as it walked off, but it was nowhere.

Hmm, I thought as Leora came up to me, warily snorting when she saw Caliya.

I peered down at the tiger, who watched the Unicorn with a steady gaze. Caliya's amber-colored eyes shone as she watched Leora.

"No, Caliya," I said to the big striped cat as she stared at the Unicorn. "No."

I walked over to Leora and brushed my hand over her snout before mounting her quickly.

"Let's go get Celio," I said as I moved a little on Leora's back, twisting around to see the enormous forest.

I instantly paused, though.

Hmm. I looked at the trees in front of me, the thick greenery.

There was no clear pathway through there, but I could make one.

All I had to do was focus.

I stared at the gigantic forest ahead of me and gazed at the massive trees.

I focused on that, concentrated on the greenery in front of me. Within a few moments, there was a loud groan echoing through the ground. I saw the trees move backward;

the roots and tendrils retreated out of the dirt, parting the way to make a path.

That's more like it. I turned my attention to the Apparition.

She looked right back at me; a smile extended across her face.

"Let's go get your Archangel," she said as she grinned. I brushed Leora lightly with my tattooed foot, and we took off along the pathway I had made into the forest.

29

Celio

cough rattled through my body as I sat on the cold ground. I supported myself from falling chest first into the black rock.

The Underworld's effect was immediate on me, which made sense since I was an Archangel.

Archangels didn't survive in the Underworld for very long.

I coughed again, and as I opened my eyes, I noticed them.

The Cloaked Spirits, the Wraiths outside the prison, that I had been thrown into by the winged, withered black creature. The prison looked like bone remnants.

I shivered at the thought, but then again, I was in the Abyss, so I shouldn't have been so surprised.

I watched the Wraiths as they drifted along the prison cell as if I was their prey. I immediately felt powerless under the gaze of these monsters.

There was nothing I could do here; I really was powerless in Hell.

Archangels didn't belong in Hell with these creatures.

I felt my wings flap behind me in my agitation as I watched the Cloaked Spirits, but then I closed my eyes. I didn't want them to see my wings anymore.

I didn't want to have them out in the open.

I shut my eyes, focusing all of my attention on pushing them back into my flesh, and, within moments, I felt them go straight into my back, soaking into my skin in the form of my tattoo.

A quick, sudden laughing startled me, breaking me out of my reverie and causing me to become more alert.

My eyes snapped open as I looked around; I abruptly saw the orange-red smoke coming closer. I knew what it was. It was the smoke that had ripped me away from Chrysanthe.

I didn't forget the shriveled, black monster that had picked me up.

Chrysanthe...

I loved her so much...

The colored haze hit me as I glared, angry at the thought of being separated from her.

I coughed yet again, choking and gagging on the nauseating smell.

It was old, musty, and disgusting.

It tasted stale, dead.

Yuck! I thought as I tasted it on my tongue.

The laughing increased in intensity as I convulsed, trying hard to get rid of the taste. The haze suddenly enveloped me.

What is this?

The smoke continued to choke me and block my visibility.

Nothing is making sense.

"We are the Ghosts."

I froze in shock as a hissing voice appeared in my ear. I inhaled quickly, exhaling as yet another, giddy, extreme laugh erupted beside me.

"Who are you?"

I glared and squinted through the fog. I spotted the Wraiths through the prison cell bars.

I would not talk to them. I won't speak to the voices.

Different ones hissed at me, and I couldn't differentiate between them.

"Who is he?", "He's pretty," and "I wonder what Thana is going to do to you, maybe feed you to the Beast." These were just some of the comments I heard.

Thana? And Beast? Feed me to the Beast?

What did this all mean? Wait.

Thana. Thana. *Thana.*

The name of the Phantom is Thana. She's Chrysanthe's twin.

Huh.

But feeding me to the Beast? What did that mean?

I gulped, quickly wondering if one of the Cloaked Spirits in front of me was somehow the Beast. I doubted it after looking at the Wraiths, though; there were way too many of them for one to be the Beast.

I sighed. All I wanted to do was get back to Chrysanthe, hug her, and tell her that I was alright.

But I had a feeling it would be a long time before that would ever happen.

I exhaled as I brought my hands up to my bare chest, crossed my arms, and attempted to settle down.

My mind was entirely on Chrysanthe as I did so.

I settled down, hoping for a moment that she was thinking about me as her face showed up in my mind.

Within moments, I fell asleep.

"elio?"

I blinked sleepily as I heard my name.

"Celio?" the voice repeated.

I slowly opened my eyes, trying to find the direction of the voice. I looked around groggily, only to see the orange haze in front of me, as well as the Wraiths.

"Celio?" the voice called for the third time.

It sounded very familiar.

"Celio? Is that you?"

I twisted my body around, inside my bone-encrusted cage, only to see Viro. He was outside of the cell, making his way over toward me. He moved even though the Cloaked Spirits were all around him and myself.

"Viro?" I said in disbelief when I saw him.

His blue eyes had lost their brightness, while his body seemed a lot less muscular and stocky. His long blond hair appeared tangled, while his beard was overgrown and matted as well.

He had always been so strong, so powerful; it was bizarre to see him in a Realm where he wasn't.

But this was the Underworld, and anyone who wasn't from the Abyss was quickly becoming weak.

"How did you get out of there?" I asked.

"I'm not out. I'm dreaming that I am, and you're asleep, too, which means you can speak to me."

Oh, I thought.

That was the reason why the Wraiths weren't reacting to Viro. It was because he was dreaming; they couldn't see him.

Which meant they couldn't see me either.

He quickly had my attention as he continued to speak.

"I need you, Celio. I need you to hide something of mine," he said. "Get out of there, and I will show you."

Since we were both dreaming, I could navigate out of this prison cell.

"Okay, Viro." I stood up and stretched out my muscles.

It was a habit I had since I loved to stretch my wings when they were out. It wasn't long before I found the cell entrance; I quickly opened it before joining Viro outside, where the Wraiths were crowded all around us.

"Let's go," he said. "We have to be in a safer place."

I blinked in surprise, tilting my head at him.

"Trust me, Celio," he said, pausing to look me in the eyes.

I nodded and followed him out of the open area.

Viro sighed as he looked at me, silently studying my face as we watched each other.

I patiently waited for him to talk, willing to wait for whatever it was he wanted to show me.

"It's the Blade," he said finally; I gasped.

"What about it?" I asked cautiously.

He was talking about the Empyrean Blade, the Blade that kept all evil out of the many Realms.

The Blade was the most powerful weapon in all of the Realms. Every Archangel and Celestial Being knew of it and its power.

"I need you to keep it safe for me," Viro said, and I stared, dumbfounded.

Viro ignored my reaction and continued.

"If the Blade gets into the hands of my twin daughter, she could... could...destroy every Realm. She could do the opposite of what the

Blade had gotten made to do. She could let evil inside the many Realms, including the Ethereal City."

I gulped.

That possibility would be horrific.

"You have to keep it safe. You are my most trusted Archangel and my daughter's true love. You have to keep it safe, Celio, so Calla doesn't find it."

"Calla?"

"My daughter's name was Calla before it got changed by Sybella, when she brought her down here, many millennia ago. Her name was changed to Thana; that is the name she goes by down here."

The more he talked, the more he made sense.

He wanted to make sure the Empyrean Blade didn't end up in the wrong hands.

"You are my most trusted Archangel, Celio, and I would like you to keep it safe."

I felt flattered that he trusted me so much and nodded in agreement.

"Okay," I told Viro and stared into his blue eyes.

"I also should mention the only way to protect it is to fully..."

"Keep it in, or as, your tattoo," I finished, already knowing what he was going to say.

He smiled before he pulled his massive red shirt up to expose his chest; sure enough, there was a tattoo of the Blade near his heart.

It had a long, curved handle, with names of enchantments written on it, while the sharp edge glowed stunningly.

Even as a tattoo, the Empyrean Blade was gorgeous.

Viro brought his hand to his chest and scraped his flesh with his fingernails. He pulled the Blade out from the handle, and it started to leave his skin.

The Empyrean Blade flashed a wonderful, white light on the tip of the edge as Viro handed it over to me; I turned my back to him, so my angel wing tattoos were visible, and I felt the tremendous power of the Blade as it entered my flesh.

I could feel the energy of the Blade as it got absorbed in my body, as a tattoo.

"And now, you have the Empyrean Blade." Viro put a hand on my shoulder as he took in my angel wings. "This Blade will help keep evil out of the Realms, and now that it's in your back, it will protect your tattoos.

I twisted around to look at him.

"I will keep the Blade safe," I said. "I promise."

When I awoke, I was immediately aware of my surroundings.

"Viro." I looked straight at the Wraiths who were crowding the outside of my prison cell. "Viro, I promise to protect it."

I turned my attention from the Cloaked Spirits to the ground when my gaze had gotten diverted to the black rock underneath me.

A puddle of water was in my cell, and I could see my reflection in it.

I can see the Empyrean Blade, I thought as I stared into the water, studying my features.

I got up and walked over to the puddle, which caused the Wraiths to drift toward me. When I looked back into the liquid, I saw the reflection of my wings. I recognized immediately where the Blade was through the pattern of my feathers.

But to someone who didn't know the pattern, there would be nothing there.

The Empyrean Blade was well hidden in my skin, disguised as my tattoo.

And now it was my duty to keep it safe.

Chrysanthe

"This is where we'll stop."

I pulled on Leora's mane gently as we made our way right in front of a cottage, which was on the outskirts of a massive flower garden. The Unicorn came to a halt.

The flowers were so bright, colorful, and abundant as I took the garden in, amazed.

The Flourishing Realm.

We had made it to the Realm of the Flowers.

"We're here." The Apparition drifted beside me as she talked, and I turned my head to the side to look at her.

I nodded before dismounting, petting Leora's neck calmly. I heard the cottage door open and looked up to see a blond Being appear; her hair was slightly tinted pink while she had a headband of flowers on. Her dress was multi-colored and flowy.

I smiled as I took in the look of her.

She seemed like she was very concerned about the Earth, almost the same way I was.

She paused as she saw both of us, and the Apparition floated toward her.

"Serenity?" the Being asked. "Serenity, is that you?"

I blinked in astonishment. Not once had the Apparition mentioned what her name was; it was beautiful.

"Altheda, how are you?"

The Flower Being, Altheda, smiled.

"Good. Just keeping up with the many flowers I have," she said, chuckling.

She turned her attention toward me.

"Hello, you must be Serenity's friend."

I smiled.

"Chrysanthe," I said, walking away from Leora and over to Altheda. I looked at the vast flower garden behind her house.

"This is beautiful." I couldn't help but marvel at the amount of foliage and color there was. "Wow."

She laughed.

"Well, they are the most powerful and precious commodities in all the Realm. And I am in charge of all of them," Altheda said. She walked over to a part of the garden before sniffing a blossom. She grinned at the smell, shut her eyes so she could absorb the scent, and turned to us.

She looked at Serenity.

"Why have you come, dear friend?" she asked.

The Apparition looked down at her feet.

"It's Chrysanthe." She looked me in the eyes. "Her love has gotten taken from her; an Archangel named Celio. He got taken from Chrysanthe by the Phantom. I told her you could help," the Apparition finished.

Altheda nodded before focusing on me.

"That, I can do," she said. The Phantom is pure evil; she is the Abyss Queen, and she must stay there. Pure, utter corruption needs to stay where it belongs. Viro commanded me millennia ago to keep watch over the Realm of the Flowers so one day I could help defeat evil at its worst, and that is what I will do."

Altheda walked over toward me, her flowy dress floating in the breeze.

'The best way to defeat the Phantom and to undo everything she has done is to find the Empyrean Blade."

I blinked.

The Empyrean Blade? The all-powerful Blade my father created millennia ago, to keep all evil out of all the Realms?

For a moment, I thought about it before it all made sense.

If I were to find the Empyrean Blade, wherever it may be, I could end my twin sister's tyranny and gain peace back to all the Realms she affected.

I looked at Altheda, hoping that she could tell us where the Blade was.

"You have to find the Empyrean Blade and use your flower, Chrysanthe."

My eyebrows furrowed. *Use my flower?*

"Chrysanthemums can help defeat the Phantom. They produce a toxin that she is allergic to; it can defeat her. I will show you the flowers in my garden and which ones can help vanquish her powers."

I blinked, stunned.

"The chrysanthemums, along with the Empyrean Blade, will be able to defeat the Phantom, Chrysanthe. Then you will be able to get your Archangel back," Altheda said, reaching her hand out to touch my chrysanthemum-tattooed wrist.

"We will defeat her," she continued as she gazed into my eyes, holding them with her blue ones. "We will make it through this."

I couldn't help but notice the 'we' in her sentence.

She was going to help us.

I couldn't help but believe her.

I stared back into her blazing blue eyes and nodded.

"Okay." I glanced down at my tattoo, and Altheda smiled. "Let's go find these flowers."

Thana

"I found him, Thana," Damon repeated yet again.

He flew around, unable to contain his excitement, and I rolled my eyes.

"Yes, I know, Damon." I reached my hand out to pet my Hellhound's coarse black fur. "I know."

I wasn't paying attention to what Damon said; instead, I was thinking of the Archangel, who happened to be Chrysanthe's love.

I kept thinking about him. The pure contempt on his face when we looked at each other.

The pure contempt, the hazel eyes that resembled liquid gold as they stared at me. The Archangel's defined, bare chest and muscled arms.

I stopped myself.

No, I thought. *No, I cannot think like that. He is my prisoner, and he is an Archangel. It is forbidden.*

But now it was in my brain; I couldn't help myself.

The way I could almost feel his black angel wings against my back as he embraced me, loved *me,* and I sensed his sweet-smelling breath, which caused goosebumps and my tattoos prickled.

A sensation of heat rose through my face at the thought of the Archangel.

"Thana, my Queen, are you alright?"

I turned around to see Gog staring at me nervously.

I shook my head quickly, coming out of my daze.

"My Queen?" he repeated.

"Yes, Gog, I'm fine," I snapped, aware my cheeks still felt aflame. It was the color of his eyes, his entire muscled body...

I gritted my teeth, snarling.

Thana, no, I thought again. *It is forbidden. Stop thinking like this.*

Vaguely, I sensed Gog coming closer to me, a confused and worried expression on his face.

He walked over to me but said nothing.

I clenched my fists and ground my teeth together as I tried to rid myself of the feelings that were boiling inside me. I felt Gog's hand brush up against mine.

Immediately, my eyes snapped downward, where his hand was touching my flesh; he instantly drew back, retreating quickly.

"Gog, I told you, I'm fine, thank you very much."

Gog nodded as I turned toward Damon, but he seemed utterly oblivious to everything.

He was still flying around in circles. He was excited at his discovery.

I growled before any more sensations could boil up and slowly took a deep breath. I forced my eyes closed to focus before opening them again and looking at Gog.

It was once I was sure nothing would disrupt my thinking that I spoke up.

"Yes, Gog? What is it?"

"It's your twin, Chrysanthe. She's looking for the Archangel. We could see her for a short while before she went off into the forest. The forest near where the Archangel had gotten taken. But now she cannot be found," Gog said. "It was both her and the Apparition that entered the woods. They said they were going to another Realm."

I squinted.

Another Realm?

"And what Realm was it exactly?"

"The Realm of the Flowers," Gog said.

I shook my head, confused. I had never heard of that Realm before.

"And where did you see this?" I asked Gog, even though part of me knew the answer already.

"In the Inferno River, my Queen."

"Take me to the Inferno River then," I said; I was becoming agitated.

"Okay, Thana." He bowed low before he walked off. I followed closely behind.

A snarl of uneasiness crept up on my face as I followed the Goblin toward the River; my insides squirmed.

I had no idea what I was going to encounter next; this made me very nervous for the first time in my entire existence.

Celio

 y hand grazed Chrysanthe's cheek, brushing away the tendrils of hair that had escaped from her braid as I studied her face. Her peacock feather tattoo took up the top part; her gorgeous blue eyes had gotten encased in the ink, while a red chrysanthemum was in her hair.

I could see her look up since her attention was on the ground, and I stroked her skin. It was then that she stared at me with such a look of love that I couldn't help it; I kissed her as my hands brushed against her flesh.

A feeling of heat rose on me as the sensation of her hands on my chest registered, and I felt my angel wings leave my back as I pulled her closer to me. I wanted this moment to last forever.

Chrysanthe pulled away from my lips to breathe, and her sweet-smelling breath drenched me once she spoke, sending ripples down my spine.

"Celio," she whispered as I opened up my eyes to look at her beautiful ones, "I love you."

My heart began to race inside my ribs, and I leaned forward, kissing her cheek.

I felt my wings rush behind me, kicking up dust.

"I love you too, Chrysanthe."

I slowly opened my eyes as I broke away from my dream, although I wanted it so badly to be real.

I wanted to be around the Being I loved, tell her I was alright, kiss and embrace her...

I knew, though, that it might be a while before that ever happened, thanks to her evil twin.

I blinked away the sleep rapidly from my eyes, trying my hardest to get as conscious as possible.

I moaned and stretched my arms out in front of me when I abruptly heard a flapping sound.

I paused and looked to see what it was; there was an owl perched up on the top of my prison cell, and I blinked again, confused.

What the...? I thought. *What's an owl doing here?*

It took me a few moments to put it together.

Wait a moment. It must be... It must be Sybella. I glanced up at the barn owl perched right on the bone-encrusted cell.

Sybella, the Oracle, could also shapeshift, and her animal was an owl.

It could have been an ordinary owl if it were nighttime, and it wasn't Hell, but it was, and I knew Sybella had gotten taken as well.

Also, the barn owl stared knowingly at me with wide, gigantic eyes and a clacking beak.

But who set her free?

I peered around my surroundings, trying to see where she must've come from, when I saw Thera in the corner of the Abyss.

I gasped as I took in her appearance.

She looked incredibly wounded; her eyes had gotten swollen shut with bruises and scrapes, and blood covered her hands and feet. Her once beautiful purple dress had gotten ruined, and she shook uncontrollably.

What the...? I thought as I saw her. *Did your own daughter do this to you?*

I watched Thera as she moaned in agony. She grasped one of her hands in the other, trying to minimize the pain she was in, but it was no use.

Her abilities didn't work in Hell, just like my wings wouldn't stay intact very long either.

"Go, Sybella," I heard Thera moan. "Go get help, go find Chrysanthe."

Huh? I thought as I heard her quiet voice.

How Thera had managed to free Sybella, I had no idea, but all I could register was the Cloaked Spirits moving along the outside of the prison cells, guarding the entrances.

They moved slowly, drifting along, and I felt a shiver rattle down my spine, but the one thing the Wraiths didn't do was register that the Oracle, one of their prisoners, was gone.

That was until I noticed one of the Wraiths go around the corner, over by the rock near Thera.

I heard the Wraith scream.

My blood curdled at the sound, and I cringed as I saw the rest of the Cloaked Spirits shriek and move away from the cells. They disappeared around the corner, to where Sybella must've been before she'd morphed.

I immediately became concerned for Thera as I saw the Wraiths disappear, their ear-splitting screams causing goosebumps on my skin. I watched in horror as Thera quickly lost her balance on the rocky surface and tripped and fell; her head hit the rock with a *crack*.

I rose from the sitting position and grabbed the cell bars. I saw the Cloaked Spirits come around the corner again, beginning to crowd Thera, who was now unconscious.

I started shaking as I took it all in.

No. No. No, Thera. No, I thought, quickly terrified for her.

But the Wraiths paid no attention as she laid on the ground, unresponsive.

They quickly soared off, away from where Thera was, and into the darkness as I stood there, in my bone encrusted cell, as their screams echoed through the Abyss.

I had to act. I had to help Thera. If I didn't, she would worsen.

I quickly looked around until I found an opening to the cell, and once I did, I opened the door, running across the Abyss. I ran over to Thera's body.

She was utterly still; her forehead soaked in blood.

I opened the door to her cell and ran to her, cradling her in my arms as I pushed back her matted hair. The movement exposed her bruise-riddled face. I felt my blood boil at the sight of it.

I gritted my teeth in anger but then spoke softly, trying to get Thera's attention.

"Thera? Thera, can you hear me?"

I looked carefully for movement, and then she spoke.

"Viro? Viro, is that you?"

She slowly opened her eyes, which looked incredibly agonizing, but then they grew wide when she saw me.

"Celio? Celio, what are you doing here?"

"Thera, I'm here to help you; you don't have to worry anymore," I said, cradling her head in my hands, pushing away a tendril of hair from her flesh, being careful of the gigantic purple bruise on her face. "We're going to get out of here."

34

Thana

A sudden high-pitched shriek echoed through the Abyss, which stopped me in my tracks behind Gog.

I squinted in confusion, bewildered at the sound, when I quickly heard it again, this time higher pitched than before.

And then I heard the Banshees wail.

I heard the sounds, and my insides instantly seemed to turn to water.

Oh, no. No. No. No. Something's wrong, I thought as I heard the excessive screaming. *Something's very wrong.*

My wings appeared, and I started running before I took off, leaving Gog alone in the darkness of the Abyss.

Morgeran was the first to greet me as I landed. I petted the coarse fur behind his ear as he pushed up against me. I looked around, pulled my wings back, and tried to locate the Wraiths; within moments, I saw one of them come near me, drifting along quickly as it spotted me.

The Wraith moved fast, screaming as it approached, and pointed a long, scabbed, bony finger toward one of the tunnels.

I stared at the cloaked figure as it continued to shriek and then understood what the Wraith was trying to show me.

The tunnel led to where I kept my prisoners, where I kept Thera, Viro, the Oracle, and now that Archangel, who was Chrysanthe's love.

The Wraith was trying to tell me that something was wrong in that area, with the prisoners.

If they had escaped...

They wouldn't *really* be able to escape Hell since they'd been here for a while. The longer they were in the Underworld, the more likely they were able to become trapped.

However, the idea still made my blood pressure rise.

I gritted my teeth in a fury, turning livid.

If the prisoners tried to escape, they would experience torture so excruciating that they would beg for death.

"Morgeran." I looked at the deformed Hellhound. "You are coming with me. Come on, let's see if anyone escaped their prison in the Underworld."

Morgeran stared at me before he walked ahead into the tunnel.

I wasn't far behind him, and I sensed the Wraith come behind me, following the both of us as we went into the pit.

I followed Morgeran hesitantly, not knowing what to expect once I came out of that tunnel.

Morgeran's snarl echoed through the Underworld as I went into the pit, and I felt the hair on the back of my neck stand on end.

He had seen or heard something wrong.

The Wraith was right behind me, but all I could see was Morgeran. A growl radiated through his chest.

The Wraith crossed in front of me as I looked around, only to see that one of the prison cells was empty.

A snarl rumbled in my throat, and I followed the Wraith as it drifted along the open area, scanning the rest of the cells, but they were all empty, too.

The Wraith screamed once more at the blank cells, and I became enraged as the Banshees screeched.

I gritted my teeth together so hard I thought they would break as I walked off, my lips curled upward into another snarl.

That's it, I thought angrily as I walked back into the tunnel. *Those Beings are dead meat.*

Celio

My ribs hurt so badly they felt like they were on fire as I stopped running. I clutched the side of a rock, trying to catch my breath.

"Celio?" Thera asked softly as I placed her on the ground. "Where do we go now?"

"Away from here," I barely answered her, still in pain from exertion.

I couldn't use my wings to fly, at least not yet. I would get caught immediately if I'd attempted to fly.

We also couldn't use the Empyrean Blade to cut through the Underworld and get free; I'd found out the hard way earlier that it wouldn't work for Celestial Beings in Hell, unless, of course, they were *from* Hell.

The Blade had started to glow stunningly in my hand as I'd asked Viro to get it out of my back before it had just turned a dull color when I waved it, trying to slice through the air. Then I'd just asked Viro to put the Blade into my back once more, frustrated.

It seemed like there was only one choice; we had to run.

So, for right now, that was precisely what we were doing. I ran, with Thera in my arms as she couldn't move and Viro following behind me.

I'd been able to go over to his prison cell quickly and set him free once the Cloaked Spirits disappeared.

Viro wasn't looking so good either, although not as bad as Thera. He only had a few scrapes and bruises and a little discoloration around his face.

Unfortunately, we were indeed getting followed now that we weren't in our cells anymore. The Wraiths were probably on alert, as were the Banshees.

Which meant we would be in trouble if we didn't move.

"We have to keep going, or we will get caught," I said to both Viro and Thera. "Now you can carry Thera. Come on," I said to Viro before he grasped her waist and cradled her in his arms softly. "Let's go."

And we took off once more.

There was very little light as we ran ahead; I was trying desperately to find a safe place to fly, but it was hard to navigate out of the Abyss.

Finally, after what seemed like forever, I found a tunnel.

But where it went, I had no idea.

"Come on, Viro." I twisted my body around to look at him.

He was still holding Thera in his arms; his hands brushed her face, and he wiped away the sweat gathered around her temple.

She winced, and I glanced down at her briefly, my heart instantly dropping to my stomach; Viro had accidentally touched the purple bruise, and Thera whimpered in agony before shutting her eyes. She moved so that she was touching his chest and her expression was unreadable.

We both knew that she was in obvious pain, though.

Thera, I thought as I watched her. *You poor thing.*

"Where does that tunnel lead, Celio?" Viro asked, breaking me out of my reverie.

I blinked and turned back to the passageway.

"I don't know where it leads, but we have to go through here; it might be our only way out. Come on, let's go."

But as the words left my lips, there was a blood-curdling shriek.

It echoed through my bones.

It was the Wraiths.

I quickly ran into the tunnel with Viro close behind, only for my heart to skip a beat once I turned a corner.

A Cloaked Spirit blocked the way so that we couldn't advance. It immediately screeched, reaching a hand out towards me, and I stopped at the edge of the tunnel. A snarl of disgust showed on my face as I felt my wings escape, blocking and protecting both Viro and Thera.

The Wraith stared at me; its cloaked head turned in my direction as it continued to scream. Its hand was still outstretched and was attempting to grab me, but I smacked it away as it approached.

I snarled at the creature and kept my wings outstretched to protect Viro and Thera.

That only enraged the Cloaked Spirit further, and I felt it grasp my shoulder with a scabbed, black hand as it screeched more. The piercing noise almost made my ears bleed.

I screamed in agony as the Wraith touched me.

The Cloaked Spirit grabbed my shoulder, twisting it with such force that I somersaulted through the air and landed straight on my back. Directly on my back with my enormous wings outstretched.

I groaned; tears ran down my cheeks as I felt my gigantic black wings crack once I hit the hard, rocky ground.

A fissure of pain shot through them. I had broken my wings, which caused me to grit my teeth as waves of agony hit me with tremendous force.

I closed my eyes and tried not to scream as I managed to bring myself back to my feet.

Oh, no. No. No. NO! I twisted my body around to look at my wings, only to feel shooting pain instead.

Viro looked worriedly at me, but at that moment, I heard the Wraith screech again, cutting off the rest of his words.

"THANA! I HAVE FOUND THEM!"

What the...? I felt all the blood leave my face as I looked up in the 'sky.'

It was the black, withered creature that had ripped me away from Chrysanthe.

He had found us.

36

"**I** FOUND THEM!"

The withered black creature flew right in front of me before throwing his wings out as he attempted to land.

I gritted my teeth as he did; anger flooded my system as I watched his gangly form hit the slick, hard rock.

Agony soared through me as well; my wings had cracked, leaving me in tremendous pain. I felt blood slowly trickling down my back as my lopsided wings hung loose.

The creature gazed at me with gigantic, orb-like, brown eyes, smirking at me as his claws clacked against the rock. He looked at Viro and Thera, who had gotten out of the tunnel. Now they were staring at the ink-black creature.

"I wonder what Thana will do to you since you tried to escape. What will you do now that your wings have gotten broken?" he asked as he turned back towards me. He extended his arm out to touch me, but I smacked his hand away, and a snarl ripped through my teeth.

"Oh, not very friendly," he commented, his eyes turning into slits as he looked at me. "Well, then I guess the Wraiths can have you... Wait...."

The creature paused, his words cut off as he saw something behind me; I couldn't tell what he spotted, but once I managed to turn around, I gulped.

It was the Wraith. It was what it was holding.

It was the Empyrean Blade.

The Wraith was holding the Empyrean Blade.

Panic rose in my chest as I held my breath. I tried not to scream out as I saw the Cloaked Spirit hold the Blade with its scarred hands.

The handle of the Blade had become deformed. It was black, and the engravings had nearly melted off the handle.

The edge of the Blade itself appeared to be disfigured also. The white light that had once shone from the Blade had disappeared; now it looked black, vile, and melted.

Nothing left my mouth as I stood on the rock in shock; sweat started to pool around my hairline as my heart pounded.

"What is that?" the creature asked, talking to the Wraith. I knew the Cloaked Spirit wouldn't talk back because they couldn't.

The Wraith held up the Blade as the creature approached the Cloaked Spirit and the deformed Empyrean Blade.

He studied it intently.

The Blade almost melted as the black creature looked at it.

"What is this?" he asked as he watched it. "I wonder if Thana would like to see this. Where was this found?" he asked the Wraith, who pointed toward my back and then to the floor.

The creature's eyebrows scrunched in confusion, but I understood as I scrutinized the Wraith.

The Empyrean Blade had fallen from my back and onto the floor. That was how the Cloaked Spirit had found it.

The creature blinked before dismissing the Wraith.

"Well, however it had gotten found, it doesn't matter now. Thana will *definitely* want to see this."

I clenched my teeth together, absolutely livid as I looked at the creature.

It was sickening seeing such a change in the Blade.

Besides the agony from my cracked wings rippling through my body, anger coursed through my system, seeing the creature watch the Blade.

There was a sudden cracking sound, and the creature twisted around.

That was when I seized my chance.

I leaped at the creature, grabbing him by the neck and slamming him to the rocky ground. I snarled as he stared at me with enormous orb-like eyes and punched him in the nose when he attempted to grab my throat.

Blood poured out of his nose as I ripped the Empyrean Blade away from him; it was right by his body, and he groaned in pain. I threw the Blade to Viro, who was still cradling Thera with one strong arm.

That was when the Cloaked Spirit attacked and threw me to the ground with a thunderous crack.

Waves of excruciating agony hit me as my wings slammed onto the rock, and at that point, I was in shock. I was uncontrollably shaking, and I felt the blood pooling around my back as I was pinned to the rock by the Wraith — its scabbed, ink-black hand kept me from moving.

But I could still see what Viro was doing.

He caught the Blade quickly before immediately inserting it into his chest.

It all happened so fast, the creature and the Wraith didn't see a thing.

The withered black creature managed to fly upward so he could be on his feet again out of the corner of my eye, gasping for air as the blood continued to stream from his nose.

He walked over to me and curled his lip upward in disgust as he grasped his nose with the side of his wing, trying to stop the flow of blood.

"Thana is going to have a great time dealing with you," he said before he screamed. "THANA, THEY'RE HERE!"

I gritted my teeth together, enraged beyond belief, and soon I heard a noise in the distance.

That was it.

We were dead.

She was going to kill all of us.

But I wasn't going to be a weakling. At least I had done something by punching the vile creature. At least I had broken his nose.

That was the kind of attitude that I was going to have when Thana came.

I was going to die, so I might as well be strong and aware until the end.

I stared at both the Wraith and the creature, and I felt anger flood my system; blood pooled around me, but I focused on the Cloaked Spirit and the creature. My body shook with emotions until I heard a voice in the distance.

"My, my, my," it was a voice I instantly recognized as Thana's. "What do we have here?"

Thana

"Damon, go and clean up your face," I snapped as I left the darkness with Morgeran behind me.

Damon looked at me with blood streaming from his nose. He opened his mouth to say something, but I cut him off before he spoke.

"Go, Damon. *NOW!*" I barked.

He glared at me and looked over at the Archangel. But he twisted around afterward and flew away into the darkness.

It wasn't until I knew he was far away that I looked at the Archangel, realizing that he was the one who had caused my messenger to bleed.

I studied his face as the Wraith took its hands off his throat and released him from its grip.

The Wraith drifted away from the Archangel and came to me.

The Archangel cleared his throat, reaching up and massaging it with his hand.

My eyebrows raised as I saw his enormous, mangled, disheveled wings and the blood puddle on the ground.

"Well, well, well," I said, causing him to look up at me. "What happened to you?"

He glared, and the amount of contempt and hate in his eyes drowned me. He kept quiet, not saying a word.

"Oh, well, I guess you want to only talk to Chrysanthe," I said, grinning maliciously when I saw him blink at the mention of her name. "Is that what you want to do? Exchange any last words with her?"

The Archangel tensed up; his teeth clenched. He was seething, and I was taken aback by the sudden ferocity emanating off of him.

I hadn't known that an Archangel could get like this, even though this same one had punched Damon in the nose.

Hmmm. I looked at him carefully, even though secretly I was still enamored with the angel.

His strong arms, those deep hazel eyes...

I tensed up at the thoughts that were going through my brain once again.

Stop it. STOP IT! I thought intensely, trying hard to get my brainwaves back on track. *You're not supposed to be feeling this way; stop it!*

It was Morgeran's black, coarse fur rubbing up against my hand that made me return to reality.

His growl reverberated through my ears.

"You are a strong Archangel," I said as I looked him up and down; he watched me. His teeth ground together hard in anger. "And if you could handle your wings almost getting severed in half, you would be able to tolerate them getting ripped off completely... I'm sure you'll feel a lot better once your wings get removed. At least nothing would hurt them anymore." I curled my lip up, revealing my teeth. Morgeran continued to growl; the sound echoed through my bones.

The Archangel stood his ground, growing to his full height as he stared at me viciously.

"Go ahead then." His eyes turned to slits.

I looked to Morgeran, who was standing still, his body poised to attack as his hackles stayed raised. He looked dangerous and vicious, and I knew he was waiting to strike.

The Archangel turned his attention toward Morgeran, and I sneered as he tensed up, knowing that he could not defeat my Hellhound.

Morgeran had gotten focused on the Archangel. Attentive to his actions. I smirked.

"GET HIM!" I screamed, and the Hellhound leaped for the Archangel's throat.

38

Celio

hana's scream echoed through the Abyss, and within moments, the deformed, wolf-like creature had lunged at me, snarling viciously as his teeth aimed at my throat.

The growl that radiated from the wolf's body was deafening as he leaped. I quickly stepped out of the way as his razor-sharp teeth came in my direction, throwing my arms in front of my face to protect it.

I didn't react fast enough, though.

The creature's teeth snapped at my arms as I threw them up, ripping into my flesh and causing me to scream in pain; I crashed to the ground, my arms going down. The fall caused ripples of agony to sear through me, but I ignored the sensation as the wolf's teeth went for my throat.

I immediately attempted to throw the creature off me, but it was impossible since he was so heavy.

He was around the size of a horse; he was massive, so it was a lot of weight on top of me as I struggled to keep him away from my face.

I had my arms underneath the creature, pushing him away from my face, snarling as he continued to snap viciously; I had the full weight of the wolf on me as he attempted to bite, causing my muscles to tire almost instantly.

NO! I thought as the wolf's teeth tore into my cheek, causing searing pain, and I screamed again.

In the distance, I heard a menacing laugh.

It was Thana; she was glad her creature was about to kill me.

Blood dripped from the wound on my face; I could smell the wolf's horrible breath, see his yellow teeth and mangled gums as he aimed for my face once more, all the while sounding vicious as he growled and snapped at me.

By now, I was really struggling to keep the creature away; there seemed to be blood all around me, and I was tiring fast.

"UGH!" I screamed as I moved my arms underneath the wolf; I punched its side with all the strength left in my body.

It yelped loudly as it fell off me and onto the rocky ground; I heard a scream as I finally managed to scramble to my feet, grabbing a nearby rock and seething from the anger that was pulsing through me.

Blood flowed from the bite on my cheek, but I just glared at Thana, who glared right back at me.

There was a vicious bark that erupted from my right side, and I turned just in time to see the wolf lunge at me again.

"NO!" Thana screeched when she seemed to understand what I was going to do, but it was too late as her creature jumped in my direction; I smashed the rock against the wolf's ribcage.

A sharp whimper escaped the creature's throat as it crashed to the ground again; the wolf's eyes closed instantly.

I watched the creature for a few moments before I looked up at Thana, who immediately screamed again as the wolf remained still. She gave me a murderous look before flying at me; the wings appeared from her back so fast that I barely saw the transition before she closed in on me. She went straight for my face as her lip curled up in rage.

"You...you killed my Hellhound!" she screeched through clenched teeth. She brought her hand and sharp fingernails toward my throat.

I was still in agony from my wings getting torn, and blood pounded through my ears. I gritted my teeth and stood my ground, not uttering a single word.

But then...

The gigantic wolf eventually opened its eyes and got up from the challenging, rocky terrain. It began yowling loudly for its master.

Thana heard the noise and looked over at the beast, overjoyed.

"Morgeran! You're okay! Good boy; you've been such a good boy. Go on now, get out of here."

Morgeran? I thought as Thana's attention had gotten diverted.

The beast limped away, but not before pausing to snarl at me.

"You poor thing," Thana spoke softly to him as he disappeared.

Meanwhile, I could feel the blood on my back drying up while blood flowed from the bite on my cheek. My wings drooped, and my face stung.

The agony was intense, but I pulled through it. I had to.

Thana's lip curled as she looked back at me.

"Now." She grabbed my shoulder roughly. "You're coming with me."

Both Thana and the Cloaked Spirit were behind me as anger and agony pumped through me with tremendous force. My bare feet touched the slippery, hard rock of the Abyss.

"I'll go in front."

Thana walked ahead of me, leading the way as I felt, to my horror, the Wraith touching my shoulder.

Thana looked behind her as I fell to my knees on the rocky surface. I screeched in pain, but Thana sneered as tears started to fill my eyes.

"I was wondering when that would happen." She smirked and glanced over at the Wraith.

I scowled at Thana as the tears ran down my cheeks.

A high-pitched screech nearly burst my eardrums as the Wraith appeared at my side. At that same moment, I felt a ripping sensation through my back that coursed through my body. It was as if I had gotten burned.

I screamed as I felt a burning, blistering feeling radiate all over me.

There was a crunching, tearing sensation, a blood-curdling shriek, and that was when I lost consciousness, letting the darkness consume me.

39

Chrysanthe

y root tattoos glowed as I stepped through the long, shining grass. I smiled at the plants around me before I looked at Altheda, who stood in front of me, guiding me through the flower garden.

Her slightly tinted, pink hair sparkled in the sunlight, while her colorful flower headband was bright.

I focused on her as we moved, being careful not to step on any of the flowers.

She stopped and pointed to the brightly colored chrysanthemums to my right.

"See these flowers? These are toxic; the chrysanthemums will help hinder the Phantom. She won't be able to use her abilities if the poison gets anywhere near her."

I nodded but then frowned.

"Will I not become poisoned also?" I questioned, worried about what would happen to me.

Altheda's blue eyes hit the light, appearing to sparkle.

"Your red chrysanthemum tattoo has helped you become immune to the toxin; I can also tint your hair a different color so that you can be protected. That is how I stay safe from the poison."

"What is the hair tint made of?" I asked.

"Petals from the flowers. Your body can grow immunity to it once it has gotten applied to the hair. I'll use a special paste as well, so it doesn't fade upon contact with water."

I nodded.

"Okay," I replied. "Are all of these flowers going to be able to help defeat the Phantom?"

"Not all… But most of them will," Altheda said. "That's the reason why these flowers are so precious. They protect the Realms by keeping them safe from harm. I will show you which blossoms will help you," she said and led me deeper into the flower garden.

Altheda was putting purple chrysanthemums into her left hand and repopulating them with her right when there was suddenly an animal noise in the distance.

We both looked up instantly as we heard the sound and saw a bird flying toward us; a few moments later, I realized that it was an owl.

"What the…? The poor thing must've gotten lost," I said as it flew closer to us.

Altheda and I both stared as the creature headed for my shoulder.

It rubbed up against my face as it made a soft call to me, and I squinted, trying to understand what was happening.

It was only after the owl stared at me knowingly and blinked that I understood.

It was trying to tell me something.

I was about to ask Altheda, but the owl flew off my shoulder.

"What was…?" I started but then stopped. To my amazement, I watched as the barn owl abruptly transformed into a blond-haired Being in a torn, dark blue dress. Her tattoos covered her.

But it was not just any Being.

I gasped when I realized who the Being was.

It was Sybella.

Sybella. Sybella. *Sybella.*

The Oracle had come from the Underworld.

She had escaped.

But how?

"Hello?" Altheda blinked when she saw the Oracle.

No answer.

"Hello?" I tried this time. "Sybella? Are you okay?"

Sybella shivered, but she didn't turn around.

She did respond, however.

"Chrysanthe, you need to help us," she said.

"I know," I said. "That's why I'm here; I'm trying to get help to defeat the Phantom, Sybella."

"Well, you need to work faster because we're not doing so well." She twisted around, and both Altheda and I couldn't help but gasp.

She looked horrible.

Sybella's cheeks had gotten hollowed out and thin, and a faded bruise on her left eye made her cheeks and forehead an awful, sickly yellow.

Her bones protruded on her body since she was so emaciated, her hair was straggly. Her bright turquoise blue eyes were now dimmed and dark; they were almost the color of the deep, dark ocean sky.

A sharp inhale of breath caught in my lungs.

My sister was responsible for doing this.

I ground my teeth together in anger.

Who knew what she had done to the others?

I couldn't let this continue. I *had* to stop my twin.

"Chrysanthe," Sybella said, breaking me out of my thoughts. "Chrysanthe, please help us." Her voice was weak, and then she collapsed.

40

I ran toward Sybella, catching her in my arms before she could plummet to the grass.

"Sybella?" I asked softly, pushing the tendrils of hair that were damp with sweat back behind her ear. "Sybella, can you hear me?"

Her eyes were closed, and she winced as she moved her head a little.

"Yes." Her voice was barely a whisper. "Yes, I can hear you; I'm exhausted, that's all. It took a while to find you."

"Well, you're in good hands now," Altheda said as she ran over to help since I was having trouble supporting the Oracle on my own.

"Come on," she said while we shared the Oracle's weight. "Let's get you inside; then you can tell us what's been going on."

"Okay," Sybella breathed faintly as we both carried her, her eyes still closed.

"Alright," Altheda said. "Let's get you to my cottage now." And we brought her to the Flower Being's home.

"Thank you," Sybella said to Altheda as she handed her some tea that had gotten made with various flower petals. "That'll help me warm up."

Sybella had gotten wrapped up in a blanket; her face looked better since I'd started to heal her. Her eyes were a lot brighter, the skeletal look and hollowed cheeks gone from her face. Even her hair seemed healthier, thicker.

Overall, she had significantly improved.

"That tea will help give you back your strength," Altheda told Sybella.

"Well, thank you," she said as I sat down in the chair across from her, across the table; she was still shivering slightly, her body cold.

Caliya brushed up against my arm. The tiger looked straight at Sybella, who had gotten focused on the tea in her hands.

I looked down at Caliya and stroked her ear as she pushed her head into my palm.

"Go on, Caliya." The tigress glanced up at me, her amber-colored eyes burning into mine. "Go on, go warm Sybella up. She needs it."

Caliya breathed deeply before walking over to the Oracle and rubbing her head alongside Sybella's body.

She smiled, petting Caliya's head.

"Aww, Caliya, you're such a good tiger." Sybella grinned. "You're such a good girl."

Caliya moaned again happily, this time rubbing her face alongside Sybella's, and she laughed.

Altheda and I chuckled at the sight, and I smiled.

"Well, Caliya seems to like you." I grinned happily.

Sybella let out a soft chuckle.

"Yes. Yes, I know," she said, scratching Caliya's chin. "She's a good tiger."

That she is, I thought and took a deep breath.

"Sybella?" I asked.

"Hmmm?"

"What happened to you in the Underworld? Is Celio there? What about my parents? Are they okay, or are they injured?"

Sybella's demeanor changed instantly. She sipped her flower petal tea before she looked at me. With a deep breath, she spoke.

"Your mother had gotten tortured when I left to find help, Chrysanthe," she said, and my heart dropped. "Your father isn't doing well, either. Both were injured when I left. Morphing into the barn owl was the only way to escape; there were prison cells in the Underworld that Thana put us in, and Wraiths guarded the cells. I transformed and flew into the air pocket which had been created when Thana came to Earth."

I listened to her and shivered as I contemplated what she had said.

Wraiths. Prison cells. The Underworld.

It all made me feel incredibly uncomfortable.

But it got me thinking.

My parents were alive, but how was Celio?

"Aside from my mother and father, did you ever see Celio? Was he there at all?"

"Yes, he was, Chrysanthe," Sybella said. "Yes, he was there. I was perched at the top of his prison cell to see him. The last time I did, he looked okay; I think he was a little heartsick." She looked me right in the face. "He loves you and wants to get back to you."

I smiled. "I always knew that we had been meant for each other."

"That you were... Heaven and Earth, together forever."

"Yes." My thoughts drifted to Celio. After a few moments, though, I shook my head and came back to the present. "You said my mother had gotten tortured when you left." I looked at Sybella. "Was there any way that she could have escaped Thana? Could any of them escape?"

"Probably," she said, shifting her shoulders. "Although they would have to distract the Wraiths."

"So as long as the Wraiths were distracted, they could escape?"

"Yes," the Oracle replied. "Yes, they could've, but it would mean that they would have to travel through the Abyss to leave. I know Celio was losing his wings already since he's an Archangel in the Underworld. The air pocket had gotten created to help Thana come to Earth, but it was small, and only little creatures could fly through it. He would be caught almost immediately by Thana. And after that, only Viro would know what would happen to him."

I took in everything she was telling me, and I blinked once she finished.

They would never really be able to escape without our help, without *my* help. The Beings I loved would never be able to escape Hell.

The only way to rescue them was to defeat my twin. To defeat Thana.

I was going to help them. I was going to get my parents and Celio out of the Underworld.

And I was going to have to do it fast.

41

Celio

 y pulse echoing through my skull was what brought me back to reality.

I opened my eyes, dazed, when suddenly I heard a clink of metal and sucked in a breath.

What was that? My heart began to pound my ribs, the reverberations pulsing through my head as I tried to keep my eyes open.

Clink. Clink.

What was that? I shook my head slightly, only to feel agony; it was as if someone had smacked it against the Abyss' hard rock.

I gritted my teeth in frustration, fighting against the fatigue overwhelming me when I quickly became aware that my arms were above my head.

I blinked again, trying to see my surroundings, but it was hard; there was little visibility.

Almost everything around me was pitch black, except for a little trace of orange light that pierced through the darkness.

I groaned and tried to keep my head clear as the orange light hit my eyes, but it was hard since drowsiness was attempting to consume me once more.

Groggily, I attempted to get my bearings. I struggled to focus on my surroundings as I felt my arms above my head. I turned to see what was holding them.

Clink. Clink.

Ahh! The more aware I became, the more I realized how much I was in deep trouble.

I moved my feet, only to discover they were trapped as well.

The drowsiness I had felt had been replaced by panic as it surged through my mind.

The orange light that was cutting through the blackness revealed I was dangling high above the rocky ground of the Underworld. My arms and feet were chained up as I hung precariously.

My heart suddenly felt like it was in my throat.

My insides felt like water as my breathing became rapid. Tremors rattled through my body as I dangled over the terrain of Hell.

"Are you having fun up there?"

I jumped slightly when I heard a voice from below me.

Sweat began to run down the side of my face; my breathing accelerated as I tried to locate Thana.

"Hello, Archangel," Thana sneered once I found her. Her sickly green eyes lit up from the orange light that sliced through the blackness. "Or should I say, Fallen Archangel." She laughed maliciously.

Huh?

Did she mean that since I was an Archangel in Hell?

I couldn't help but wrinkle my face in puzzlement as Thana took a few steps forward. Her eyes were wide and crazed.

Whatever it was that she was talking about, it couldn't have been good.

I focused on what was in front of me, but then my heart dropped as I saw blood dripping from the object.

I focused on it; the detail of it cut through with the light.

Blood continued to drip from it, making me feel incredibly uneasy.

Quickly, my insides twisted and felt like liquid. I noticed the black feathers, each individual one until the orange light moved and showed ... wings.

They were wings.

The object in front of me turned out to be black angel wings.

Panic raced through me, and I began to hyperventilate as I looked at Thana. Then I saw an evil grin across her face.

NO! I struggled frantically, trying to feel my wings but only feeling pain.

Agony ripped through my body as I struggled against the chains holding me.

But I didn't care.

I struggled, but that just caused the chains to rip into my skin.

I took a deep breath and tried to calm myself, twisting my head to the side and looking around. I saw that there was a sudden ripple on the ground as if someone had thrown a rock.

I realized that it was water.

It continued to ripple, and that was when I spotted my reflection in the liquid.

But what I saw in the water made me feel like I'd gotten pierced in the heart. Stabbed in the heart with an arrow.

It was the Mark. It was the outline of wings in deep, dark, red blood.

My wings...

My breathing became rapid; I thought I would pass out as I looked at the black feathers.

My wings...with blood dripping from them...

I felt like I had gotten pierced in the gut. I screamed so loud it felt like my vocal cords were getting sliced. *"NO!"*

42

Thana

**O!"** The Archangel's scream ripped through the silence as I watched him writhe in both agony and anguish.

A menacing smile spread across my face as it all hit him; he didn't have his wings anymore and only had a Mark.

He had Fallen.

"NO!" he yelled as I turned and left the darkness, leaving him alone.

I didn't care that the Archangel had lost his wings; in fact, I immensely enjoyed thinking about how the Archangel's life had gotten ruined. All because of me.

I walked through the tunnel, and as I left, I saw Damon perched on the ground, looking up at me with a worried expression.

I saw his nose was no longer bleeding.

"You look good, Damon," I said as I noticed his clean face.

"Thank you, my Queen. Now what?" he asked, looking up at me with wide, orb-like eyes.

"Now, we go to the Inferno River," I said. "To see if Chrysanthe is anywhere."

I needed to find her; it was unsettling not knowing where she was. So, I would have to use the cursed Waters to discover her location.

It was going to be interesting.

"My Queen? Is everything alright?"

I ignored Gog as I brushed past him and instead looked at the Waters of the Inferno River. Damon followed closely behind me.

I *needed* to find Chrysanthe.

"Thana?" Gog asked again, and I bristled in agitation as I looked at him, furious that he was talking to me.

"Gog, stop, alright? I'm fine; I need to do something essential."

There was another way to find her.

I leaned forward and looked into the murky water, seeing the ripples wave through the liquid. "Show me Chrysanthe," I demanded.

I waited as the Water rippled once more, but then nothing showed as I stood over it expectantly. It was just the murky fluid of the Inferno River.

I snarled, and my eyes narrowed in anger.

I turned my attention to Gog.

"Gog?" I asked. "How could this happen?"

The Goblin turned and looked at me.

"She's in an area that has gotten protected from the powers of the Water. Enchantments have guarded her, so only certain Beings can see through them or go there. It has gotten forbidden to anyone in Hell."

"I wonder why." I clenched my teeth.

Chrysanthe was planning on destroying me. Why else would she be in a forbidden area where I couldn't see her?

The entire thing had me enraged and unnerved.

I vowed to find out what she was planning.

Chrysanthe

I jumped slightly as Altheda's icy hands brushed past my neck, causing water to drip onto my skin.

I shivered as I felt the sensation.

"I'm sorry!" she said. "I didn't mean to startle you."

Altheda was tinting my hair blue, using some unique flower petals so I would become immune to the toxins they contained. She made sure the hair paste could glide through my mane to lock in the protection. That way, whenever I encountered the flowers, I would not be poisoned.

I took a deep breath as Altheda continued tinting my hair. I sat at the table across from Sybella and Serenity. They had been out exploring the rest of the Realm before they returned and settled down with us.

Sybella played with Caliya and sipped her flower tea as she stroked the tiger's face. Caliya moaned happily when Serenity suddenly spoke up and twisted her body so that she faced me.

"I can take all three of you to Hell since you need to get Viro, Thera, and Celio back. I can take you to the entrance," she told me. "But I cannot go into the Underworld with you; a spell prevents me since I am an Apparition. We would also have to go back to the Psychic Lake again. We would have to do this to determine exactly what is going on with your parents in the Abyss. Your parents as well as your love," Serenity continued. "We need to check on them before we go to Hell to see how they are faring. I will be able to take you there," she repeated.

"Will it be a long trip?" I asked and swallowed as Altheda continued with my hair.

"No," Serenity said. "We would be at the Lake within a few mornings. I'll then be able to fulfill my duty and take you to the Underworld finally. I'll be able to go to Heaven once I've helped you."

"You must really want to go there." I suddenly felt sympathetic toward her.

Serenity must have spent millennia being a Floating Soul. Never being able to move on.

It must've been a troubling predicament, being where she was.

She couldn't go to Heaven as she had sacrificed herself on purpose, and couldn't go to Hell because she had gotten destined for the Afterworld.

Until she finished her duty, which was to help me, she couldn't go anywhere. She had gotten stuck between the Worlds.

"There we go," Altheda said, breaking me out of my thoughts. "Now, all you have to do is wash your hair to remove the excess paste."

I turned around to face her.

"Where do I go now?" I asked.

"There's a body of water outside; I'll show you. Also, I'll get you some new clothes for tonight."

I was about to say thank you when Serenity spoke up.

"I'll help, too," she said, her body floating above the table. She glanced at me before speaking to Altheda.

"You help with her hair; I'll help with her clothes," Serenity stated.

Altheda nodded.

"Okay," she said before turning back to me. "I'll show you where the water is."

And then I followed her outside.

When I reached the body of water deep within the forest, I sighed. I was able to relax for the first time in a long time. Altheda brushed her fingers through my hair, removing any excess paste.

"Throw your head forward," she told me, scrubbing my hair clean.

The excess water had gotten rinsed out when she was complete, and my blue-tinted blond hair settled at my elbows.

I saw my reflection in the moonlit water and smiled.

"Now," Altheda said, "you are immune to the toxins of these flowers."

"The Phantom can get defeated now?"

"Yes. The Phantom can be defeated."

The grin took over my entire face; I was ecstatic.

Finally, there was a way to defeat my twin.

We could put an end to all the death and destruction she had caused.

I was going to get Celio, Thera, and Viro back, and my sister would pay the ultimate price.

Celio

 y lungs felt as if they were going to burst as I struggled to get to the surface. I was suffocating as I tried to reach the open air.

I kicked as I pushed through the liquid. It was so heavy and thick that it felt like I had gotten enveloped by it.

Come on, Celio, I thought, kicking again. Make it to the surface. Come on; I must breathe.

I felt myself getting propelled upwards.

I threw my arms out in front of me as I swam through the goo-like substance. I had to get to the surface before I drowned. I pushed myself up further. Nearly there.

I felt it when I finally was able to get to the open air.

I was about to rejoice that I had made it out when I quickly gasped in oxygen, becoming alarmed.

Something...something was wrong.

There was a problem as I tried to breathe.

I tried to inhale air into my lungs, but I was breathing in liquid — it covered my lips.

What the...? I thought as I felt the fluid ooze into my mouth; the taste of it caused me to gag. Ugh.

My vision was blurred. A thick coat of film covered my eyes, and I couldn't see anything in front of me.

Panic raced through me as my heart pounded against my ribs.

No. No. No.

I choked on the liquid as I attempted to blink, but it was futile.

I couldn't breathe, and I couldn't see.

I began to asphyxiate, immediately lost my balance, and fell on the ground, not realizing I'd fallen on a bunch of sharp brambles and branches until I felt blood dripping down my wrists and arms.

But the pain was masked by the panic of not being able to breathe.

I was slowly losing my battle to stay alive. I coughed, trying to pass the liquid, but it was no use.

I tried to glance at my surroundings, but all I saw was black.

The liquid had saturated my body.

But then I somehow noticed a female Being standing above me, with a hungry, malicious look on her face.

It was Thana; her eyes pierced through mine as she sneered at me.

I couldn't even glare at her as I felt myself begin to fade away.

I was dying as I stared at her, looking as her smile spread across her face. I felt the life slip away from me.

That was when I felt my body finally give out. My head hit the ground as my body finally shut down, and I entered complete oblivion.

I gasped as I was jolted awake. It felt so real, but after a few moments, I realized that it was a dream. A nightmare, really.

I took a few deep breaths to slow my heart rate and realized I was trapped in the chains of the Underworld still.

My hands were still high above my head, my wings hanging in front of me, to torment me about the fact that I had a Mark.

My heart raced as anger poured through me. I thought back to what Thana had done to me and what she was likely to do to Viro and Thera.

And I knew she would soon pay the price for what she had done.

45

Chrysanthe

 cold breeze brushed my face, causing my skin to tremble as I struggled to see what was in front of me.

The night sky was black as ink as I stepped forward blindly, trying to locate something to grasp. There was nothing to help me navigate my surroundings.

A snap startled me as I made my way a little further; I heard the rustle of leaves.

Huh?

I shook my head, confused before I understood where I was.

I was in a forest.

My eyebrows furrowed as I looked down, trying to see my bare feet, but I couldn't. It was too dark out to see anything in front of me.

"Chrysanthe?"

A voice floated through the forest, and I twisted my head toward it.

It was Celio.

"Chrysanthe? Chrysanthe, where are you?"

"I'm over here!" I yelled back.

I couldn't see him, but maybe he could see me.

"Chrysanthe?"

"Celio! Celio, I'm over here!"

I stopped walking so he would be able to pinpoint where I was. I heard his heavy breathing and his feet crushing leaves within a few moments.

"Chrysanthe, I'm coming!" he yelled as I heard him run. "Just stay there!"

I stayed where I was, and soon, I felt his fingertips graze my arms as he reached me.

"Celio." I smiled as I felt his arms around me.

The moon cut through the trees, and I saw half of his face light up.

"Chrysanthe," he breathed as he leaned toward me. He brushed my cheek with his fingertips. "I missed you."

He kissed me in a way that made my heart rate spike.

For a few moments, the only thing heard in the quiet forest was our heavy breathing as we became entangled. I eventually broke away from Celio.

But he brought his mouth to mine for a second time; my insides went numb as the sensations boiled inside me.

Celio, I love you so much...

His breath soaked my face as we broke apart once more. But then, I felt my gut twist uneasily. I knew something was wrong.

"Celio?"

His breath started to smell strange as it saturated my skin, his body feeling different.

"Celio?" I asked again, becoming slightly unnerved.

What was going on with him?

The right side of his face illuminated in the brightness, his hazel eye watching mine. The other half was shrouded in darkness.

"Chrysanthe, I'm sorry."

What? *I thought as I watched him, watched the color of his eye glow in the pale light.*

Why was he sorry?

There was a quick flapping sound; I noticed Celio's wings behind him.

There was something wrong with them, though, and it took a few moments for me to notice what it was.

They looked ripped in places, and the feathers had gotten torn out in strange angles.

Huh? *I focused my attention on his face again, which had gotten contorted into a pained expression. I placed my palm softly on his cheek.*

My heart sank at the sight of it.

What was going on here?

"Chrysanthe, I'm sorry," *Celio repeated, and his body shrunk under my right palm.*

I shook my head in confusion. But then the moonlight shifted so that I could see the other side of his face.

I gasped, unable to process what I saw, and felt a sob close my throat.

"No. No," *I mumbled, and Celio's pained expression grew.* "No...."

My eyes widened in fear. My intestines twisted as I took in Celio's face.

The left side of it made it look as if Celio was decaying. Bone and teeth were exposed.

"No. No. No," *I shrieked as I took it all in.* "No..."

Celio stared at me, the decaying portion of his face becoming more deteriorated as the moments went by. His right eye was no longer hazel; instead, it was becoming a disgusting, rotting brown that was verging on black.

"Celio..." *I choked out as I watched his face decaying before me.* "Celio, no..."

He attempted to flap his wings, but he couldn't. He was too weak, and they crumbled.

"Celio...."

His skin continued to disintegrate, and it spread to his face. I felt his frame shrink further under my palm.

I took my hand off his chest and started to hyperventilate as panic coursed through me. His frame changed as I stared, and within a few moments, he looked like a rotting corpse.

I took a step back, petrified at what he was turning into, and it quickly became apparent that he was beyond saving.

Tears flowed from my eyes, and I screamed as Celio gagged. He held his hand out and attempted to grasp mine before he collapsed face-first into the dirt.

His crumbling, rotting body stiffened, and his wings broke down into the soil as a sob choked me, preventing me from taking in air.

I couldn't believe it; I didn't want to.

Celio was dead.

The screech that erupted from my throat was enough to make me hoarse. I bolted upright immediately; my body was drenched in sweat as my scream killed the silence.

I looked around, still on the edge of panic, when I saw the Oracle calmly approach me.

Sybella crouched beside me. She took a steady breath before speaking.

"What is it, Chrysanthe? What happened?" She put her hand over mine.

"It...it was Celio," I stuttered, still trembling. "He... He died...in my dream."

She stared at me as if she was thinking about something. She leaned forward and looked me directly in the eyes.

"It was a dream, Chrysanthe. Remember that. Celio is still alive; we all know it. All you need is a good night's sleep," she said.

I saw orange striped fur out of the corner of my eye, and I felt a smile make its way on my face.

It was Caliya.

"Here," Sybella said and focused her gaze on the tiger. She stroked her ear affectionately as Caliya looked at me. "Here's someone that will keep the bad dreams away."

Caliya looked at me with her amber eyes before she padded softly in my direction and went to lay down beside me.

I instantly felt calmer as I pulled the blanket up to my chest, feeling the tiger's warmth as I burrowed myself in the sheet.

My eyelids grew heavy almost as soon as I got comfortable, but I heard a few words getting said right before I fell asleep.

It was Sybella, talking to both Serenity and Altheda.

"It's the Archangel," Sybella said to both of them. "He is being tortured."

46

My eyelashes fluttered as I slowly woke up, shaking away the drowsiness from my brain. There was a breathy snore next to me.

I looked over at Caliya, who was fast asleep beside me, and studied the up-and-down movement of her chest as she breathed. She threw a gigantic paw in front of her as she stretched, extending her claws so I could see each one individually.

They looked razor-sharp and lethal.

I leaned down and rubbed her ear affectionately before I stood up, stretching.

It was still dark outside, which meant that I was up a little earlier than Altheda and Sybella. Serenity, of course, didn't sleep since she was an Apparition.

I yawned, brushed my hair with my fingers, and walked over to make some tea. I opened the tin and removed some of the tea petals before putting some into a cup.

When I found where the water was, I poured it into the cup and held it to warm up the liquid.

Thanks to my powers, the fluid became hot, and I smiled again as I sipped the drink, enjoying the feeling as it registered in my body.

"It's good, isn't it?"

I blinked and looked over my shoulder to realize that Serenity was right beside me.

"Hey," I said. "Yes. Yes, it is."

It suddenly hit me how she couldn't have tea or anything because she was a Floating Soul. I wondered what that must've been like for her. To not have anything to eat or drink.

"She was right," Serenity said, interrupting my thoughts.

Huh? I thought and then realized she was talking about Sybella.

My heart sank.

"Sybella was telling the truth? Celio really is being tortured?"

"Yes."

'How...how...how do you know this?" I demanded between breaths, trying not to cry.

"The Oracle. She saw a vision after you fell back asleep, proving she was telling the truth. I'll let her explain it herself." Serenity turned to the Oracle who had seemingly come out of nowhere.

My breathing was rapid, and my heart pounded inside my chest as I tried sipping the tea, but my hands were shaking so badly that I had to put the cup down.

Now, my love and my parents were all getting tortured.

I had to get them out of Hell; I had to.

And I had to do it fast.

My eyes were fixed on Sybella as she ran her fingers through her lengthy hair, blinking away the sleep still taking over her. She took a deep breath and looked at me with a look of concern etched into her face.

Sybella took another deep breath before speaking.

"I have a lot to tell you, Chrysanthe." She took a seat opposite me.

"Chrysanthe," she said slowly, and I felt my heart skip a beat. "You know I have the power of seeing into the future, but as I was in the Underworld, my powers didn't work. No Being's powers will work unless they are actually from Hell or have been there for a *really* long time."

She took another breath before continuing.

I didn't like this. It was making me feel more anxious. But I knew I needed to understand what Sybella was about to tell me.

"Chrysanthe, not long after your nightmare and saying Celio had gotten tortured, I had a vision about him."

My hands were still shaking badly; I couldn't pick up my cup of tea yet.

I placed my hands underneath the table and hit fur with my fingertips.

I grasped Caliya's fur anxiously as I waited for the Oracle to finish what she was saying.

She looked me straight in the eyes before she said, "Chrysanthe, Celio died in my vision."

Thana

Restlessly, I paced around the rocky Abyss; my mind had gotten focused on Chrysanthe.

I knew she was planning on defeating me; I knew that she was up to something. I just needed to know how she was developing her plan. It was eating away at me, not knowing.

I gritted my teeth so tight I thought they would break, and Damon observed me from the rock he had gotten perched on when there was suddenly a familiar voice that echoed in the darkness.

"Thana? Where are you?" Gog's voice reverberated around the Abyss.

"I'm over here," I replied loudly.

I stopped walking and waited until I heard the Goblin run up to me.

He sounded out of breath as he made his way over. His breathing was ragged and croaky as he appeared, and he clutched his side.

"Thana," he started once he was able to catch his breath, "it is important news that I am bringing you."

I waited as he gulped in more oxygen, calmly waiting for him to continue.

"It is the Empyrean Blade; it is here, in the Underworld."

I blinked as I absorbed what he said, and my heart rate abruptly spiked.

The Empyrean Blade. It was here. The very Blade that could help or hinder me, depending on who was wielding it.

It could either keep evil out of the many Realms or let it into them...

"Are you certain of this, Gog?" I had to make sure he was right. This would be my only chance.

The Goblin nodded. "Yes, my Queen."

I abruptly remembered who oversaw the Empyrean Blade.

My father.

Since my father, Viro, was King of all Celestial Beings, he oversaw keeping the Empyrean Blade safe.

And if he was here, that meant that the Blade was here as well.

"Thank you for telling me this, Gog," I said before making my way to where the cells were.

"You're welcome, my Queen."

A malicious smile formed on my face as I thought of how I would soon have the Empyrean Blade.

And I would let evil into all the Realms by using the Celestial Object.

"Where is it?" I asked as I entered through the tunnel leading to the prison cells.

I didn't hear a response as I turned the corner. I could only see the Ghosts and the Wraiths crowding both prison cells where Viro and Thera had gotten put.

The Wraiths twisted and looked to me while the Ghosts drifted away.

My parents had gotten separated on either side of the rocky terrain. When I turned the corner, I saw both of their faces pale. I walked over to Viro's prison cell.

Thera looked as if she was about to cry, her face still a purplish-blue mess. Viro gulped, his face cut up with scrapes.

"Where is it?" I demanded again as I studied Viro's demeanor.

He wrinkled his eyebrows in confusion.

"Where is what?"

"The Empyrean Blade. Where is it? I know you have it, Viro."

I hated his actions. He was pretending like he didn't know where it was at all when he possessed it all along.

Viro shook his head, not realizing the more he didn't cooperate, the more trouble he would encounter.

I clenched my teeth together and took in his appearance. He was emaciated compared to how fit he used to be.

The tattoo on his collarbone poked through the top of his shirt.

It looked like a knife, the edge of it poking out.

It took me a few moments, but then I realized that's exactly what it was. It was actually the Empyrean Blade.

I snarled and rushed at the cell, grabbing the bones that were keeping my father from me.

"Is that not the Empyrean Blade?" I growled and pointed to the tattoo. My blood was boiling.

Thera was crying while Viro stayed quiet.

I seethed when Viro didn't answer me; I quickly ripped the cell open and got into my father's face. I was so close that our noses almost touched.

"You really think you can outsmart me?" I snarled and watched Viro's blue eyes dimming.

I grabbed the flesh by his collarbone with my bare hands and grasped the Blade inked to his skin. Swiftly, the Empyrean Blade left his flesh, and I felt pain as I grabbed the sharp edge, but I ignored it and shoved my father away.

He gasped as he flew backward, and I sensed he was watching me.

Blood dripped from my hand as the Blade cut into my palm, and I stormed out of the cell, not saying another word as I grabbed the handle of the Blade with my other hand.

Slamming the door to the cell roughly, I walked away, but not before noticing the Empyrean Blade was disintegrating in my hand. The Blade edge was black and melted, oozing dark slime, and the handle had turned black also.

I growled heavily. Eventually, everything I touched would dissolve.

But then I stopped, realizing what that meant. It was responding to me; it was listening to me.

That meant I was its new master.

I possessed the power of the Empyrean Blade.

48

Chrysanthe

A chill rattled my spine, which caused me to shiver as the Oracle's words repeated in my brain. *'Chrysanthe, Celio died in my vision.'* The words wouldn't leave me.

My jaw had dropped as Sybella said those words. My eyes felt as if they were going to pop out of my head.

It was difficult to process what she had said; my mind couldn't contemplate anything.

Since Celio was being tortured and could potentially die, I was ready to go to the Psychic Lake again. I was ready to see how they were faring. I also wanted to see what was going on with my parents and my love.

My heart raced at the thought of them getting tortured and a lump built in my throat. I heard a noise behind me, and I turned to find Sybella, her eyes wide and bright.

"I know you're scared, Chrysanthe, but we have to do this. My visions are not always correct; the future is always changing."

I paused; I had never thought of that.

Sybella put a comforting hand on my shoulder.

"Chrysanthe, we are going to have to go to the Psychic Lake no matter what, but I don't know whether or not my vision will come true. It quite possibly could be wrong altogether; I don't know."

"Let's make sure it doesn't come true," another voice said, and I looked to see Serenity floating into the room.

If only I knew how to do that. I studied Serenity's gaze. *If only I learned how to change the future.*

As Serenity said, it took a few mornings to reach the Psychic Lake.

My heart was in my stomach the entire time.

What if it had gotten confirmed that Celio was going to die? That my parents were being pulverized to a pulp by their daughter? By my sister.

The way I felt rubbed off on Leora, my Unicorn, as she kept nudging me and snorting. She wanted to get petted regularly. I sensed she knew I was nervous; I was tense and stressed as I took in my surroundings. At night I dreaded the moment I would have to shut my eyes, afraid I would have horrible nightmares.

But they never came.

The first morning on the Psychic Lake journey, I had woken up early, only to find Sybella up and sitting on a rock. Her blond hair billowed in the breeze; her turquoise blue dress rippled with the wind. Her tattoos shone, and color bounced along her skin in the sunlight. Her back had gotten turned from me so that I couldn't see her expression.

"Chrysanthe?" she asked, and I twisted around on Caliya, whose gigantic striped body had become my pillow.

I yawned and focused on the tattoos that adorned her skin.

"Chrysanthe?" she repeated and turned to face me.

Her eyes were a brilliant blue, her face the color of the inside of a peach.

Everything appeared normal. Sybella didn't look as if she'd been in the Underworld.

I lifted my head off Caliya's chest as she stretched out her long claws sleepily, and Sybella smiled.

"I need to talk to you," she said, focusing her attention on me as I slowly propped myself up.

"About what?" I asked, suddenly hesitant.

"It's about your parents and Celio."

"What about them?" My heart raced; I wasn't sure I wanted to know her answer.

"It's Celio; he has the Mark. I had another vision as I woke. Thana has taken his wings."

49

Thana

"My Queen?"

"Yes?" I didn't look up from the Blade in my hand.

"I have more news for you."

"What is it, Gog?" I asked as my fingers moved over the metal.

"It's Chrysanthe; I found her. She's going to the Psychic Lake, along with the Oracle and another unfamiliar Being. An Apparition is also with them. I saw them in the Inferno River, my Queen."

My heart skipped a beat.

"When did you see this, Gog?" I turned to face him.

"I just came from the Inferno River, Thana; I came as soon as I saw her."

"Good, Gog." I seethed with anticipation. "Thank you for the information."

The Goblin bowed his head deeply and disappeared into the darkness. I was left alone with Damon, who had gotten perched on a rock behind me.

Gog had found her. Now I knew where she was; I could bring her to Hell.

I looked at Damon, and he met my gaze, his body tense. A smile formed on his face.

"Come on, Thana!" he yelled, his voice echoing through the Underworld. "I can go find them!"

"That's *exactly* what I want you to do," I said to him, a grin beginning to form on my face as well.

Damon's eyes lit up as he absorbed my words.

"Damon, go and find Chrysanthe, the Oracle, the Apparition, and this other Being. Find them and bring them to me. The Wraiths will go with you, as well as my crow tattoo, and make sure they *all* come to Hell."

Damon nodded understandingly.

"Yes, Thana."

I took a deep breath and brought my right hand up to my heart. I scraped at my crow tattoo, and it came alive. The crow perched on my left arm and looked at me with small black, beady eyes.

It cawed and looked at me before I leaned in close.

"Go find Chrysanthe," I told my ink animal. It cawed again and took off into the darkness.

I stared as my crow flew away and turned to Damon.

"Follow the crow, Damon. Go find her."

His bat-like wings sounded awkward as he took to the sky, but then I saw him straighten them out and fly after the crow.

It didn't take long for me to find the Wraiths. They were still crowded around the cells that contained my parents.

They looked up as I entered, their hooded heads twisting in my direction when they sensed me. I ignored the helpless stares from my parents and approached one of the Wraiths. I extended my arm and allowed my skull tattoo to become visible.

The Wraith brought a black, scabbed hand out toward me.

I grabbed the hooded figure's arm and repeated an incantation I had memorized from when I had tortured the Oracle. The magical words had the power to protect the Wraiths while they were on Earth so that they wouldn't evaporate into smoke.

I held onto the Wraith's arm and stared straight into where the hooded figure's eyes should have been. "Go find Chrysanthe," I said with as much force as possible.

I repeated the incantation for all the Wraiths. Then I watched as the hooded figures floated into the darkness after my crow and Damon.

They are going to find you, Chrysanthe. And they will bring you to Hell. Good luck attempting to escape.

Chrysanthe

"What about my parents?" I asked Sybella, a lump building in my throat.

"They are still getting tortured, and Thana stole the Empyrean Blade from your father. Forcefully."

My heart skipped a beat.

This was not good news. My twin could let all evil into the Realms at any moment if she wished.

"Thana has the Empyrean Blade, Chrysanthe," Sybella said.

That Blade could release all evil.

"What about...?" I started to ask but trailed off when I saw Sybella's face in the early morning light.

She was staring off into the sky, her blue eyes almost liquefied as she became unfocused. I quickly realized she had another vision.

Caliya rubbed against my arm as I watched Sybella return to me.

"Oh, Caliya." I stroked the tiger's ears. "It's okay."

Even though I'd just said that the look on the Oracle's face was enough to make my heart stop.

"We have to leave," Sybella said instantly; all the blood had drained from her face. "We have to go. Now," she repeated. "It's Thana; she's onto us," she said with urgency.

Her blue eyes widened in fear before she quickly stood up from the rock on which she was sitting.

"We must leave now," the Oracle told Serenity, who had floated right up to her. "It's Thana; she's following us with the Wraiths as well as her messenger and her ink animal."

The Apparition absorbed the information quickly before she turned toward me.

"Go wake Altheda," she said. "We have to leave this very moment before your twin arrives."

I nodded before going to where the Flower Being was sleeping, curled up in the grass.

I leaned over her as I crouched down on my knees and shook her shoulder gently.

She opened her eyes groggily and focused them on me.

"What is it?" she asked.

"We have to leave now. Thana is onto us. We must go."

Altheda gulped as she rose to her feet.

Maximus, the Winged stallion, had returned. She got onto him and looked toward Sybella.

"Let's go; we have to find a place far away, so Thana can't find us. The Wraiths and her messengers are moving fast."

I heard a whinny, as well as a snort, and noticed Leora making her way over to me.

"Hello, Leora," I said as she pushed her head into my body. "Can you take me far away from here?"

As if in response, the Unicorn snorted, and I chuckled.

"Okay, girl," I petted her mane, and she bowed low so I could get on her. "Come on," I grasped her mane gently. "Let's go."

I looked at Sybella, Serenity, and Altheda, who were ready.

Sybella had morphed into the barn owl in just mere moments. She clacked her beak impatiently, and I nodded understandingly.

"Alright, girl," I said to Leora. "Let's get out of here."

And we all took off, in the opposite direction, away from the Psychic Lake.

We were on the move all day, and were exhausted by the time it was dark.

"We can stop here for the night," Sybella said once she had transformed back into herself.

Finally, I thought. *A place to rest.*

I slowly climbed off Leora as she pushed her snout into my stomach, wanting to get petted. I ran my hand over her mane, praising her.

"Good girl, Leora. Good girl."

I petted her for a few more moments before I spotted an area nearby where it looked comfortable enough to sleep. I went to it and let Leora graze as I got myself comfortable on the ground.

A rumble echoed through the night, and I saw Caliya, who had followed closely behind us.

"Come on, Caliya," I said, looking at her amber eyes watching mine. She rumbled, and the noise reverberated through the darkness. "Come on, girl. Come sleep over here."

The tiger ran over to me and almost barreled me over with her sheer force.

The rumbles echoed as she rubbed her head against my chin affectionately, and then a few moments later, she was lying on the ground, her tail twitching in the air.

"Good girl, Caliya." I settled down with my head on her massive chest.

I was exhausted from the long day, and it wasn't long before my eyes drifted closed.

Good night, Caliya, I thought before my mind shut off. *Good night, World.*

But what happened when I was unconscious, I did not expect at all.

51

"Chrysanthe? Chrysanthe, is that you?"

My eyelashes fluttered as I recognized the voice speaking to me.

Wait a moment...

"Chrysanthe?"

I opened my eyes to see Celio leaning over me; he touched my cheek as a smile formed on his face.

"Celio," I said lovingly, feeling my skin that he had touched get warm. "Celio, you're here."

But when I focused on his face, his eyes, I realized something was seriously wrong.

His body wasn't healthy and stocky anymore, and his eyes lost their hazel color. His cheeks and face looked paler; his features seemed almost skeletal — much like Sybella before I healed her, and my heart dropped into my stomach.

I knew what was going on now.

"Chrysanthe?"

Celio sounded worried.

Perhaps he had seen my face fall after seeing what he indeed looked like, now that he was in Hell.

"Chrysanthe?" he repeated, and this time I looked at him through the orange haze surrounding us.

I saw the scars marking his arms and legs, as well as the scar on his cheek.

He was getting so weak, being in the Abyss, that was for sure.

"I know, Chrysanthe," Celio said, looking at me once my eyes went up to his face. "I look pretty bad, don't I?"

I didn't answer him, instead watching his dimming ones.

"You know, I didn't think this would work," Celio said, causing me to refocus.

"What?"

"I didn't think that I could get you in my dreams again, but it turned out all I had to do was think of you." His lips curled into a smile.

Celio…

I grinned back, walking over to him, and wrapped my arms around his body.

I closed my eyes as I hugged him, feeling his warmth when suddenly my arms felt something strange on his back.

I gasped, and my eyes opened instantly. When I looked up at Celio, there was a grimace on his face.

"Celio?" I looked at the Archangel, but he wouldn't make eye contact with me. "Celio, what's going on?" Again, he didn't meet my gaze.

It was several moments before he spoke.

"Chrysanthe," he said slowly. "Something happened to me. Something bad."

I stared at him and absorbed his words.

I brought my hands to my sides, but not before I moved my fingertips along the skin of his back. I stopped and twisted my head to the side once my hands grazed Celio's flesh, feeling the bizarre texture of his skin.

As I turned my head to the side, Celio's eyes closed instantly, his jaw clenched, and he took a deep breath.

"Celio?" I asked, my voice shaking slightly. "What's going on?"

He opened his eyes, piercing me with his steady gaze, before leaning forward and kissing me. Kissing me in such a way that kept me wanting more, even after we broke apart.

Our eyes met again, and that was when Celio twisted around to show me his back.

I let out a scream.

I couldn't stop the horror on my face as I took in his flesh.

His back was raw and bloody; it looked and smelled horrible.

That's when I saw the bloody outline. The place where his wings once were.

I heard him sigh; a deep exhale that soared through his lungs.

I held back the tears that were threatening to escape my eyes.

"Oh, Celio," I sighed and walked closer to him. I observed the Mark on his skin. "Thana did this to you, didn't she?"

He stayed silent for a few moments before responding.

"Yes, she did. She tortured me… and… and…took my wings."

I heard a hitch to his breathing and realized that he had begun to cry.

"Chrysanthe, I don't have my wings anymore. I have the Mark; I failed my duty, and now I've Fallen. Chrysanthe… Chrysanthe…"

Celio trailed off; I extended my arm out and touched his flesh to quiet him.

"Celio." I touched his right shoulder where the top portion of his wings would be and felt him shudder. "Everything's going to be okay." I knew that wasn't true, but I was trying to calm him down.

"It is?" he asked.

"Yes, it is. Everything's going to be fine," I lied. "Look at me; turn around, Celio."

He turned and met my gaze.

I leaned forward and kissed him. When we broke apart, I ran my fingertips along his face and brushed away his tears.

"Everything will be okay, Celio, I promise," I said as he stared at me.

"Okay," he mumbled, and I felt him nodding.

"Alright." I kissed him again lightly before bringing my hands back down to my sides. "Now," I said, looking at him steadily, "where are my parents? We need to find them so that I can get you all out of here."

Celio looked at me, his gaze powerful as he watched my eyes. It took a few moments before he spoke.

"They're over here," he said. "Follow me."

And with that, he walked off, me following him as we navigated the Abyss.

"Chrysanthe? Chrysanthe, is that really you?"

My mother's voice echoed through the rocky terrain of the Underworld as Celio and I finally reached the prison cells. I had to stifle a scream as I saw her appearance.

"Yes, mother; I'm here," I managed to splutter through the horror building inside me. "I'm here." My eyes found hers, and I couldn't help but stare.

"I know," Celio said, hearing how frightened I was at the sight of her.

Her face was puffy and bruised, while her right eye was almost swollen shut. She was completely unrecognizable, so beaten up, that it was not very comforting.

I tore my eyes away and instead looked at Celio, who was right beside me.

"*Where is my father?*" I asked quietly, but then I heard footsteps and realized he was walking toward me.

He didn't look good either. His red shirt was in shreds, scrapes and bloody bruises covered him, and he also had a swollen eye.

But he didn't look as bad as my mother did. Not at all.

"*Chrysanthe,*" he said as he walked over to me. "*Chrysanthe, we need your help.*"

"*I know,*" I said. "*I already saw Celio's back; he has the Mark on him, his wings are gone, and now you two have been tortured. I know my twin has got to be defeated.*"

"*She has the Empyrean Blade,*" my father said quickly.

"*I know,*" I replied. "*And now, we must stop her and get it back. I promise I won't let anything else happen to any of you. We will defeat her; I promise.*"

It wouldn't be easy, though.

"*Chrysanthe,*" my mother called from her prison cell, and I looked up as our eyes met. "*Chrysanthe, you can do this.*"

"*I know I can,*" I said. I ran up to where Thera was and unlocked the cell.

My mother scrambled from it before hugging me tightly. She had more strength than I had expected.

"*You can do this, Chrysanthe. I know you can.*"

I turned around, looked at Celio, my father, and then at my mother.

We were going to defeat Thana. And we were going to do this together.

Suddenly, a scream pierced through the Abyss, and I looked around, puzzled.

What the...? I thought, but then I heard the loud screech again. I glanced over to Celio and my parents and saw they were fading away, their bodies slowly becoming transparent.

I gasped.

"Bye, Chrysanthe," was all I heard from Celio right before I awoke.

My surroundings changed from the Underworld to the green surroundings of the Earth.

Only, when my eyelashes fluttered as I awoke, I saw a Cloaked Spirit heading toward me, screaming.

Oh, no...

We had gotten caught.

I heard Caliya wake up instantly, and a roar burrowed in the back of her throat as I heard her growl. She stood as soon as I propped myself up on my elbows, standing right in front of me. She roared, and the sound shook my bones.

The Wraith refused to back down, instead drifting right toward me with the speed of a flying arrow. It ignored Caliya's swipes and shoved her massive body to the ground with a loud *thud.*

Caliya roared again and got up as the Wraith closed in on me, about to grab my shoulder, when I saw the tiger leap at the Wraith's back, grabbing onto it with her strong jaws.

The Cloaked Spirit shrieked as it felt Caliya grabbing it and sent her flying to the ground once more.

"No!" I screamed as I saw the Wraith draw its sword from its belt, its gaze fixed on Caliya. "No!" I yelled again as I ran over to the Wraith and wrestled the blade from its hand.

The Cloaked Spirit was powerful as I attempted to grab the weapon, but as it threw me to the ground, on my back, I heard a voice.

"Well, well, well." I looked up to see a shriveled, black creature staring straight at me. "You're not going to come easily, are you?"

52

I snarled at the shriveled, black, emaciated-looking creature perched above me. I was still on my back, and ripples of pain coursed through my body.

I seethed, disgusted, and Caliya growled, a loud, thunderous noise that reverberated throughout her body.

"Well, I guess none of you like me," he smirked, his gigantic eyes wide as they fixed on me. "But that doesn't matter. All Thana wants is you and your friends."

I scrambled to get up, my shoulders sore from the impact of colliding with the Earth.

Caliya managed to come up behind me, so I leaned against her to stand up. It took a few moments, but I was finally able to do so.

"That Wraith really did hurt you, didn't it?" the creature sneered, and my blood boiled.

I glared at him before Caliya attacked. The tiger leaped away from me and straight at him, swiping at the black creature in midair with razor-sharp claws.

He screamed and took off, but it was too late; the tiger knocked him to the ground with a mighty swipe of her paw, forcing him to the ground with a *thump*.

Caliya growled as she pinned the creature to the grass, roaring when he tried to escape.

"HELP ME!" He screamed in terror. *"HELP ME!"*

The tigress kept him pinned beneath her gigantic paws. *"GET THEM!"*

I gazed at the other Wraiths heading my way, and Caliya roared, swiping at the Cloaked Spirit that drifted near her.

The black creature wriggled free of Caliya's grasp.

"GET THEM!" he repeated as he flew into the sky, and within moments I was surrounded by the Wraiths.

Caliya's roar was deafening as the Cloaked Spirits approached her, and she swiped at them with her massive paws as they shrieked, attempting to grab her fur as well as my skin.

The tiger tried her hardest to keep them away from both herself and me. But there were too many of them crowding us.

The Wraiths grabbed my shoulders; I slapped them, trying to get them off me, but it was no use.

One of the Wraiths hit me in the face, knocking me to the ground and causing blood to pool from my lip. Caliya roared thunderously, the noise shaking the terrain, but there was nothing she could do as another Wraith blocked her from me.

Another nearby scream caught my attention, and I saw Serenity squirming free from the black creature who had grabbed her.

There was more commotion as a barn owl flew off, and Serenity took off into the woods.

Within only a few moments of the Wraiths appearing, everybody had dispersed, escaping. The horses, Maximus and Leora, had cleared the area the moment the Wraiths had approached and fled into the woods.

I was pinned to the ground by the Cloaked Spirit once more. I felt its scabbed, black hand grasp my shoulder, and

I screamed in pain as it twisted my flesh. I shut my eyes as I felt the agony.

The Wraith screamed amidst Caliya's roar. I quickly felt weightless as the Wraith clung to my shoulder. The Cloaked Spirit dug into my skin so tightly it felt like it would fall off.

Caliya got torn away from me as I felt myself flying, and then, after a few moments, the Wraith let go with a bloodcurdling screech.

I slammed into the ground and opened my eyes as I attempted to remain calm.

That was when I felt the rocky terrain digging into my back.

My heart sank as I scanned my surroundings, only seeing darkness and death around me.

The Wraiths, the black, gangly creature, and a large black wolf that was half decaying and had blood-red eyes that stared right through me.

My heart stopped.

I was in Hell.

Thana

A high-pitched shriek caused my head to snap upwards, diverting my attention immediately.

My heart raced a few moments later when I realized it was the Banshees. It meant they had heard or seen something.

Damon, I thought instantly. *Damon and the Wraiths...*

And then my heart skipped a beat.

Chrysanthe. They found her.

My breathing increased. They had found my sister.

I quickly stood up, released my wings, and flew off to another portion of the Abyss.

"Chrysanthe?" The Archangel mumbled as my footsteps echoed through the Underworld.

He must've become delirious.

"Chrysanthe, is that you?"

"No, no, it isn't," I replied as I turned the corner. The Archangel hung from the chains, high above the ground, and stiffened immediately as our eyes met; his muscles locked into place tensely. He looked exhausted.

"I bring good news," I said, watching the Archangel's face as he slowly twisted his head. "You're getting out of here."

 228

I needed him once I saw Chrysanthe; I needed her to know his horrible state. I needed to torture her with it.

I twisted my head around and whistled. I looked into the darkness until I heard fabric moving in the distance.

A Wraith drifted toward me.

I glanced at the Archangel, who appeared apprehensive when he saw the Wraith beside me. I ignored him and turned my attention back to the Wraith.

"Let him go," I commanded the hooded figure. "Set him free."

The Wraith stared at me for a few moments before moving its black, scabbed hand to its belt; it removed the sword and drifted to the Archangel, cutting the chains binding him.

The Archangel tumbled to the ground as the chains broke, clinking against each other as they hit the rocky floor, along with the Archangel.

He shut his eyes in pain when he hit the floor chest first, clenching his teeth to avoid crying out.

His skin was almost translucent, the bones in his face protruding from his skin. He had gotten severely weakened.

It was evident that Hell was no place for an Archangel.

I watched as I approached and roughly pushed him up off the ground.

"Come on." I grabbed him by the shoulder. "Let's go; we have to leave."

I looked at the Wraith in front of me as I felt the Archangel's eyes focus on me intently.

"Lead the way," I told the hooded figure. "Show me Chrysanthe." I let go of the Archangel's shoulder so he could walk on his own, although he stumbled along.

He pierced my gaze as our eyes met again; although his eyes had dimmed, his look still made my heart skip a beat.

"Come," I told him, attempting to ignore the feeling he gave me. "We must follow the Wraith; Chrysanthe is here."

I twisted my head around so that I looked at the Wraith moving along the rocky ground. The Archangel followed closely behind me.

I heard Morgeran's snarl rip through the Underworld, the sound grating every nerve in my body as I caught sight of him; his hackles had gotten raised, his black, coarse fur stood on end.

I stared at the wolf's rigid form and watched his body language, catching movement out of the corner of my eye; it was Chrysanthe, shaking in fear.

Before I could say anything, the Archangel's voice shattered the silence, making me jump.

"CHRYSANTHE!" He yelled, making me turn around. "CHRYSANTHE!"

I elbowed him in the ribs to cut him off.

"Shh!" I snapped, but Morgeran had already turned his attention toward him.

Morgeran growled, a deep vicious sound as he snarled with his teeth exposed.

He stopped when I looked at him, but he kept his gaze on the Archangel.

The Archangel watched Chrysanthe, who was still shaking in fear. Her vivid blue eyes had gotten latched onto the Archangel's; it was enough to make my blood boil, seeing how much they cared for one another. Even from across the Abyss, it was apparent that they loved each other.

Morgeran continued to stare at the Archangel, and I walked behind him, pushing him forward.

He stumbled but regained his balance quickly before making his way to his love. I shoved him into her arms.

I stared at Chrysanthe and smiled, watching her eyes widen in horror as she saw the Archangel's body. Her focus diverted to his back, where the Mark was.

"Celio... Celio..." She touched his back and saw the bloody red imprint of the wings no longer on his flesh.

Chrysanthe's face became ashen; her voice shook with fear.

"No, Celio, no!"

54

Chrysanthe

"*NO!*" I screamed as I touched Celio's back, feeling the indentations where his wings used to be. "*NO!*"

I grasped his shoulders gently, careful not to hurt him, and he looked up at me; his eyes were sad as they locked with mine.

"I'm sorry," I said to Celio, my heart breaking at the sight of the bloody outline. "I'm so sorry."

I knew he had lost his wings because of my dreams, but I hadn't been prepared for the sheer sight of the bloody Mark.

It was carved deeply into his skin, appearing incredibly painful.

My hands roamed Celio's flesh as he started to stand; my palm slid from his back to his heart. He kept his eyes fixed on mine once he regained his balance.

Slowly, I regained mine, not once taking my eyes off Celio. Once I was on my feet, I turned to look at Thana and the black wolf that was snarling at us, its blood-red eyes staring.

The growl of the wolf was deafening. It was a sharp, cutting sound that slashed through the quiet that had once surrounded the Underworld.

It shook my bones as I stood beside Celio. I did not want him out of my sight since I had only just gotten him back.

I accidentally took a step backward, right into Altheda, who for a moment I forgot was even there.

She calmly put her hand on my arm; I looked behind me, only to come face to face with Thana, who had a malicious sneer taking over her features.

I flinched at the sheer intensity of the expression. It looked purely evil.

I clutched Celio's arm, determined not to lose him again, and that was enough to make Thana laugh.

"Don't worry, twin sister," she said sharply, the words cutting like a knife. "I'm not going after your lover. Not anymore." She winked at Celio.

I felt him shudder, and Thana laughed again.

I watched as she stopped and brought her hand up to her chest. And then I spotted the new tattoo beside the crow's wing.

What the...? But the color drained from my face, and Celio gulped loudly.

Thana grinned as her eyes began to change; she touched her skin. I blinked, unsure of what I was seeing.

Her pupils expanded and dilated, and she chuckled when she saw the looks of horror on both of our faces.

She scraped her long, black nails down her chest.

I gasped in horror, though, as I saw what she pulled from her skin, and I felt Celio grasp my arm hard.

The black handle... The oozing, sharp edge...

It was the Empyrean Blade, or what had remained of it.

Thana's eyes dilated again as she removed the Blade entirely out of her flesh. She held it in her hand.

She wore a triumphant smile.

"Well, my sister." Thana paused to look me in the eyes. "Look what I found."

Thana

The Archangel gulped for a second time as I stood there, in front of Chrysanthe and him, balancing the Empyrean Blade on my palm.

They both were watching me nervously.

Morgeran walked toward me, his eyes fixed on Chrysanthe and the Archangel, and he paced around them as I toyed with the Empyrean Blade.

You're not getting out of this one, I thought as I heard a vicious snarl erupt from Morgeran. *You will not.*

I grabbed the handle of the Empyrean Blade and strode over to where they were.

They held each other as I approached, and their eyes locked. I could smell their fear as they continued to look at each other.

I growled to bring their attention back.

Wait a moment. A thought suddenly struck me.

Either I could have Morgeran end Chrysanthe and her Archangel lover with one command or finish them both myself.

I clenched my jaw and smirked.

My lip curled up in disgust as I raised the Blade, ready to finish both my twin and her angel lover when I quickly heard a loud screech echo from the Abyss.

I turned to see an owl flying through the darkness.

Morgeran leaped off the ground and attempted to grab it with his strong jaws, but he failed.

The owl flew to the side of the wolf as it escaped Morgeran, but I watched in horror as the bird of prey then made its way toward the black wolf again, its sharp talons extended.

I didn't have a chance to scream out before the barn owl attacked him; its talons went straight for the wolf's red eyes.

The Hellhound yelped in agony and snapped his teeth blindly as blood streamed from his face; the barn owl flew upward before descending a second time towards his bloody head.

This time the owl grabbed his ears with its talons, causing Morgeran to yelp again and leap backward.

His ears had gotten ripped, and blood poured onto the rocks as he whimpered.

The barn owl screeched as Morgeran howled in pain; blood drenched his flesh, and a scream finally got released from my throat.

The barn owl soared into the darkness and disappeared. Morgeran yelped a third time, alone in the Underworld.

I couldn't bring myself to react to what happened for several moments. Shock overwhelmed my body.

No. No. No. I looked at Morgeran's defeated body. *No, don't cry.*

It was then my muscles loosened, and I could move.

I ran over to Morgeran.

He didn't look good at all.

Blood streamed from his forehead and ears, causing the fluid to run down his muzzle and his face. Both his ears had gotten torn due to the attack.

You poor thing, I thought as I heard Morgeran cry. *I'm so sorry. When I figure out why that barn owl attacked you, I'll... Wait a moment.*

The owl attacked Morgeran right as I was about to finish Chrysanthe and her Archangel lover. That meant the owl had come for a reason.

The owl had come to protect them, both of them, from me. Morgeran had just been its target.

What was so special about a barn owl? How come an owl came to save them? What was...?

It suddenly hit me.

I finally understood what was happening.

I had, for some reason, forgotten about the Oracle, who I had abducted along with my mother and father. I suddenly just now remembered that she possessed shapeshifting abilities.

She could transform into an owl.

The very owl that had attacked my Hellhound.

I ground my teeth, livid.

It was all Chrysanthe's fault; she had the Oracle come to save her. She made the Oracle maim my Hellhound; it was *her*. All of this was *her* doing.

I silently and slowly crept up behind her and her lover, raising the Empyrean Blade in the air.

My sister would pay for this.

Another loud screech erupted through the Abyss, and Chrysanthe jumped, only to turn around and spot me with the Blade raised.

She flinched away from the Blade, recoiling, and I snarled at her as I saw how cowardly she was.

Tears escaped her eyes, and she let out a scream, but I ignored her.

"You're going to pay for this," I seethed; I was ready to finish her. I needed to end this.

"Goodbye," I growled as I raised the Blade high and brought it down in a quick motion.

What I expected was for the Blade to hit flesh.

What I didn't expect was for her lover to jump in front of Chrysanthe. Right in front of the Empyrean Blade.

56

Chrysanthe

The screams that erupted from my throat were so loud that it seemed like they weren't mine.

My heart pounded against my ribs so forcefully that I could feel it in my head, blood seeping into my skull. My hands trembled severely.

My breathing hitched, and my eyes widened as they fixed on Celio. On the blood from the wound made by the Empyrean Blade.

"No, Celio, no!" I continued screaming.

I heard a menacing laugh in the distance and looked up to see, through tear-stained eyelashes, my sister grinning. The Empyrean Blade oozed black slime on its sharp edge, and it dripped slowly to the Underworld floor.

I tried not to pay attention to that.

My eyebrows creased as I stared at Thana, taken aback by how evil she indeed was.

She didn't care about anything.

She ignored the fact I was distraught before cutting through the thin air with the Empyrean Blade, slicing through the Abyss with ease.

I stared in horror as Thana approached the gigantic, wounded wolf. She guided the black creature to where she had sliced through the Underworld before grabbing it roughly and grinning at me once more.

"Goodbye," Thana sneered before both she and the wolf disappeared.

What...? My mind raced until I heard rough breathing. I looked down to see Celio watching me with now dimming hazel eyes.

"Chrys... Chrysanthe," he stammered, bringing me back to reality. "Chrys... Chrys..."

"No, Celio, shh." My voice hitched. "Shh."

Celio collapsed and lost his footing before he fell toward the ground. I caught him before he could hit the rocky terrain.

I held him tightly in my arms, crying as I brushed my fingers along his face, trying to push the strands of hair out of his eyes.

Celio, Celio, no. I started to panic as I watched the blood pour from the wound in his chest. I locked eyes with him, never wanting to break his hazel gaze. *No.*

I didn't notice Altheda behind me until I felt her hand on my shoulder.

She brushed Celio's forehead with her palm gently and slowly moved her hands along the wound; I saw her place some flower petals on his injury, hoping it would help.

Instead of getting better, though, the wound continued to bleed, and I held my breath.

"Chrysa... Chrysanthe... I love you..." Celio gasped as he touched my cheek, brushing his fingers through my hair.

"I love you, too, Celio," I said through tears and stroked his skin. He attempted to smile, but it was weak.

Altheda grabbed my hand and held it tightly as I continued to watch the blood pooling around his torso.

No, Celio, no! I watched his face and felt his hand grazing my cheek once more.

"Chrys… Chrys…" Celio stuttered, and he blinked as his eyes locked with mine again.

My chest hiccupped with sobs that rattled through me, and I pushed his hair from his eyes again.

I couldn't speak as Celio's breathing slowed.

Fresh tears flowed as Celio took his final breath, and his body stilled. Within moments, a bright, white light radiated from the wound where the Empyrean Blade had made its mark. The light became blinding, leaving Celio like the sun's rays, illuminating his body.

The light quickly receded. And Celio's body was gone.

He was gone.

I took a deep breath and attempted to steady myself as Altheda held my hand. But the tears continued to escape as an anguished scream left me.

It was too painful.

Celio was dead.

And my sister was to blame.

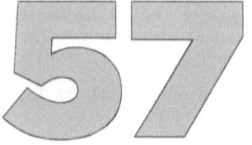 

Thana

I opened my eyes as my body stopped spinning; I felt my feet hit the grass, meaning I was on Earth.

A smile crept onto my mouth and my eyes drifted toward Morgeran, who was beside me.

Dried blood pooled around his eyes, drifting down toward his torn-up muzzle and open jaw.

Oh, Morgeran, I thought while looking at him. *You poor wolf.*

The Hellhound moved his head into my palm, wanting to get petted. I stroked his rough ears before taking in my surroundings.

I couldn't help but beam, but that soon changed to sickness as I looked at the Earth; the grass was sickeningly green and healthy, while the sky was bright blue.

My blood began to boil at the sight of it, of how *perfect* it all was; it was disgusting to me.

Drip. Drip. Drip.

I noticed the dark puddle on the green grass slowly turning it black.

The Blade was still in my hand, now empty of color as it oozed black slime onto the ground, and I grinned.

I suddenly realized just how much power I possessed, enhanced by the Empyrean Blade. I was no longer in Hell.

Destroying everything was going to be fun.

I spotted the black slice in the Earth from where the Empyrean Blade had ripped through and snarled. I was ready to let loose Hell on Earth.

Gripping the Blade tightly, I sliced through the air again.

Within mere moments there was a chorus of blood-curdling shrieks. It was the Wraiths; they were joining me on Earth.

Good luck dealing with all this, Chrysanthe. I laughed as the hooded head of one of the Wraiths poked through the slit. *Good luck.*

As soon as the Wraith hovered over the sickeningly green terrain, it instantly became dead.

It was incredible how fast the Earth was changing; within moments of the Wraith entering Earth, the ground immediately morphed and disintegrated into nothing.

Things worsened as Wraith after Wraith hovered through the hole. The ground turned into mush beneath my feet, and the sky darkened as my powers began taking control.

The ear-splitting screams of the Wraiths echoed through my eardrums as they made their way onto Earth. They dispersed from me, quickly hovering over the terrain as they took off, leaving the rotten landscape in their wake.

The Banshees came next; pale, wispy women with silver hair and dead, black eyes. They wore torn, black dresses that had gotten ripped from their time in Hell.

Their skin tone made them all appear translucent; their black eyes looked hauntingly creepy.

With a loud wail, they took off into the distance.

Morgeran sat and observed me.

"Let's go, boy," I said as the Empyrean Blade continued dripping on the ground. "Let's go destroy the rest of Chrysanthe's world."

58

Chrysanthe

I couldn't recall when I finally could breathe or when the tears finally stopped, but my eyes felt raw. My head pounded like it had gotten smashed against a rock.

Altheda's hand touching mine was what broke me out of my tears; I looked up to see a look of sympathy on her face. She tried to keep her emotions in check, but it was hard for her as she bit her lip, trying not to lose control in front of me.

An anguished scream echoed behind me suddenly, and it took me a while to discover that my mother had made the sound.

"Mom!" I yelled as I scrambled into the depths of the Abyss, Altheda close behind me. "Mom, I'm coming!"

"Mom? Dad?" My broken voice echoed through the Underworld; the sound bounced off the nearby rocks. "Where are you?"

"Chrysanthe, over here!"

My father's voice floated through the Underworld.

"Over here; we're over here!"

I crossed to where his voice was before I came to a prison-like cell.

I let out a gasp as I took in the disheveled appearance of my parents.

One of my father's eyes was black and blue, his skin smeared in bruises, while my mother looked incredibly beaten up. I wondered how she was still conscious.

"Chrysanthe, Chrysanthe," my father rasped, breaking me out of my reverie. I studied his features.

I noticed the desperation in his eyes.

I stared at him through the bone-encrusted bars of the cell, watching him, before words poured from my mouth.

"I'm going to get you both out of here."

Altheda stood beside me, and she reached into a crossbody bag, grabbing a few multicolored flower petals before holding them out.

"Hopefully, this'll work," she said. "The flower petals should be able to dissolve the bones of the cage."

"What?" I asked in disbelief.

But she paused before resuming her task.

Once Altheda had a significant amount of red, blue, yellow, and white petals, she approached the cage. She looked down at her palm, where all the petals had gotten clustered. Then she blew them in the direction of the prison cell.

I watched in amazement as the petals flew from her hand, and that was when, to my utter astonishment, the front of the cage evaporated into thin air.

It was hard to comprehend what had just happened when my father lunged forward and engulfed me in a bear hug.

I was sure my bones were going to break from the strength of the hug, but I welcomed it as he held me close to him.

He eventually loosened his grip.

He put his hand on Altheda's shoulder, and they shared a smile.

"Thank you. Thank you so much." His blue eyes fixed on hers.

"You're welcome, Viro." Her expression engulfed her entire face.

My father turned and glanced at my mother, who looked like she was in excruciating pain. Her purple dress was tattered, while dirt covered her bare feet.

It was all enough to make me feel like I was going to vomit, the way she'd gotten treated.

How could my own sister, my mother's *own blood,* do this to her?

How could my sister do this to Thera?

It was an unsettling sight, looking at my mother's swollen and battered face.

My father ran over to her before lifting her off the ground with ease.

Viro carried her toward me.

I couldn't help but wince as I saw my mother's face; it had gotten so beaten up.

I reached out and touched her hand; she blinked slowly before her eyes focused on mine.

"I'm so sorry, mother. We're going to get out of here. I promise."

Viro and Altheda watched me closely.

"Come on," I said, motioning into the darkness. "This way."

We reached the area where Thana had disappeared, and I took a deep breath, staring at the long, black slit she'd created with the Empyrean Blade.

It was only when my father gasped that I let out the breath in my lungs. His eyes widened as he stared in horror.

"I know," I said. "We have to stop her."

"Does she still have it? Does she still have the Blade?" my father desperately questioned.

"Yes. Yes, she does."

"Then we must leave now; the amount of power she has could destroy every single Realm."

I nodded, not sure what would happen next.

"We must leave now." He stood beside the slit in the thin air, with my mother in his arms. "Follow me," he said before he turned into smoke right before my eyes.

Altheda and I looked at each other.

"I'm right behind you, Altheda."

She disappeared into smoke like my father and mother. I took a deep breath before I stepped up to the gap in the air.

I could hear water dripping off the rocks.

I felt a strong force pulling me forward then and quickly felt lightheaded as I got swept out of Hell.

I was dust in the wind as I traveled through the Realms, but I clenched my teeth and squeezed my eyes shut as I felt my body blow through the air.

I could handle this; after all, I had to save the Earth.

I had to save the Earth from destruction.

I had to save us all.

59

My feet hitting the grass and the abrupt halt of the spinning sensation made me open my eyes.

I took a deep breath of fresh air into my lungs and took in my surroundings.

It was apparent that Thana had been here.

The once green grass had gotten destroyed. The dirt on the ground was now black, slimy mush.

My heart raced, and I started to hyperventilate. My body shook uncontrollably.

I shuddered at the sensation of the ground beneath me. I looked to see my feet drenched with black, oozing slime.

My lip curled upward in disgust. I looked in the distance and saw the state of the trees that were in front of me.

They were utterly lifeless and charred; the branches had splintered into pieces.

I was positive Thana had been here now.

If only I knew where she was.

"Chrysanthe?"

I heard Viro's voice in the distance and saw him come toward me.

"There you are," he said, leaning forward as he hugged me.

"Where's Mom and Altheda?" I asked as soon as I pulled away.

He pointed behind him.

"Your mother is resting on a rock nearby. We could use your help healing her, and Altheda is keeping her company."

"Is there any way Altheda could help heal Mom with the flower petals?"

My father shrugged.

"Maybe, but we need to get back to them right now, heal your mother, and then stop your sister before she destroys everything."

I nodded in agreement before I followed him into the broken, repulsive landscape. I was determined to stop Thana, now that I had seen what she had done.

And she would pay for it.

"Chrysanthe," my mother said; a smile formed on her face as she saw me walking across the dead terrain.

Altheda was beside her.

"Chrysanthe, how are you?"

I studied her appearance — her bruised, battered face — before I answered her.

I saw a knowing look in Altheda's eyes from my peripheral vision as I watched my mother.

"I'm good. I'm just going to feel better once Thana isn't going to obliterate Earth and all the Realms."

"Calla, you mean. Her name is Calla."

How could you be so gentle in your thoughts of my sister? I thought as I nodded wordlessly, with no emotion. *She attacked you and killed...killed Celio.*

At the thought of Celio, fresh tears began to fill my eyes which threatened to choke me. A hand grasped my shoulder, and I look up to see my father standing there, a concerned look in his blue eyes.

"I forgot to say this earlier, Chrysanthe, but we are both so sorry about Celio. We knew something was wrong when we didn't see him with you and Altheda. And then we saw your eyes…" he trailed off as tears poured down my cheeks once again.

Viro leaned forward, kissing my cheek. "I'm so sorry, sweetheart."

"It's okay," I replied to my father in a thick voice. "At least now, he's out of Hell."

"Chrysanthe," my mother piped up, and I looked up at her through tear-stained eyelashes.

It was difficult looking at her and seeing her face swollen.

"Chrysanthe, I'm sorry, too. An Archangel like Celio didn't deserve to die the way he did," she said. "I'm so very sorry."

I struggled to keep myself from falling apart as I looked in my mother's blue eyes, which were surprisingly piercing, given her condition.

Thana was going to pay for this.

Thana, not Calla. No matter how much my mother wanted to protect her by saying her real name, it still wasn't going to save her.

Thana would pay the ultimate price.

I took a deep breath and shut my eyes before focusing on my mother, but I had to hold back a growl.

There was even bleeding in her mouth, and her left eye was yellow and green and looked putrid.

"Shut your eyes," I told her softly.

Ordinarily, my mother would be able to heal herself, but right now, she couldn't move her arms around without agony.

It made me livid as I brought my hands up to her face.

But I remained silent.

Within moments of my fingers on her flesh, I felt a warm sensation radiating from my palms. The purple swelling started to fade and quickly disappeared. Her skin color returned, and as the healing finished, a cooling sensation took over.

I smiled.

"That's much better," I said. "Do you feel okay?"

"Yes," my mother replied. "Much better."

A bone-chilling growl suddenly tore through the clearing, and I froze, my entire body locking into place.

It was the cruel laugh that made me whip around immediately. It was then that I came face to face with my evil twin.

Out of my peripheral vision, I saw Viro seething; his knuckles were white against his flesh.

But Thana's attention had gotten focused solely on me and my — our — mother.

"It won't work," my twin almost laughed.

Mom gasped, and I turned to look.

Then I was horrified.

The swelling on her face had returned. However, this time her right eye had gotten swollen shut.

A lump formed in my throat and threatened to strangle me as I saw my mother.

A black oozing slime started to spread over her flesh, constricting her skin.

No. No. No, Mom.

She let out a blood-curdling, gut-wrenching scream as her eyes, once a piercing, ocean blue, turned black.

They became empty of any color.

A laugh broke me away from the appearance of my mother, and I twisted around to see my sister's face contorted into an evil smirk.

"Now *that's* how you torture someone," she laughed. "And here I thought you were smart."

My ears were still ringing from my mother's screams, but all I could focus on was Thana. Then I saw the Empyrean Blade she was still holding.

60

I stared at my twin sister as I seethed, grinding my teeth so hard I thought that they would break.

I could still see the Empyrean Blade dripping the black ooze onto the once gorgeous, green terrain out of the corner of my eye. But I couldn't look at it; I didn't want to take my eyes off Thana, who watched me with disdain.

"Go on, Chrysanthe," Thana taunted. "Try it."

But I knew better.

Her resulting malicious laugh echoed through the air, followed by a deep, vicious growl.

It was her Hellhound.

It snarled, exposing its teeth. As it approached me, I could see that most of the skin of the wolf's muzzle had gotten torn off.

Tendons and sinew were exposed entirely, causing the demonic creature to look even more frightening.

I stared at the creature, and I knew, in my gut, that it was going in for the kill.

Thana laughed cruelly as she looked at the beast with love; the animal barked at me.

Me.

Me, of all Beings.

But that was my mistake.

Because within that moment, the beast lunged at me, its teeth headed straight for my throat.

I scarcely had time to protect myself before the beast lunged, but the animal never reached me. There was a sudden flash of black-striped, orange fur as Caliya leaped from out of nowhere.

I watched in amazement as Caliya, with a thunderous roar that seemed to shake the Earth, pinned the enormous black wolf to the dead, decaying ground. She swiped at the beast's face with her long sharp claws.

They hit their mark, and the wolf howled in agony. Thana screamed, unable to watch as Caliya tortured her creature.

She approached them, her long black nails extended toward Caliya. I wondered if she was going to harm her, but a loud thunderclap made her jump.

I glanced over at my father, who was utterly livid as he stepped in front of me protectively.

"Do not touch the tiger," he commanded as he glared at his daughter.

"Okay, then," was all she replied as she whistled.

I scrunched my forehead in confusion before I realized two Wraiths appeared through the dead trees, hurtling toward Caliya. I quickly understood what was going to happen.

"NO!" I screamed as the Wraiths approached, and I knew they would kill her.

I needed to save her.

I immediately threw my hands up, causing the ground to crack underneath the Wraiths. They screeched and stopped when lightning struck them.

Thana turned at Viro.

She yelled in frustration and was about to say something when Viro cut her off.

"You will *not* continue this," he spat. "You will return the Empyrean Blade. *NOW!*"

But my sister just laughed maliciously.

"Really? You think you can defeat me? I'm the Queen of Death, thanks to you. There's nothing you can do to make me give up this Blade."

"Is that so?"

Now it was my turn to talk.

"There's nothing that can make you give up that Blade?" I asked, stepping forward carefully as I spoke. "Not even to save your precious wolf?"

Thana paled as she kept her eyes on me; her dark brown hair blew slightly in the breeze between us.

"You can't kill Morgeran. You can't kill him; he's a Hellhound. He belongs in Hell; he's already dead."

"Then why is he here? Anything in Hell *stays* in Hell. If he's here on Earth and not where he's supposed to be, he can get killed."

She glared at me.

"You wouldn't!" she growled.

"You doubt me?" I smirked.

I twisted to glance at Caliya, who still had the beast pinned.

Caliya looked at me with piercing, amber eyes. Her claws scratched Morgeran's face, and he whimpered. The tiger looked at me, waiting for a command.

"Kill him, Caliya."

The roar that erupted from the tiger was enough to shake through my bones and drown out Thana's scream. Caliya closed her jaw around the wolf's throat, cracking it with a loud crunch before the wolf turned limp, lifeless, in between Caliya's front paws.

She carelessly stood up afterward, ignoring Morgeran's carcass.

Thana shook violently, and her eyes narrowed.

"You...You...You..." She stammered, but I cut her off.

"And that's how you torture someone," I echoed her own words as she glowered at me.

"Now," I said, watching her gaze. "Are you going to give up the Empyrean Blade? Or no?"

"You're going to have to take it from me," she seethed, her teeth gritted into her skull.

And with that, she disappeared, evaporating into black smoke.

61

I glanced over at Viro, who was still by my side.

My father was furious, his face red with emotion.

"She... She'll..." he started to say, but he got cut off as a sudden moan resonated behind him.

We both turned to see my mother; her eyes were entirely black. Slime still covered her bruises, penetrating them.

She cried out as she fell to the dead ground beneath her.

It was apparent that she was unable to see. Her vision had gotten taken from her.

"Thera?" my father asked as he approached and knelt to help her. "Thera, can you squeeze my hand? It's me, Viro."

She moaned yet again, but she was able to apply some pressure to my father's hand.

"Good, Thera. That's very good."

"Viro..." My mother's voice started to break. "Viro, I'm blind."

My blood ran cold. My father immediately looked at me.

"Thera... Thera, it will be alright, my love." He turned his attention back to my mother. "You're going to be fine."

Altheda, who had been quiet until this point, approached my mother and grasped her other hand.

"Thera, it's Altheda," she said softly. "I'm right here; I'm going to stay with you, okay? Everything's going to be alright."

"Okay," Thera stammered.

My heart raced as I thought about how panicked she must've been feeling. I would make Thana pay for this. She would suffer as she had made us suffer.

"Chrysanthe," Altheda turned her gaze toward me, away from Thera. "Chrysanthe, here, take this bag. It contains the flower petals that will defeat *her*. Throw them on Thana whenever she gets too close to you, and they will paralyze her. She won't be able to use her powers then. After that, you can take the Empyrean Blade from her."

I knew what she meant.

I would have to kill Thana.

"Chrysanthe?"

I looked up at the sound of my name. I had been putting the crossbody bag Altheda gave me over my shoulder, ensuring the petals were safe.

"There you are, Chrysanthe," I heard again. It took me a few moments to realize it was Serenity.

She found us again.

She drifted towards us, and a sigh of relief escaped me as our eyes met.

"Are you alright?" Stupid question. She couldn't be hurt.

"I'm okay. You?"

"I'm good, but my mother isn't. She's gotten blinded by Thana, who has disappeared."

Serenity glanced over at Thera.

"We must find her." There was a sense of urgency to her voice.

She noticed the wolf's dead body, who lay on the ground, abandoned.

Serenity suddenly became serious. "Chrysanthe, what is that?"

"Oh, that's Morgeran, Thana's wolf. Caliya killed him."

Serenity quickly became agitated. "Chrysanthe, anything from Hell is already dead." She looked at me. "You can't kill a creature that's already dead and decaying."

I shook my head, confused.

"Then what was the loud crack before? I thought the wolf had certainly gotten killed."

"It was the wolf," Serenity said. "You just didn't kill the creature. That Hellhound is still very much alive. The only way you can completely send it back to Hell, along with Thana, is to use the Empyrean Blade."

I was surprised by her explanation, but then I was interrupted by the wolf; it had begun to breathe again.

I watched in amazement as the Hellhound moved its head before opening its blood-red eyes.

It glowered at me, growling before it stood and walked off into the gloomy woods.

I watched the wolf disappear; Serenity interrupted my thoughts.

"Chrysanthe, Thana is the Queen of Death; she rules Hell, and there *always* needs to be someone there to rule. If not, the Souls of the Damned can escape the Underworld, like what happened here. Although it would be far worse having no ruler."

It would? Not that I voiced my concerns.

Right now, everything looked bleak and dead; I didn't know how it could get any worse.

Serenity took in the Earth. "She needs to go back. Permanently," she said.

I nodded.

"That shriveled black creature, her main messenger, is also *not* what he appears to be," Serenity said. "He wasn't always like that," she repeated. "He was once mighty, so powerful he was part of the Heavens, but he quickly fell."

I didn't completely understand what she was saying.

"How do you know all of this?" I asked.

"He's the reason I'm an Apparition, Chrysanthe."

I froze, taken aback by her statement. I glanced to my father, who watched Serenity.

"Chrysanthe, I fell in love once. With an Archangel, the same as you. Although your love story is a lot nicer." She sighed.

I absorbed her words, needing to know more.

"The Archangel was very charming; his name was Xander and he was a Protector of the Souls. And he was very handsome. He told me he loved me once, and that was all it took. I told him I loved him, too."

Serenity gave a small pause.

"But being so naïve was my undoing. Little did I know that Xander would trick me into thinking I could live with him in the Afterworld. He told me I could join him in the Afterlife if I ended my own."

Serenity sighed heavily.

"I remember him laughing and being so cruel once I became an Apparition. He told me I was weak and that he was more powerful than I was. But it was when I was an Apparition that I realized my mistake. He never loved me, had never cared for me. He left without a trace just a few mornings later."

"What happened to him?" I asked curiously.

It was Viro who answered.

"I shrunk his wings, removing feathers as a warning to Xander. I warned that I would take his wings if he fell completely."

"He ignored Viro," Serenity piped up. "He was ejected from Heaven and tossed into Hell, where your sister discovered him. She morphed his wings before they could be taken, and now he's a messenger for her. He even changed his name from Xander to Damon."

I had so many questions, but it was not the time for them.

"If we find Damon, can we defeat Thana?"

Serenity nodded.

"Certainly, but we must not waste any more time. Thana could be anywhere, destroying the Realms as we speak. We *must* find her."

I turned around to face my father, who was still holding my mother's hand.

"Dad, you have to come with us. We need as much strength as possible to defeat her. Altheda," I faced her. "You take care of my mother."

I focused my attention on the dead forest.

"Caliya!" I yelled.

I quickly saw the tiger bounding towards me, her pawprints creating tracks in the terrain.

"Come on, Caliya, let's get this done."

My father now stood beside me.

"Okay," Serenity nodded.

"Let's go defeat Thana."

And we walked into the unknown.

62

Thana

A growl erupted from my throat as I materialized.

I was seething as I stomped through the terrain, but then I blinked rapidly, confused.

I couldn't see the Wraiths anywhere.

Where are they? I thought as I looked around for them but to no avail. *I need them.*

I tried whistling, but within a few moments, there was no response.

Where are they? I need them.

I had an important task for the Wraiths.

A Banshee drifted past me, her dark dress tattered and torn while her eyes were black and emotionless. Her pale, white complexion made her look haunted.

The Banshee stared before she shifted her focus behind me and wailed.

Huh? I thought as I rotated to see what she saw; my heart began to smash against my ribs.

It was Morgeran.

My Hellhound was here.

Morgeran whined and wagged his tail gently before running toward me. He brushed his face against my side.

"Morgeran, good boy. Good boy." I brushed his rough, coarse fur. "You've been such a good wolf."

Chrysanthe was wrong, I thought as I petted Morgeran. *Chrysanthe was wrong, and I knew it.*

Even though I had screamed when her tiger had *tried* to kill him, I did that for effect. To make Chrysanthe believe she had won.

But I knew he was okay.

I knew Morgeran was a Hellhound, and he couldn't get killed. Morgeran was no ordinary wolf; he helped drag and keep certain Souls in Hell, so he would always be safe.

Safe as long as I kept the Empyrean Blade away from Chrysanthe.

If she got her hands on it, she could kill us for good.

I needed the Wraiths.

I glanced to Morgeran and whistled softly, which immediately grabbed his attention.

"Go find the Wraiths," I said to him. "Go find the Wraiths, Morgeran."

The Hellhound blinked before he ran off into the emaciated landscape.

I watched him leave, intensely hoping he would find them.

Drip. Drip. Drip.

I glanced down at the Empyrean Blade that was in my hand, which had gotten coated in black ooze.

Come on, Morgeran. Come on.

I needed to hide the Blade so Chrysanthe couldn't find it.

And I had to do it fast.

I started to turn around, but I instantly felt my blood run cold as I did so; I had come face to face with Chrysanthe, my father, and an Apparition.

I was frozen in shock, surprised that they had found me, but then my shock dissolved as I snarled; my lip curled upward as I stared at my twin sister.

Chrysanthe wasn't fazed by me snarling at her, but I knew she saw my shocked expression.

"Thana, give us the Empyrean Blade. We don't wish to fight you."

Yes, you do, I thought as I stared into my father's blue eyes. They were so angry they looked like aqua-colored flames.

"I've already told you," I said as I glanced between my father and sister, disgust boiling inside me, "you're going to have to take it from me."

And then I disappeared into black smoke and evaporated into dust.

As I did, I heard a growl erupt from Viro that was enough to shake through my bones.

I was not sure where I landed. Wherever it was, it was near the Wraiths and Morgeran.

Morgeran had finally found the Wraiths, who had gotten grouped together as they waited for me.

The Hellhound watched as I materialized, and approached me so I could pet him.

Hey, Morgeran. How are you doing, boy? I thought as I put my hand on his fur.

He whined, pushing his head into my hand.

Good boy, Morgeran.

But then I was distracted by the sound of thunder rumbling in the distance.

I turned my gaze toward the sky as the clouds changed. They grew darker and more ominous as lightning began to erupt across the sky.

I growled as I heard the Wraiths screaming.

One of them pointed toward the trees behind me, but when I looked, I couldn't see anything.

I looked back at the hooded figure, who screeched so loud that my eardrums ached.

Morgeran growled, the Hellhound sounding vicious as his red eyes blazed. His ears pinned back as he walked ahead of me, and he snarled as he caught sight of something.

Hmmm...

Both Morgeran and the Wraith spotted something as I stood there, squinting. I still couldn't see anything.

That was when I suddenly had an idea.

I glanced at my crow tattoo before I scraped my fingernails along my flesh.

I knew what I had to do.

If *I* couldn't see anything, then I would send out my crow tattoo to find whatever it was that had grabbed Morgeran's attention.

There was a weird sensation as the crow abruptly morphed and perched on my arm.

Caw. Caw. Caw.

"Go and find out what's going on," I said to it; I made sure it understood my command. "Go now."

And the crow took off into the fog.

64

Chrysanthe

Viro's knuckles were white against his flesh as he snarled again. He looked beyond enraged; his blue eyes blazed as he looked up at the sky and brought his hands in front of him.

With a flick of his wrists, a roar of thunder echoed through the air, booming across the landscape.

I watched my father in silence. The air crackled around us.

"If she doesn't give us the Blade, then she'll have to deal with this," he said, referring to the thunderstorm.

Another crackle of thunder split the sky, followed by lightning. I stood back as Viro continued to wreak havoc on the atmosphere and spotted Serenity floating in my peripheral vision.

She was stoic as we both watched Viro, and within mere moments of him changing the sky, I felt raindrops dripping on my flesh.

"Come on out, Thana," my father growled; the words scraped through his teeth as they clenched tightly. "Come out, come out, wherever you are."

As he said that, lightning lit up the atmosphere, and thunder erupted.

Caw. Caw. Caw.

My brows scrunched together in confusion as my attention quickly got diverted. My eyes darted to the dead forest behind me before I looked at Serenity.

Caw. Caw. Caw. Caw. Caw. Ca...

The sound of the crow got cut off, and it quickly let out a shriek. I looked up at the trees to see a barn owl locking eyes with me.

Sybella? I watched the owl move its talons away from the black crow that had gotten pinned to a tree branch.

The crow continued to flap its wings, but all it could do was let out a weak caw.

A blood-curdling scream ripped through the clearing, causing Viro, Serenity, and I to pause.

Wait a moment. I recognized that noise. *Thana.*

"I think we found her," Viro said, glancing at Serenity and I.

I nodded. "Yeah," I said. "I think we did."

A screech abruptly erupted from above me, and the barn owl flew off the tree branch where it was perched and down in my direction, her talons out as she aimed for the Earth.

There was a brilliant white light that surrounded the owl, and within moments the animal got soaked in the illumination; the barn owl disappeared, revealing Sybella.

The Oracle looked at all of us before she focused her attention on where the scream originated.

"You're right," she said. "That was Thana; she's weak. I have wounded her crow. She'll be angry now, though. Harming a tattoo like her crow will be excruciatingly painful; she'll have a Mark now. But she is weakened, so we can finally defeat her."

I studied her blue eyes.

"Are you sure?" I asked.

She nodded.

"Let's go find her." I began walking off as I felt the raindrops on my skin.

We were going to defeat my twin sister, the Phantom, finally.

We were going to do it together.

Thana

Thunder tore across the sky as I fell to my knees. It felt like a knife had stabbed my chest and sliced it open.

What is going on here? My thoughts raced as I crumpled to the decayed terrain. *What is happening to me?*

"My Queen?"

I sucked in a breath in shock before Damon landed beside me, his claws covered in dirt.

"Thana, what's...?"

But Damon trailed off as he saw the searing pain that engulfed my face.

I growled at him. I'd needed him before, but he hadn't come. And yet, now that I was in pain, he had come straight away.

The growl became embedded in my throat as I felt another wave of agony wash over me.

"Thana?" he asked. "Thana, where's your crow? Where's your tattoo?"

My head immediately snapped to my chest. Damon recognized my look and backed away.

But I was fuming.

It was Chrysanthe's fault.

She had gotten ahold of my crow.

A burning sensation coursed through my body once again, and I stayed on my knees. Another scream escaped me and echoed through the silence.

"Thana, what's going on here?" Damon asked, startled.

I just glared at him through anger and pain.

"Damon, go get my crow tattoo. Leave me be."

"Yes, my Queen."

Damon then flew into the fog that drenched the Earth.

A raindrop hit my cheek as lightning continued to illuminate the sky. I frowned at the atmosphere as I heard Morgeran approach me. He rubbed his muzzle into my face.

I knew Viro and Chrysanthe were coming for me, though.

And I was going to go up against them.

Morgeran's growl ripped through the clearing, which quickly brought me out of my thoughts.

I opened my eyes, still dazed from the agony burning through me, only to see Chrysanthe, Viro, the Oracle, and the Apparition heading in my direction.

I locked eyes with Chrysanthe, and she stared me down, challenging me. I growled, despising the fact that she was doing this.

I stood, and Morgeran looked behind him with his blood-red eyes focused on me. I reached my hand out and petted him.

Lightning took over the sky, making me more threatening, but then Viro raised a hand to the atmosphere; his eyes had turned into slits. Thunder shattered the silence, which caused me to jump. The Wraiths behind me screamed.

I gritted my teeth, seething, and my blood boiled.

So, that is what you've decided? I thought. *Okay, then.*

I threw one of my hands up and sent a ripple through the Earth. It caused a fissure in the terrain between Chrysanthe and my father.

Mud oozed in the fissure as the Oracle glared at me. I suddenly spotted thick, black wings appear from behind her.

She started to rise into the sky and took off into the angry atmosphere.

I blinked, suddenly realizing the Apparition was also missing.

I couldn't see her.

It bothered me that I didn't know where she was.

Rain dripped on my face, and I felt a Wraith come up beside me as Morgeran came to my other side. My hand still gripped the Empyrean Blade as it dripped and oozed slime.

The Wraith held out its scabbed hand, and I instantly knew what it wanted.

And I agreed.

Quickly glancing to make sure Chrysanthe or Viro couldn't see what I was going to do, I twisted toward the Wraith and gave it the Empyrean Blade.

The Wraith nodded and placed the Blade deep within the black fabric that surrounded it.

"Keep it safe," I said to the hooded figure.

It nodded and took off into the woods, screeching.

However, as I turned back behind me, I realized what had happened had not been done privately; Chrysanthe and Viro glared at me.

They had seen everything.

66

Chrysanthe

I stood on the disgusting terrain, rooted to the spot with my mouth agape.

I couldn't believe what I had just witnessed.

Thana had given the Empyrean Blade to a Cloaked Spirit, and who knew where it would take the Blade?

The ground continued to split; there were gaps between my father and I.

Viro's face was beet red as he just glowered at his daughter. I'd never seen him so upset.

A sound of disgust erupted through his throat, and he fumed as he gave his daughter a threatening look. I knew then that Thana was going to pay for what she'd done.

Viro raised a hand and caused the rain to pound, resulting in the Wraiths screaming and taking off, hiding in the forest.

Lightning took over the sky amidst the downpour, and rain pummeled the ground. I heard Thana scream in anger.

I was shocked by her reaction as she had brought this upon herself.

Meanwhile, Viro appeared furious as he threw another hand up toward the sky. I watched in amazement as he flicked his wrist and caused a massive gust of wind to blow toward my twin. The blast of air completely knocked her off her feet, throwing her onto her stomach.

The screech that echoed through the air from Thana, despite the rainfall, was one of complete and utter agony as the mud crept into her wound.

She snarled, enraged, as she stood, soaked.

She sneered at Viro as I saw her wings appear, and she quickly became airborne, flying high in what appeared to be black mist.

Thana flew over to Viro and stopped in front of him; she grinned maliciously before she threw her hands out in front of her, causing the black mist to engulf my — our — father, who just glared at his daughter.

But then I screamed as I saw what she was going to do, to which Viro was oblivious.

He was so angry that he didn't see it coming.

"*NO!*" I shrieked as the mist went in his direction. It quickly overwhelmed him, and he collapsed.

Instantaneously, the weather cleared up, no longer pouring down rain; it immediately stopped, revealing an overcast sky.

Since Thana was in the atmosphere, she was still messing with it, which was why the sky was so gloomy.

"*NO!*" I screamed again as I saw the weather clear up once Viro became unconscious.

"Chrysanthe," Thana said, her lip curling into a sick smile. "Did you really think you could defeat the Queen of Death?"

I glowered at her, quickly feeling my blood pressure rising. I shivered from the wet clothes that clung to my body.

Thana continued to smile.

"Did you really think you could defeat me?" She smirked, watching my father's body.

His long blond hair was tangled and his beard scraggly. His body was still weak, and his frame not as stocky as it was before he was in Hell. The shirt he wore still seemed oversized and tattered, while the rest of his clothing appeared bulky.

"Did you really think you could win this fight?"

I tore my gaze away from my father to look at my sister. She faced me while still airborne and gave me an evil look.

I couldn't take it anymore as she floated. I threw my hands up and growled.

I screamed, frustrated, and created a column of air that knocked Thana off balance.

She somersaulted in the sky and snarled. I lifted my left hand, causing Thana to fall and slam into the Earth with tremendous force.

After that, I scanned and inspected the terrain; I lifted my hands and focused hard.

Within moments, the landscape beneath me began to repair itself.

I smiled internally, not daring to show emotions around Thana, but hesitated when I saw my father still unconscious.

"No, no, no. Dad." I scrambled toward him and knelt beside his body. "Dad," I said softly, running my hand across his face, brushing his hair back from his temples. "Dad, can you hear me?"

No answer.

"Dad?" I asked again desperately.

He moaned, the mud smearing over his face as he moved. When he opened his eyes, though, my blood turned cold.

His eyes weren't their usual bright blue; instead, they were an intense murky white color. His pupils were gone, and his expression vacant and emotionless.

My father just watched me, wide-eyed. He sucked in a quick breath and gasped as he closed his eyes again.

I soon realized that his breathing had become shallow.

"No. No. No." I shook my father to try and keep his focus on me.

"Dad? Dad?" Panic was rising inside me.

There was no response as he lay on the cracked ground; the mud smeared across him.

I heard a piercing shriek in the distance, which caused me to turn. But as I did so, the overcast sky began to turn black.

The blackness rushed toward me, and I quickly realized they were crows, gathered together in the sky. There also seemed to be an orangish tint that appeared to be fog.

The orange fog raced toward me, and that was when I heard the voices.

The voices that echoed when Celio had gotten stolen from me.

A cackling laugh filled the air as the orange mist advanced. The darkness flew closer, and my heart pounded. I didn't know what was going to happen next. I had to defeat Thana, but I was alone. I wasn't afraid to admit that I was scared.

The voices began to speak.

"We are the Ghosts," they said. "We have come to take over the Earth, as well as collect the Soul that has gotten poisoned."

Caw. Caw. Caw.

The crows surrounded me.

Caw. Caw.

My thoughts were elsewhere as I focused on what the Ghosts had said.

What? I felt my blood freezing.

A Poisoned Soul.

They had come to collect my father.

The crows cawed around me.

"NO!" I shrieked, and I flung myself over his body to protect him.

"But first," the voices echoed. "The Poisoned Soul will kill you, Chrysanthe."

"What?" I voiced my confusion.

I heard a gasp and turned to see my father sitting rigidly. He looked right at me as his lip curled upward in a snarl.

Tears gathered in my eyes as I took in his murderous expression. Thana was going to use my father against me.

The tears started to trail down my face as I saw his when I gasped; his hands had abruptly wrapped around my throat, choking the essence out of me.

67

I struggled for breath as my father's fingers cut off my airway. Panic coursed through my veins, and tears streamed down my cheeks.

His fingers pressed into my windpipe; I could feel myself slipping away.

"Kill her," the Ghost's voices seemed to chant. "Kill her now."

No… I couldn't die at my father's hands. Viro's eyes were large and milky, his look incredibly frightening and bizarre as he continued to choke me.

"Kill…"

Their voices were mocking as my own father suffocated me.

"Hey!"

A loud shout erupted through the clearing, which stopped the Ghosts.

The crows halted, and Viro paused, although his hands stayed tight around my throat.

A roar shattered the landscape, and that was when Viro's hands left my neck. I coughed violently as I took in breaths, the air crashing into my lungs.

Ahhhh…

I saw Caliya running in my direction. Her amber eyes blazed as she snarled; she leaped straight into the crowd of crows and Ghosts.

Caliya roared as she swiped at them with her paws until they dispersed, scattering into the wind.

Then she made her way over to my father and snarled at him, her sharp teeth showing.

Caliya, no. Please don't hurt him. I watched her demeanor change before she left my father and walked over to me.

"Chrysanthe!"

My head snapped to the side.

"Chrysanthe, are you okay?"

Serenity appeared, but she looked concerned.

"I've been better," I replied, still taking in gulps of air. "Thank you for saving me. What's going on with my father?" I asked, desperately wanting an answer.

Serenity drifted toward me carefully, wary of Viro.

I finally regained my balance and lifted myself from the ground. My father's eyes followed me as I did so, and a voice echoed from a distance.

"He's been poisoned."

Sybella was slowly flying toward us; her gigantic, black wings flapped behind her as her turquoise blue dress rippled in the breeze.

"He's gotten branded to spend the rest of his days in the Underworld," Sybella said as her bare feet hit the terrain. "He's possessed, which means he also has to do whatever the Ghosts command him to do."

"Which is why Viro tried to kill me." I took a deep breath; I still hadn't recovered from that.

Sybella nodded. "Yes, you are correct."

"So how do we save him from this?" Serenity asked. "There must be something."

"There is something," the Oracle said, "but it's tricky to find, and it's not in this Realm."

Not in this Realm.

"Which Realm?" I asked Sybella.

She looked me dead in the eyes.

"The Afterworld."

For a moment, my eyes went to my father, who still looked at me with his possessed ones.

"So, how do we get the Empyrean Blade? I saw Thana give it to the Cloaked Spirits."

"We're going to have to track one of the Wraiths down and take it back," the Oracle answered matter-of-factly. She looked at me as she answered but then paused as she saw me. "Chrysanthe, you need to get your throat fixed; it has gotten riddled with bruises."

It was true. My throat ached from where my father's hands had squeezed, hoping to end my existence. I could still feel his hands around my neck, and I rubbed it gently.

"Hold still, Chrysanthe." Sybella took a step toward me. She put a tattooed hand on my throat and spread her fingers across my flesh as a sensation of heat radiated from her palm. I could feel my neck healing, and the burning sensation in my throat disappeared.

"Now, we must find the Blade and overpower Thana," she said once she had finished healing me.

And I agreed with her.

I was finally ready to end all this tyranny.

I was ready to get the Blade back.

To save my father.

So that I could return things to normal and save the Realms.

I was more than ready.

 sudden, abrupt noise in the distance caused us to stop and turn around.

What was that sound?

My head snapped up as the noise echoed again, and that was when I saw black, bat-like wings flapping nearby before disappearing behind a tree.

My heart began smashing my ribs.

We had found him.

It was Thana's messenger; I knew it.

The creature that caused Serenity to become an Apparition.

"You... You... You..." The Floating Soul stammered, although I barely heard her.

I could see how upset she was.

"I'll get him," Sybella piped up. "He'll be useful if we are to find the Cloaked Spirits and retrieve the Blade."

I nodded.

We desperately needed the Blade in order to save the Realms from my sister.

Sybella's wings appeared, and she got bathed in bright light as she took off into the skies.

"Bring him to me," I whispered.

A screech filled the air, followed by a cracked yell.

I looked up to the sky and saw Sybella flying toward us with Thana's messenger grasped in her claws.

He looked haggard as Sybella approached us and dropped him to the ground. He groaned as he stumbled, and his eyes widened once he saw Serenity.

"Oh, no," he said as he retreated from us.

"Oh, yes," Serenity smirked.

He stared at her in horror.

"No. Please, n-"

He got cut off as Caliya jumped at him; she roared as she tackled him to the ground. Her claws cut through his flesh.

"Good girl, Caliya. Good girl," I praised her. "We got him."

Sybella transformed back into her Being self and approached Caliya.

"There's no need for all of that," she told the messenger as she locked eyes with him. "We need you to tell us where the Wraiths are."

"I'm not going to be able to tell you that; the Wraiths could be anywhere by now," he rasped.

"If you can't tell us where they are," I interjected, "there is no need to keep you alive." I looked at him knowingly, and his eyes widened in fear. "Now," I asked again, "where are they?"

But as he opened his mouth to speak, I heard a moan in the distance.

It was Thana; she was waking up.

Thana

Another moan escaped me as I came around.

I was groggy and struggled to regain my balance.

Pain radiated from my side; there was a steady pulse from my rib cage. Not to mention my body felt like I was on fire.

My eyelashes fluttered as I reclaimed my surroundings.

Once my eyes opened, though, I started to understand what was happening. Everything hit me at once.

I rose to my feet, only to spot Chrysanthe, the Oracle, and the Apparition in front of me. My father sat on the decaying ground, his eyes a clouded white. Chrysanthe's tiger had Damon pinned beneath its gigantic paws.

"No," I growled.

But Chrysanthe and the Oracle watched me while the Apparition's gaze had gotten fixated on Damon.

My attention turned to Damon, but as I started to speak, he cut me off.

"Don't say *anything* to them!" he screamed while the tiger growled at him. "They want the Blade; they want to know where the Wraiths are, don't say anything!"

The tiger roared, annoyed, and cut off the rest of his words.

I knew that was what they wanted.

They trapped Damon in hopes of getting information from him.

The information they needed to defeat me.

They would *never* get it.

"What are you going to do now?" I challenged. I stepped toward them. "You know you can't kill me; I am the Queen of Death."

Chrysanthe scowled at me.

"Plus," I added lazily, "I poisoned *our* father."

Chrysanthe trembled in anger.

"Oh." I grinned menacingly. "So angry."

"Just remember how you got knocked unconscious in the first place," Chrysanthe said cuttingly, and I immediately felt the grin leave my face.

You...You...You...You will pay for that.

I felt pain burning through me at the thought.

It was as if invisible flames licked at me, causing my breathing to buckle slightly.

The fact the crow wasn't on my chest still caused me extreme discomfort.

My eyes closed as the knife returned and carved my flesh, little by little....

Caw. Caw. Caw.

My eyes flashed open. I glanced up to see a crow fly out of the decimated trees toward me.

Caw. Caw. Caw.

The ink animal flapped its wings awkwardly as it neared.

I inhaled sharply and noticed blood dripping from the crow's wings.

My crow had gotten wounded by Chrysanthe, and that caused me to suffer.

But then I realized there was something in the crow's beak.

It was the Empyrean Blade.

70

Chrysanthe

y eyes widened as I saw what the crow was holding.

I watched as the ink animal and the Blade entered Thana's flesh, the tattoo spreading across her chest as her eyes became dilated.

"This. Is. Your. Fault," she spat between clenched teeth after the crow went into her skin.

I stayed silent. It was my fault. I was the one who aimed to destroy her. To take her life and save the Realms. And to avenge my family and Celio.

"You will pay for this," Thana said as she snarled. "Damon, come here!"

Damon struggled to break free from Caliya's grasp; eventually, he could, but not before he tore his flesh on her claws.

Thana screamed in frustration, raising her hands, and the already deteriorated landscape cracked again.

She brought her hands up and down quickly. The movement caused roots to spring from the ground and hold Sybella and I in their grasp. The black slime oozed beneath our feet.

Thana's eyes pierced mine as she smirked.

No...

"Now you're stuck," she said lazily, "so, I guess I can kill you." Caliya roared from behind me, but Thana just smiled wider.

"Your precious tiger cannot protect you now, Chrysanthe," Thana laughed.

I noticed Sybella was struggling to break free of the mud, but to no avail. The harder she fought, the more suctioned she became.

"Can't get free, can you?" Thana asked maliciously.

Sybella narrowed her eyes and growled.

"I'll make sure there's a special place in Hell for you, Oracle, don't worry," Thana said. "You're the reason I'm the Queen of Death; you're the reason why I oversee the Underworld." Her green eyes locked on Sybella. "I'm going to enjoy killing you, Oracle. I mean," Thana paused and exhaled, "I'm going to have fun killing *both* of you, but I'm mostly excited about wiping out your existence."

It was beyond entertaining for Thana to cause harm and unnerve other Beings.

"So now that you both are trapped," she said, "I can execute the two of you." Her expression was savage as she grinned at us.

Sybella showed no emotion on her face as she stared back at Thana, but I sensed she was trembling.

"Now," Thana said and exhaled. "This is going to be fun."

The words scraped through her teeth.

Thana's eyes shifted to behind me, and I followed her gaze to look at my poisoned father, who looked around blindly.

It was then that I realized what was going to happen, and my stomach churned as my heart raced.

Thana was going to use my poisoned father to harm us.

There was nothing I could do as Thana whistled towards Viro, which grabbed his attention.

He turned and gazed into her eyes; his look was completely crazed.

"Kill the Oracle, Viro," Thana uttered.

My father made his way over to Sybella and I, walking smoothly over the terrain.

I tugged on the roots holding me, trying to escape, but it was no use.

Caliya growled loudly and snarled. She tried to follow my father but was unable to move through the wet dirt.

Now we all were stuck.

With our hands trapped, there was nothing either of us could do as he approached Sybella, preparing to wrap his hands around her neck.

The Oracle shrieked, but Viro's hands continued toward her.

"Dad, no! Please don't!" I cried out. Tears rolled down my cheeks as I saw Sybella's frightened face.

But at that moment, Viro's hands went up to her throat. He began choking the essence out of her.

I struggled to breathe as I watched my father's horrifying expression.

No, Dad. No!

But Sybella was being strangled.

She couldn't scream or anything since her airway had gotten blocked. All I saw were the tears running down her cheeks.

And there was nothing I could do to stop it.

"NO!"

"Shut up!" Thana screamed angrily. "There's nothing you can do now; he only responds to me."

My heart raced as I struggled against the roots. I needed to reach Sybella. I needed to save her. Her face was entirely red since she was suffocating, and I couldn't take it anymore.

"NO!"

An abrupt shriek shattered through the clearing, causing Viro to pause.

Sybella coughed, immediately trying to gasp in oxygen as my father's hands left her throat.

That was when Thana was distracted.

Her attention was diverted when, out of nowhere, Serenity soared toward her, knocking her to the ground.

Thana growled in frustration as she got to her feet, furious that her concentration had gotten broken.

"Don't touch them," Serenity snapped, her teeth clenched. "You will *not* touch them again."

"Oh, and you're going to stop me, are you?" Thana challenged.

I watched in amazement as Serenity answered.

"Yes, I will, you Dead Hellion. I will protect them from you."

71

Thana's eyes widened incredulously at what Serenity said.

Serenity's eyes narrowed as she stayed in the air, her gaze not moving off Thana. "I will *always* protect them from you."

I watched in astonishment as Serenity stood up against my twin, but that was when I heard a screech in the distance, and my head snapped up.

The Wraiths.

They had returned.

I felt the blood drain from my face as the Cloaked Spirits drifted toward Thana.

They were so frightening that a cold shiver ran down my spine.

Thana looked at the Wraiths. "Kill them both," she said, loud enough so we could hear.

"No." I continued to struggle further against the thick roots.

My heart raced, and my breath quickened as the Wraiths drifted toward us.

But the harder I struggled against the roots, the more tired I became.

I couldn't escape.

No.

The Wraiths continued to advance toward Sybella and I; one of them extended out its black, scabbed hand toward me as it tried to grab my arm.

A shriek erupted from my throat as the Earth decayed further, as the Cloaked Spirit came closer. Thana laughed, and I quickly realized her green eyes were wide in anticipation.

"USE THEM NOW!"

Huh? I looked at Serenity, who floated above me.

"DO IT NOW!"

I smelt the dead, decaying Ghouls approaching; the smell was like rotten meat left out in the sun.

It was disgusting. Nauseating.

But then, I looked at my tattoo; I focused on my chrysanthemum and saw it was bright and shining against my skin.

Serenity's words resounded through my head. *Use them now.* I suddenly knew what she meant.

I'd gotten my powers back.

As the deathly scent of the Wraiths washed over me, I closed my eyes and focused on summoning my powers.

I opened my palms, angling them toward the ground, and the roots holding me let go.

Wait a moment.

The Wraiths screamed as they prepared to kill us, drifting closer and closer...

I threw my hands out and yelled; some roots took hold of them.

The Wraith's hair-raising, blood-curdling shrieks were enough to make my ears bleed as they got trapped. I turned to Sybella and released her before there was yet another screech in front of me.

Thana looked furious when I turned my attention to her, her green eyes fierce.

"*YOU WILL DIE!*" she screamed, appearing wild and untamable.

I held my ground, seething at her.

That was when I knew I was ready to face Thana.

72

Thana was enraged; her expression was livid as her green eyes were violent and crazed.

She was unhinged.

With a quick flick of the wrist, she released the trapped Wraiths. The roots turned black, the mist surrounding them.

The Wraiths retreated.

Thana threw her hands in the air, and I watched the dark mist swirling around her. She controlled it, and I knew she was going to use it to engulf me.

I blocked it just in time to stop it from choking me. With a screech, I threw my own hands out and sent the tree roots hurtling toward her.

The mist blurred my vision, but then I heard a gagging sound.

The fog suddenly faded, and I turned to see Thana choking from the tree roots around her neck.

Part of me wanted to save her as I saw her green eyes grasp mine, searching them. The other part of me tightened the roots around her neck.

A quick scent of rotting meat filled my nostrils, followed by a smack, and I got shoved to the ground.

I looked up to see that a Wraith was beside me. It had pushed me out of the way and gotten Thana free. As I watched it, I knew it was going to kill me.

The Cloaked Spirit was inches away. Ready to take my soul.

But I couldn't move, couldn't think, as it slowly put its hand on my face. My stomach buckled at the odor, my flesh ice-cold under its touch.

I felt my skin immediately starting to decay as the Wraith touched me.

An animalistic screech filled the air quickly, causing me to flinch away from the Cloaked Spirit. As it moved away, the icy sensation dissipated. The owl attacked, its talons grasping the creature, and I ducked out of the way as the owl plummeted from the sky.

I hadn't even seen Sybella transform after I'd released her.

Meanwhile, the Cloaked Spirit screamed and drifted off into the woods. I heard Thana's voice through the air.

"NO!" she shrieked at the top of her lungs, and her wings unfolded.

Not this again. I stumbled through the mud, the wet dirt clinging to my flesh and clothing. Thana hovered above me, and then I spotted black clouds that seemed to be rushing through the skies.

Wait.

Caw. Caw. Caw.

I understood what was happening, realizing what Thana was going to do.

Caw. Caw.

Thana sensed my panic as the crows blocked out the sun.

"And now," Thana sneered amidst the moving darkness, "you're going to die. "Get her," she growled to the crows, her tone low and vicious, "poison her and bring her to me."

She thrust her arms out and directed the crows at me.

I stared in horror as the combination of black mist and birds soared toward my body.

Caw. Caw. Caw.

The last thing I remember was hearing the cawing overwhelming me and a prolonged, drawn-out, piercing scream before I collapsed and disappeared into unconsciousness.

73

A lightheaded, dizzy sensation overwhelmed me as I opened my eyes groggily, attempting to grasp my surroundings.

My head pounded, and my mouth was incredibly parched.

I blinked, gathering everything around me when I realized that an orange mist surrounded my body. I was also lying down on a hard, black rock.

No, I thought as I glanced down at the terrain. Oh, no.

I was in Hell.

Again.

No. No. No.

A sudden, abrupt cold sensation rattled my spine, and I twisted around to see a Banshee staring at me. Her pitch-black, eyeless sockets bore into my soul as I watched in horror.

Her black dress swayed as she floated; her skin was so pale it was almost translucent, and her white hair was a tangled nest.

Banshees were genuinely terrifying creatures. Anything in the Underworld was frightening.

The Banshee continued to stare at me, watching me with her soulless eyes before she drifted off into the vastness of the Abyss. Then she screamed, the sound echoing through the atmosphere.

Wait a moment.

That meant that someone else was here.

Banshees only responded when someone entered the Underworld, someone who had just died.

"Chrysanthe?"

I jolted at the sound of my name and pushed myself up onto my elbows as I tried to get a better view of my surroundings.

All I could see was the orange mist coming from the Inferno River.

"Chrysanthe? Are you there?"

That voice sounded very familiar.

I took in the water only to see it rippling and murky.

It took a few moments to notice the hard rock jutted straight out of the Inferno River.

I noticed the tall but skinny frame of my father, who had gotten perched up on the rock.

He looked in my direction but couldn't see because of the orange mist.

"Dad!" I yelled. The sound carried through the Abyss. "Dad!"

"Chrysanthe, is that you?"

I immediately got to my feet and ran through the fog.

"Dad, I'm here!"

I made it to the edge of the Inferno River, just as my father twisted toward me. His eyes locked with mine, and I discovered that they had returned to their bright blue.

"Dad, hold on!"

I held out my hand and stretched across the River, only to see the faces of the Dead, drowning in the water.

One of the Dead reached out from beneath the liquid, a freakish smile on his lips.

He reached up with his left arm. He reached out of the Inferno River.

But as soon as his hand seemed to hit the surface of the liquid, it was gone. His hand evaporated and turned into mist.

That was when it hit me.

The Dead surrounded my body. The mist had gotten built from the Dead.

"Chrysanthe! Chrysanthe, help me!"

I quickly looked up at my father, tearing my eyes away from the Dead in the water. They started to crowd him.

"No, Dad! No!"

I threw my hand out again, trying my hardest to ignore the Dead mist that floated in tendrils above the liquid.

"Dad, here! Grab my hand!"

I grabbed the edge of the rock with my other hand to steady myself.

"Come on!" I yelled.

My father focused on my hand.

"Come on, Dad!"

Viro blinked and reached out, grasping my hand.

I was ready to smile as Viro grabbed my skin, but as I started to pull him across the fluid, I realized to my horror his eyes had once again turned clouded.

The screech from the Banshee engulfed my ears as I watched my father in terror.

The fog surrounded us.

The taste of it made me gag, and my stomach churned as I tried hard not to vomit.

Dad!

I felt my father's grip lessen, and I heard the splash as he hit the rancid water.

The Banshee's screech almost made my ears bleed as I watched my father get pulled under the Inferno River.

The Banshee's wail rattled through my bones as I watched, helpless, as my father drowned before me.

I couldn't contain the pain as it ripped through my body.

I jerked awake and wrenched myself from the nightmare. I realized then that something was wrong.

I realized I couldn't see. My vision was horrible, and everything around me was just large unfocused blurs.

I couldn't get my bearings, and panic filled me as I collapsed into the mud, feeling the wet dirt sink into my face as I lost consciousness once more.

74

Thana

I felt a smile creep up on my face as I watched Chrysanthe collapse, her skin and hair becoming caked in mud.

I walked over and crouched to look at her.

"Try to kill me? Like you could ever do that. You've gotten poisoned, and now you have to do whatever I say, *sister*." I spat the final word. "You have been branded to stay with me in Hell. You will *never* see anyone you love ever again. At least, not in the way you wish. Now," I smirked at her, "all I have to do is drag you and our father to the Underworld."

I stared at her for a few moments before I began to stand, but then I heard a feral screech that diverted my attention. I saw the barn owl soaring toward me, lightning-fast. I didn't have time to brace or defend myself as it descended, and I gasped in agony as it dug its talons into my chest and tore my skin. I screamed as blood poured from the wound, and the owl took off, blood dripping from its talons.

Wait a moment.

It was the Oracle; the owl was the Oracle.

And her next target was me.

A sudden shriek caused me to look back into the sky, ignoring the pain still ripping through me. I looked up to see the Apparition rushing to Damon, who flapped erratically. He was trying to warn me.

"N-!" Damon started to scream again, but the Apparition cut him off as she flew right at him. He somersaulted in the sky and slammed to the blackened terrain with a hard *thump*.

There was nothing I could do as the owl targeted me again, talons still out. I was helpless as they sliced through my skin once more. My skin felt as if it was on fire as blood continued to flow.

I dropped to my knees beside Chrysanthe as I became dizzy almost instantly from the blood loss.

I could only watch, helpless, as I saw the Oracle fly toward me a third time, and I glanced down through the mess of bodily fluid to see the Empyrean Blade poking out from my flesh. My skin no longer absorbed it.

NO! I thought, but there was nothing I could do as the Oracle soared toward me. She grabbed and tore at my flesh and took hold of the Blade, yanking it from my body.

I couldn't hold back the blood-curdling, agonizing scream.

I heard a commotion next to me, only to see Chrysanthe stirring.

I could see her poisoned eyes as they watched me; pale, milky, and clouded. Her pupils were missing.

Once again, I heard the Oracle screech, and I saw her swooping toward me *again*.

I braced for more pain when I saw the Oracle drop the Blade by Chrysanthe.

I fumbled for the Blade; I needed to have control of it. However, I couldn't reach it as the Oracle transformed back into her Being self and crouched beside Chrysanthe; she took hold of the Blade.

Tears built in my eyes as pain radiated through me.

I managed to see through the agony. The Oracle had gone into the crossbody bag that Chrysanthe had on her. It took mere moments to see that the Oracle had gotten flower petals out of the bag.

I breathed heavily as I struggled to remain conscious, the blood now pouring out of my chest with each beat of my heart.

No. No. No, was all I kept thinking as I fought the haze that was beginning to engulf me.

But then I suddenly felt utterly frozen, paralyzed, as I looked at the Oracle; she had thrown the flower petals on me, which had me immobilized.

I put it all together; it was the poison.

Those flowers were poisonous.

NO! I screamed internally as I stared at Chrysanthe and the Oracle, completely rigid, unable to move.

Chrysanthe stared between the Blade and I. The Oracle watched me as she held out the Blade to her.

"What are you going to do?" I asked, my breathing ragged by this point. "Kill me?" My body had gotten weakened, and I didn't have the energy to fight back. Blood congealed on the wounds, and the pools below me started to harden and discolor.

Chrysanthe took a final look at me before she took the Blade from the Oracle. She studied it for a moment before grasping it tightly. Pushing herself onto her knees, she hovered above my body, looking me dead in the eyes before she quickly plunged the Blade into my chest.

75

I gasped as the Blade plunged into my chest, and pain soared through me. Darkness consumed everything as my body convulsed. Blood gushed from the wound and pooled around, and I started coughing as a burning sensation tore at my throat.

Only once I managed to look down. I realized how deep the Blade had gotten, up to the hilt in my rib cage.

Chrysanthe, no. Chrys....

I looked up to see Chrysanthe when I could feel the Oracle's gaze on me. I resented her for taking away my choices. She was the reason I'd become the Queen of Death, and I would never forgive her, or my parents, for allowing that to happen.

Anger consumed me as my body weakened and started to fade into the darkness that shrouded me.

I couldn't escape the burning pain of the Blade as it roared through my body.

A glowing light erupted from the Empyrean Blade, and it pulsated inside me. Chrysanthe gasped, and I noticed she had dropped it. The cloudiness in her eyes disappeared, her pupils returned.

I managed to look down at my chest, only to see my crow tattoo morphing into a cardinal with deep red feathers, and my skull tattoo changing into a sunflower.

My eyes struggled to adjust to the bright light, and I squinted rapidly.

"Thana," Chrysanthe breathed, taken aback as she watched me. "Your eyes...they're light blue now."

My stomach buckled at her words.

Somehow, I knew what was happening. I was becoming Calla. The Being I would have been if I had not gotten forced into Hell.

My dress started to repair itself as my hair morphed — the blood disappearing, the knots untangling and becoming smoother.

"Chrysanthe..." The word barely escaped. "Chrys..."

I could see my dress had become navy-blue through my clouded vision while the black mist surrounding me evaporated.

"Chrys...."

I coughed her name once more before finally giving into the fire that ravaged my body and disappeared into oblivion.

76

Chrysanthe

 fire-like sensation radiated from the Empyrean Blade, causing me to drop it to the ground with a *thump* as pain soared through my shoulder.

Ahh, I thought as I felt it. *Ouch.*

I looked at my arm, feeling the burn go deep within my skin, and noticed a scar that had gotten etched into my flesh.

It intermingled with the Realms to create a strange pattern.

What the...? I thought, but the rest of the thought got cut off as I winced; my right arm trembled.

"You've gotten scarred," a voice said, and I turned to see Sybella beside me. "That burn is from the Blade. It scarred you since you got poisoned," she said.

"Is there a way to remove it?" I asked.

Automatically, I wanted it removed. I wanted to erase every memory of what had just happened from my mind.

I mean, I had just killed my *own sister*. I knew I had to do it, but I still felt terrible about it since I was supposed to be caring for all Creatures, the Protector of the Earth.

The fact that I'd just killed my sibling made me feel awful.

I shook my head to get rid of the thought before turning back to Sybella, who answered my question.

"There is a way, but it is in the World Beyond."

The World Beyond.

"The most important thing, though, is that Thana is gone." Sybella sighed in relief. "It's all over, Chrysanthe."

I turned my attention to the landscape around me, the terrain beneath my bare feet, the mud that seeped between my toes.

Thana.

She was gone.

"It's all over, Chrysanthe," Sybella repeated.

I had finally defeated Thana, and all of the creatures from Hell had returned to the Underworld. They had gotten banned from returning to Earth, their only place being in Hell.

Thana had gotten banned from Earth for the rest of her existence.

It really was over.

My gaze shifted to Serenity, who smiled down at me.

We had done it. We had defeated Thana. Together.

It also meant that Serenity had completed her final task; she had helped bring me to Hell to defeat the evil that was Thana.

Serenity was free.

An abrupt, blinding light suddenly soared through the atmosphere and illuminated the sky.

The light was healing the Earth; grass grew and turned to a luscious green, tree branches strengthened and blossomed, fissures mended, and flowers grew back between the cracks. I heard a feral noise and turned to see Caliya free from the Earth and running toward me.

I shielded my eyes from the light as I turned back around, but then I noticed a figure in the distance.

Thick black wings protruded from the figure, and my breath caught.

I instantly knew who it was.

Celio.

He had returned to me.

I was rooted to the spot as I saw Celio rematerialize.

He had come back.

"Celio," I said, looking at his smiling face before running to him and throwing my arms around his body. "Celio, you're alive."

He was silent as he held me, and I breathed in his sweet-smelling scent.

I buried my head in the crook of his neck.

"I thought...thought you were...were dead," My words choked. "You were gone..."

"I'm back now." He rubbed my back gently before pulling away and looking at me. "I'm here now." He stroked my tears away with his fingers.

Celio was all I could focus on as he slowly ran his thumb over my bottom lip.

"Chrysanthe," he breathed as his mouth met mine.

Celio gently grazed his fingers across my cheeks as he kissed me.

I loved him so much.

Soft fur against my hip caused me to break away from Celio. Caliya brushed up against me, moaning.

I pet Caliya, rubbing her ears. I had missed her, and I was so grateful she hadn't been taken away from me. Serenity and Sybella came over to me and smiled.

I grinned back at them before I remembered my father. My father. My mother. Altheda.

I needed to get to them.

"Chrysanthe?"

I turned at the sound of my name, only to see my father walking across the landscape.

His body had returned, and he was healthy once more. As he approached, I noticed the same mark on his arm.

"Viro," I ran over to him and wrapped my arms around him tightly. "Dad, I missed you."

"I missed you too, Chrysanthe." He hugged me. "Are you okay?" he asked as he broke away from my grasp and brought his hand to my face.

"I am now."

"Chrysanthe," he beamed. "My lovely daughter."

"Mom. Altheda," I remembered. "We have to find them."

"Let's go." Viro looked across the clearing before glancing at Serenity and Sybella. "Let's go this way."

I took a glance at Celio before I felt his hand on my arm.

"Come on, Chrysanthe," he said. "Let's go find Altheda and your mother."

"Okay," I said. "Lead the way."

77

"Mom?" I asked, walking over to her. "Are you feeling better?"

"Chrysanthe." I saw tears streaming down her face as she ran to me and enveloped me in a hug. "Chrysanthe, you're okay."

"Yes. Yes, I am."

I pulled away to look into her eyes.

The swelling on her face was gone entirely.

She had gotten healed now that Thana had gotten defeated.

My mother's eyes were her natural blue, and her long brown hair cascaded down her back.

"Mom," I said as she placed a calming hand on my shoulder. "I'm glad you're better."

"Me too," she smiled.

"Thera?"

I twisted at the sound of my father's voice. He stood on the terrain, watching my mother.

"Thera," Viro said lovingly as I stepped away from my mother, allowing my father to embrace her. "Thera, you're healed."

"I am," she said as she returned his loving gaze.

"I'm glad you're safe," he said softly before he kissed her.

"I'm glad you all are." Thera turned to me, immediately focusing on my skin. "What happened to your arm?" she asked as her eyes drifted to the burn.

Thana.

The Empyrean Blade.

We had to explain what had happened, even though she still loved Thana.

"Chrysanthe? Viro?" Thera asked again, her fingers brushing against my father's skin. "What's going on?"

"They've gotten branded as a result of defeating the evil that tried to harm the Realm," Sybella spoke up. "They'll have a permanent scar now."

I was confused — she had told me there was a cure, but I didn't mention this in front of my mother.

Celio, the Guardian of the Spirits, would know what to do.

But right as our eyes met, I heard Thera's breath catch.

"Celio," she said softly. "You're here. But...But... How? I thought you were dead."

It was Sybella who spoke again. "A life for a life. The threat has gotten removed, so he got returned."

"Wait, Thana... Calla," she corrected herself, "was the threat. Does that mean that she's...?"

"She's gone, Mom." I felt myself tearing up as I watched her; I knew what Thana meant to my mother, regardless of whether she was evil or not.

"My Calla, my daughter..." she sniffed and wiped at her eyes.

"Mom, she was going to destroy the Realms," I said tenderly.

"I know," she said. "She was just...my daughter..."

"I know," I echoed her words.

"Calla..." she said, her words trailing off.

"I'm sorry," I told my mother.

"You were doing your duty and protecting your Realm. It will just take a while to sink in."

I sighed. I was the reason my mother was upset, and I hated that. "I'm glad you're okay," I said; I leaned forward and hugged her. My father stepped closer, and I wrapped my arms around him also. "I'm glad everyone's alright. The threat is now gone."

Thana.

She couldn't hurt us anymore. She had gotten trapped in Hell for eternity.

We were finally free.

"Chrysanthe?"

I pulled away at the sound of my name and saw Serenity's eyes fixated on me.

"Yes?"

"Does this mean I'm free?" she asked slowly.

"It does." I glanced to my father, who had spoken. He smiled.

"You are free, dear friend. Any friend of Chrysanthe's is a friend of mine, and since you helped my daughter on a very long and dangerous journey and succeeded, you are most certainly free."

Serenity's smile took over her whole face.

She was no longer going to be a Floating Soul.

"Thank you, Viro," she said before gazing at me. "Thank you, Chrysanthe."

"No, Serenity, thank you. Without you, Celio and I would've never found my parents, and this could've ended a lot differently. Thank you for helping us."

"Yes, thank you," Celio spoke up from behind me.

"You're welcome," she said as she drifted over and held her hand by my cheek. "I will never forget this."

"Neither shall I," Viro stepped forward and looked at her. "From now on, you will be accepted into Heaven."

Serenity's face glowed, and even though she was a Floating Soul, tears filled her eyes.

"Thank you, Viro," she said, sniffling as emotions threatened to close up her throat.

"Goodbye, Serenity," Altheda said.

"Bye, Altheda." She smiled.

A glow took over her body quickly, and that was when Serenity disappeared into the light.

She was finally in Heaven.

"Bye, Serenity," Altheda and I said together. "Enjoy the Afterworld."

I sighed before I turned around to look at Celio.

"Now," I said, grinning at the Archangel, "let's go home."

78

"Home? Do we even have a home now? I mean, to get back to?"

I hadn't thought of that since both my parents had been in the World Beyond. Now, I didn't know what would happen at all since my father and I were both scarred.

I knew from Sybella the only way to get rid of the scars would be in the Afterworld. I just didn't know if my parents could get accepted in the World Beyond since Viro had gotten poisoned.

I looked around at Sybella in hopes she could provide an answer.

"Viro and Thera, you both cannot return to the Afterworld. Since you were affected by Thana, the effects would appear as soon as you reach Heaven."

"What are the after-effects?" Thera asked Sybella.

"You both would burn up in the Everlasting Light that surrounds the Afterworld," Sybella said. "Both you and Viro were tortured by the Queen of Death and marked by her, which means that if you were to enter the World Beyond, you'd both burn up immediately."

She took a deep breath as Thera and Viro exchanged glances, but then Viro looked at Celio, who was behind me, his hand resting on my shoulder.

"Could you help, Celio?" Viro asked but then continued before Celio could say anything. "You could help us." He looked at the Archangel, who appeared to be dumbfounded.

"I don't know about that..." Celio started but trailed off when he saw me watching him. He had to help my parents.

"There's always a possibility," Sybella glanced at my mother and father. "He is, after all, an Archangel. He can return to Heaven."

Celio could help my parents; he could get the cure so they could enter the Afterworld once more.

That meant he could also help me.

"Is there a cure for this at all?" Thera gestured to my scarred arm. "Or are my love and my daughter going to be cursed with this scar for eternity? Am I going to be permanently branded from what happened with...with... Calla?"

"There is a cure, but it is tough to find," replied Sybella. "It's in Heaven, and only then can the effects be removed."

Celio looked between us all. "Of course, I will help you."

Viro and Thera smiled at Celio.

"Well then," Sybella said as she looked up at the sky for a few moments before bringing her gaze back to my parents, Celio, and I. "I think I need to make you Beings a place to stay. I do believe I can make you a little cottage here so you can be comfortable until you return to the Heavens."

I smiled as I looked at my parents, who would be living in the home.

I'd made my place to stay in a treehouse that had been constructed long ago, deep within the forest.

I was happy for my parents; they would have a place to live and sleep until they could return to the World Beyond.

"Thank you, Sybella," Viro said before focusing on my mother and kissed her cheek.

"Yes, thank you," Thera echoed.

"Anything I can do to help you both," Sybella embraced my parents before turning around; she threw her hands out.

I watched in awe as a stone cottage quickly formed, complete with a beautiful flower garden.

Altheda gasped.

"They're so pretty." She was mesmerized by the flowers.

"Altheda," Sybella started after looking at her, "I'm going to have to return you to your Realm."

"I do need to go back," Altheda said. "There's nobody there, but I placed a protective spell on it before I left. But yes, I do need to get back."

"Well, thank you so much for your help, Altheda. I couldn't have found Celio without you." I smiled at her, thankful for the support she provided.

Altheda's pink-tinted blond hair blew in the breeze as she nodded and beamed.

"The most important things are that you found your love, and you defeated the Queen of Death," she said. "I'm glad that your Realm is safe now."

She hugged me.

"And now," she said, breaking away from my body and glancing at Sybella, "I do believe I must leave now."

"Bye, Altheda," Viro and Thera said together. "I hope you get back to your Realm safely," Thera said.

"I will." Altheda and Sybella started to walk into the forest when Celio whistled. A snort followed a whinny.

It was Maximus; he could help Altheda return to her own Realm.

"Oh, thank you, Celio," Altheda watched Maximus as the Winged Horse approached her. The stallion rubbed his muzzle on Altheda's shoulder. "It always helps to have a horse to get back to your Realm."

"That it does." Celio grinned. "I wish you well on your journey."

Altheda approached the stallion, who automatically bowed and allowed her to get on him.

"Hope everything goes well with you," Altheda said. We watched as Sybella was engulfed by light when she transformed into the owl.

Then they both took off into the forest. Moments later, I saw Maximus flying in the sky, followed by the barn owl.

"Chrysanthe?" Viro asked. I turned and ran to my parents, embracing them.

"I'm so glad you both are safe," I said, feeling Viro's hand against the back of my head as he held me close.

"You saved us." Thera pulled away from the hug to look at me. "We love you, Chrysanthe, more than you'll ever know."

I grinned at my mother and father.

"I love you both, too," I replied.

"Well, we have to go look at our new cottage," Thera said as she gave me another quick hug.

"Enjoy it," I said as they walked away; they made their way to their new house, inspecting the flower garden.

It wasn't until they were out of earshot that I turned around to Celio.

"I have to go, too." His voice had gotten filled with disappointment.

"Well, you are the Guardian of the Spirits, and now that the threat is gone, you can return to the Heavens," I said.

"I also have to save Viro and Thera's lives," he said.

"That too," I looked into his hazel eyes. "But with that one, I think you could use a little help."

Celio blinked.

"I think I can help you," I replied.

"You can?"

"Of course, it never hurt to ask. I'll ask Sybella once she returns if I can help." I brushed Celio's cheek with my fingertips, and his eyes fluttered.

"That'll be good," he said before he kissed me.

Butterflies seemed to riot in my stomach; my breath had gotten immediately taken away as Celio embraced me.

When we eventually broke away from each other, I saw him pick something up from the ground. It took me a few moments to realize what the item was.

It was a yellow chrysanthemum, the very flower I was named after.

One had started growing where we stood.

He tucked the stem of the flower behind my right ear, sending tingles down my spine.

"A gift for you."

"Thank you, Celio," I said, smiling.

"It goes with your tattoo very nicely. It's very bright and colorful."

"Thank you," I said again before I looked at him steadily.

"Well, I have to go," Celio said before sighing. "I'll miss you."

"I'll miss you, too," I breathed into his lips, before I pulled away from him.

I looked into Celio's eyes that blazed and were bright hazel.

And then I stepped backward as he released his wings and propelled himself into the sky.

I don't know how long I was standing on the grass, watching where Celio had gone into the atmosphere.

I played with the chrysanthemum behind my ear before I finally sighed.

It was time for me to go home.

Home to my treehouse, where there was a bed waiting for me.

Home, to where I could finally rest, knowing that my parents were safe.

I glanced around at the now gorgeous foliage that surrounded me—the colorful trees, the flowers, the green grass.

Everything, it seemed for the moment, was back to normal.

"Time to go home."

A familiar rumble quickly echoed through the forest, and I saw Caliya bounding toward me; I laughed as she brushed her fur against my body.

"Oh, sweetheart." I petted her as a rumble went through her throat. "You're a good girl, aren't you?"

She moaned loudly and wrapped her tail around my legs.

"Oh, Caliya, you're so good. Do you want to come home with me? Do you?" She let out a happy rumble.

"Alright, honey." I pet her once more. "Let's go home."

And I walked off into the forest, Caliya following close behind me.

Glossary

Chrysanthe- (Chris-an-th)

Caliya- (Ka- lee-ya)

Celio- (Seal-e-o)

Viro- (Vi-ro)

Thera- (Ther-a)

Altheda- (Alth-eh-da)

Sybella- (Sigh-bell-a)

Thana- (Than-a)

Calla- (Kal-a)

Damon- (Day-mon)

About the Author

Elizabeth Wittekind has always had an imagination. Growing up loving the fantasy genre in books and movies, she one day was inspired to write her own novel. *Ethereal Imprints* is her debut.